A FAMILY AFFAIR

A Family Affair

Cheryl Mildenhall

HEADLINE
Liaison

First published in 1996
by HEADLINE BOOK PUBLISHING

A HEADLINE LIAISON paperback

10 9 8 7 6 5 4 3 2 1

ISBN 0 7472 5387 0

Typeset by CBS, Felixstowe, Suffolk

Printed and bound in Great Britain by
Cox & Wyman Ltd, Reading, Berks

HEADLINE BOOK PUBLISHING
A division of Hodder Headline PLC
338 Euston Road
London NW1 3BH

A Family Affair

Chapter One

'Hello, someone's been spending big.' The young woman behind the counter smiled as Sophie entered the patisserie weighed down with carrier bags. With only a slightly sheepish grin on her face Sophie nodded enthusiastically and dislodged a few hair pins from her unruly honey-blonde hair in the process. Hooking her foot around the leg of the nearest chair she pulled it away from the table and sat down heavily.

'I found myself lured into Jamieson's and got carried away,' she said, dumping the bags on the empty seat next to her before reaching up to fiddle with her hair. 'I thought I deserved a few early Christmas presents and for once, I don't think Piers will be complaining about my extravagance. He'll be too knocked out.' Her grin broadened as she reached into one of the bags and pulled out a basque that was barely more than a wisp of ivory lace. 'What do you think of this?' she added, standing up and holding it against her shapely body.

Thankfully there was no one else in the shop to witness her shameless display but even if there had been the odd customer, it was no guarantee that she wouldn't have done exactly the same thing regardless. Caution was not one of Sophie's strong points. Nor tact. Nor diplomacy. She was impulsive and hotheaded. She never looked before she leaped and rarely thought before she spoke. Sometimes she got into trouble but more often than not her disarming smile and charismatic personality blinded people to her faults. She was the girl with laughter in her sea-green eyes and the sunshine in her hair. Not only that, it was coming up to Christmas and so she was feeling extra carefree.

'What are you doing for the holidays?' Sophie asked, nodding as Carole the waitress pointed to the coffee pot. 'Yes, please, and I'll have a baguette to go with that – cream cheese and cucumber.'

Carole brought the sandwich and coffee over to Sophie's table and sat down opposite her. She tucked a strand of mousy, chin-length hair behind her ear. 'I'll be spending Christmas sprawled out in front of the TV with a box of chocolates. How about you?'

It didn't escape Carole's attention that her favourite customer positively smirked.

'Piers has suggested a romantic week away at the cottage,' Sophie said smugly.

Carole laughed. 'Piers – romantic?'

Pretending not to be affronted, Sophie adopted a condescending expression. 'He's not a complete bastard, you know.'

'Isn't he?'

Carole glanced down at the table cloth and began to gather up imaginary crumbs. She regretted her remark instantly and wondered if Sophie was actually aware of the 'real' Piers, the one who regularly visited Crispin's Wine Bar and tried to pull every girl there. Usually without success. He might be rich. He might be a successful something in the city. But basically, Piers was a prat.

It was lucky for her that Sophie was in too much of a good mood to take offence.

'I'll ignore that remark,' Sophie said, biting into her baguette and sending real crumbs everywhere. 'Now, while I eat this, take a look at the stuff in the other bags and tell me what you think.'

Six hours later, at home in their Pimlico flat, Piers' reaction was uncannily familiar.

'Someone's been overtaxing our flexible friend,' he observed.

Sophie glanced up and smiled, loving the way his auburn hair stuck up all over the place. It looked so endearing in comparison with his sober black-and-grey pin-striped suit.

'I think you'll get as much pleasure from them as I will,' she said confidently. 'Just hang on here and I'll give you a private fashion show.'

As she scurried off into the bedroom with her packages, she missed Piers' heavy sigh. He recognised the logo on the bags and therefore knew Sophie had been buying expensive lingerie. And the combination of Sophie and expensive lingerie meant that she would be expecting a bit more than a cup of cocoa and a chaste goodnight kiss. Shit! He was absolutely exhausted and about as ready for sex as a eunuch. All he wanted was to sleep for a week.

'Well, what do you think?'

Sophie twirled around in front of him, startling him from his reverie. She was dressed only in a black silk g-string and matching strapless bra, her generous, creamy breasts spilling over the inadequate cups like froth on a cappuccino.

'Erm, lovely,' he said, trying to avert his eyes. He didn't want to get a hard on. He wanted to sleep. Sophie walked up to him, leaned forward and shimmied right in his face. Oh, hell! From the vague stirring in his Turnbull & Asser boxer shorts it looked as though she was going to get her own way after all.

'Darling, it's all right. Really. I understand.' Sophie reached up and stroked a stray lock of hair away from Piers' forehead. Still hovering close to him, her eyes searched his face carefully, looking for clues. This was not the first time he had been too tired to make love. In fact, it was not even the first time that *week*.

Piers sighed and wished she didn't have that annoying habit of making him feel terrible about something that wasn't his fault. Worse still, she was always so damned nice about it.

'It's work, you know,' he murmured tiredly, 'everyone trying to cram too much in before Christmas. Christ! I hate holidays. All the disruption they entail.' He banged his fists upon the navy-and-white striped duvet, making Sophie jump.

She couldn't understand his dislike of holidays and weekends. Although she loved her work she lived for time off. Time to think. To plan. To dream . . .

'Remember this year it will be different though, darling,' she said, snuggling against him again and reaching under the duvet to stroke his flaccid cock. 'Just the two of us, all alone at the cottage. No relatives. No bickering. No worrying about who'll be first to crack under the strain.'

'It's usually me,' Piers mumbled, looking a bit more cheerful.

Sophie smiled as she felt something harden under her palm. 'That's right, but not this year. This Christmas is going to be perfect.'

It was a nice thought and Piers felt the tension drain out of him. All but one vital part of him began to relax and he found himself smiling as Sophie ducked under the covers and began to tantalise him with her lips and tongue. Kicking back the duvet, he reclined against the pillow, hands clasped behind his head as he glanced down at the young woman with the magic mouth.

By now she had managed to coax him into full erectness. Totally naked, she knelt beside him, her long blonde hair trailing over him, completely obscuring his groin. Although he couldn't watch her mouth at work, he could feel her. Feel the wetness of her lips surrounding his cock stem, sliding rhythmically up and down as her fingers caressed his balls.

His belly clenched and he felt the heat rise quickly inside him. Now was the time to act. Now, before it was too late. Pushing her roughly aside he rolled her over and plunged straight in. Thank God she was already wet. He hated having to do the equivalent of what she had just done for him. It was bad form, he knew, to dislike cunnilingus but he did, and it was becoming more and more difficult to hide his revulsion.

Unlike Sophie, most of the women he met these days demanded nothing less than full gratification.

Sophie writhed beneath him feeling ever so slightly disappointed that he was inside her so quickly. Oh, she was pleased that her clumsy ministrations had achieved the desired effect – for a moment back there she'd been convinced that lovemaking was definitely not on the cards. But now she knew otherwise, she wished Piers could show a little more finesse.

During countless idle hours in the tiny, backstreet bookshop where she worked she read avidly of lingering caresses, butterfly kisses and delicate, tantalising licks. In books, heroines basked in the glory of their bodies, knowing from the appreciative comments and embraces of their lovers that they were truly beautiful and desirable. Why couldn't it ever be like that in real life? Sophie wondered regretfully.

She was sure she was in love with Piers and he with her, yet sometimes – in fact, if she was honest with herself, increasingly often – she yearned for more. That indefinable 'something' that seemed to be beyond her grasp. Piers was practical and pragmatic, far removed from the smouldering, swashbuckling heroes she lusted after in the books she adored with a passion. She wished that just for once he would surprise her. Throw all caution to the wind and ravish her the moment she stepped through the door. Or perhaps pitch her over his knee, pull her knickers down and spank her soundly for some half-baked misdemeanour.

Her fantasies aroused her, causing her to remember the erotic passages she had read recently. The wicked lord of the manor who had demanded his innocent housekeeper's virginity, ignoring her plaintive cries as he stripped and plundered her body. Or the coarse pirate who, having discovered a female stowaway on his ship, kept her in his cabin as his personal sex prisoner. Shuddering at the very idea of the pirate's rough, calloused hands extracting every ounce of passion from the captive heroine, Sophie's arousal grew in leaps and bounds.

She sensed herself blossoming, her eager sex opening out like a precious bloom to welcome the friction of Piers' body against hers. Wrapping her legs tightly around Piers' waist, she felt the wily serpent of desire slithering around inside her, its forked tongue setting fire to her insides.

'Mm, oh, yes,' she moaned.

In her imagination Piers' cock was not yet inside her. Instead, his head was nestled between her thighs, his soft, petulant mouth covering her secret flesh with delicious kisses and wet little sucks. Purely by the power of her own inspiration she could feel her arousal intensifying. Her clitoris swelled and began to throb, the gentle pulsing growing in tenor, gradually building to a delicious crescendo. In her feverish mind Piers had been replaced by an uncompromising sultan who had plucked her from the harem and was now subjecting her to his lascivious whims.

Raising her hips, she ground herself against Piers' slightly softening body. The sultan was urging her on with a stream of erotic obscenities. Sophie tossed her head from side to side, trying to block her mind to the images while all the time her body responded with increasing enthusiasm.

'More, more,' she gasped, bucking her hips wildly until the three of them – she, Piers and the sultan – all climaxed. As Sophie crested the final wave of desire, the image of the sultan receded and she descended back to earth just as Piers gave a final gasp of release and came to a shuddering halt.

For two whole days Sophie floated on air, then her pink cloud darkened to a stormy grey.

'What do you mean, we can't go to the cottage?' she demanded as she clenched her fists and glared at Piers.

She had spent her entire lunch hour trawling around the packed supermarket buying enough provisions to last them a week, then carted the whole lot home on the bus. Consequently, his casual shrug almost incited her to violence.

'It can't be helped, sweetheart,' he said in a tone of voice that, to Sophie's keen ears, was deliberately intended to sound resigned. 'The bank needs me. They are relying on me to do a good job. And successful negotiations on behalf of the bank mean certain promotion.'

'But not at Christmas!' Sophie wailed. 'It was supposed to be *our* time, Piers. For the first time in the two years we've been together, this was supposed to be you and me.'

Resisting the automatic temptation to correct her grammar he shrugged again, his expression becoming wary as Sophie's face suddenly brightened. It was unnerving the way she did those quick mood-change things. They always caught him off-guard.

'I'll come with you,' she said, allowing her imagination full rein. 'So what if we don't end up enjoying a white Christmas? We'll have a hot Florida Christmas instead. Turkey and all the trimmings under the shade of a palm tree.'

Piers frowned. 'You can't come, Sophie.'

'I can. I can get the time off and I've got the money. Just.'

'All right. I'll put it another way. I don't want you to come.'

'What?'

He sighed. 'I didn't mean it to sound like that.'

'Like what?'

'Like I don't want you to come with me.'

'But that's exactly what you just said.'

'I know but— oh, good Lord!'

With a heavy heart Sophie watched as Piers began to pace up and down the tiny sitting room of their flat. Three steps forward. Turn. Three steps back. Run fingers agitatedly through hair. Turn. Three steps forward . . .

He turned to look at her. 'You'll be bored.'

Sophie shook her head determinedly. 'No, I won't. I make friends easily.'

He was starting to feel defeated. It was true. Everyone wanted to get to know Sophie. She was that kind of woman.

'OK. It will distract me if you're there,' he said. 'Instead of concentrating on business I'll be worrying about you.'

'Bullshit!' She countered crossly. 'You never worry about me. Well, sod off to bloody Florida on your own then. And— and— I hope you get airsick.'

It was a pretty feeble retort, she knew, but she didn't trust herself to say what she really thought. If she did Piers might walk out and never come back. Glancing up at his red, stubborn face she realised that, for once, the prospect of losing him didn't make her stomach cramp the way it used to, and she instantly felt guilty. In a flash she crossed the room and wrapped her arms tightly around him.

'I'm sorry, darling,' she crooned. 'I didn't mean it.'

There was a long pause during which she held her breath and then Piers sort of smiled.

'I should bloody well hope not,' he said, shrugging off her embrace. 'Now, do you mind if I borrow your new suitcase?'

After a lot of persuading, she agreed to spend Christmas at the cottage alone. It wasn't that she worried about being on her own in the middle of nowhere. Left to Sophie by her grandmother when she died, the cottage was so cosy and welcoming. Often it felt more like home than her own flat. And the Cotswolds would be lovely at this time of year.

She could just picture the views from the cottage. Acres and acres of rolling fields all covered in a deep layer of snow. Lone walkers with their dogs – their fluorescent kagoules making pretty patterns against a stark backdrop. And clumps of fir trees, their branches, like outstretched arms, decorated with the sparkling raiment of a heavy frost. Moreover, she would be surrounded by the special hush of winter – a heavy silence broken only by the occasional echo of dogs barking in the distance, or the mournful hoot of an owl.

To a true romantic like Sophie the prospect was almost too idyllic for words.

'Yes, I'll go,' she'd said in the end and smiled inwardly. For once her decision had not been made to placate Piers but solely to please herself.

* * *

A couple of days later and a hundred miles away, someone else was viewing the prospect of Christmas in the Cotswolds with a good deal less enthusiasm than Sophie. Charles Abbotson-Carruthers, or simply Chas as he preferred to be called, was dreading being cast in the role of mine host yet again. If it was left up to him he would buy a ham, a whole Stilton and a case of good claret and spend the entire holiday indulging himself – alone.

Unfortunately, it wasn't up to him what he did with his own time because he had Charlotte to contend with, and what Charlotte wanted, Charlotte invariably got. God, sisters were a pain! Even step-sisters. Just because she was two years older than him, Charlotte seemed to think her elder status gave her the right to dictate how he should behave and to have the final say in everything.

Most of the time he kept quiet and just let her get on with it. So what if she didn't like his long hair, his penchant for listening to rock music and playing his electric six-string guitar really loudly? And who gave a fuck if she thought that, at thirty-two, he should be thinking about growing up and settling down? Charlotte didn't approve of him and the way he chose to live. Well, bugger her – and her pretensions! Immediately, his reckless thoughts made him grin. He had to admit, it was a lot easier to be rebellious when big sis wasn't actually around.

Outside in the paddock Chas' chestnut mare, Rachel, was waiting patiently for him, her head bent as she tried to nibble a few blades of frozen grass. Most people commented that Rachel was a strange name for a horse and he would chuckle inwardly, remembering how he had named her after an ex-girlfriend whose features, he realised after they had split up, were astonishingly equine.

That was the trouble with the sort of women he invariably got to meet. Debs and socialites most of them. All teeth and hair and strong-jawed faces. There was no doubt about it, inbreeding had a lot to answer for.

Swinging himself up onto Rachel's back, he headed in the

direction of the lane. Although his denim-clad thighs clasped the horse as tightly as possible, his grip on the rein was loose. It was more of an effort to ride bareback but he loved the freedom of it – the lack of constraint for both himself and his steed. And he loved to feel the movement of another living, breathing thing directly beneath him. It stimulated him in a way that made him long for a stray woman to cross his path. One who wouldn't mind having her skirts pushed up to her waist and her body plundered remorselessly. A generous, free-spirited woman who liked to commune with nature in all its forms. Ah, well, he mused, leaning forward to pat Rachel's silky neck, he could dream, couldn't he?

Heathrow was even more hellish than usual. Sophie hated the airport at any time of day but she had hoped that, being so early in the morning, it would not be quite as busy as it was. With Christmas only two days away the place was absolute chaos. Harassed travellers streamed aimlessly across the road, hampering her passage and frightening her with the thought that she might actually run one of them over. And lines of traffic, kamikaze taxi drivers and carelessly parked cars provided a multitude of additional hazards.

Consequently, it took a great deal of effort for her to smile at Piers as she wished him goodbye. It still rankled that he had chosen to go to Florida without her and, although she was looking forward to going straight on to the cottage, it was small consolation. The idea of spending Christmas alone terrified her. She had never done it before. Face it, girl, she thought ruefully, in the past two years you haven't even spent a whole night alone. For all his faults Piers had always been there. No matter how late he stayed out at night – watching the movements of the yen or whatever – he had always come home eventually. Now he wouldn't be around at all, she was dreading it.

As usual, Piers seemed oblivious to her mood.

'Bye, darling,' he said, blithely ignorant of her downcast

expression. 'You've got all my numbers, haven't you?' Leaning across from the passenger seat he dropped a light kiss on her cheek.

Fighting back the tears that prickled at the backs of her eyelids, Sophie nodded.

'I wish you didn't have to go,' she said in a small voice.

Glancing sideways, she noticed that not only was Piers ignoring her, he already had one foot out of the car door.

'I'd better be off. You know what the traffic wardens are like around here.'

Through a mist of tears she watched him slide out of the car, take his suitcase – correction, *her* suitcase – out of the boot and walk towards the terminal. Just before he reached the automatic doors he stopped and turned. Just at that instant he looked less than cheerful.

Gratified that, now it came to the crunch, Piers looked miserable about leaving her after all, Sophie forced a smile and blew him a cheery kiss. In return his expression brightened, then he waved and was gone, swallowed up in a tide of people with places to go and people to see.

Sophie stared into the depths of the glass doors idly contemplating the reflection of her car, a nippy blue Peugeot 205 cabriolet. It was only a small car, but without Piers seated beside her the compact interior suddenly seemed vast and empty. With a heavy sigh she put the car into gear and flicked on the indicator and waited to pull into the stream of traffic.

It should have been blatantly obvious to anyone with half a brain, she thought some five minutes later, that she wanted to pull away from the kerb. Another car was waiting patiently behind her ready to nip into her space and the traffic was hardly moving. Yet for all that, it took several more minutes before a taxi driver displayed some seasonal spirit and let her edge in front of him.

Away from the airport the roads were much quieter. Dawn had only just started to break, the black sky lightening to a dull grey streaked with red.

'Red sky in the morning,' she mumbled glumly as she pressed her foot down a little harder on the accelerator. The sight should have cheered her but it didn't. Now she was on her way, the sooner she arrived at her destination the better.

As she entered the picturesque village of Chipping Brampton her spirits began to lift at long last. The sky was brighter, the wintry sunshine lending a warm glow to the walls of the Cotswold stone houses that lined Main Street. Passing the Post-Office-cum-general-store on her left, she noticed that it was already doing a brisk trade. No wonder. Not only was it the only shop in the village but with its leaded windows frosted with fake snow and decorated with coloured fairy lights, it looked very festive and inviting.

Farther along, at all four corners of the crossroads, groups of old ladies had stopped for a natter, their thickly padded bodies separated by tartan shopping trolleys. While along both sides of the street, young mums pushed babies in buggies with one hand and kept a firm grip of excitable toddlers with the other.

Just for a moment Sophie felt a pang that she didn't have a baby in a buggy, then she came to her senses just as quickly. Babies weren't part of her plans just yet. At twenty-six she still had plenty of time.

Chas glanced up as he heard the unfamiliar sound of a car coming down the lane. He had been sketching the old pump which under current conditions made an intriguing sight – its black iron body glistening under a thin layer of frost while its old bent nose dripped with icicles.

Pausing with pencil in mid-air, he listened to the sound of the car coming to a halt and one of its doors opening and closing. Then he watched with only half an eye as a young woman dressed all in red emerged from around the side of the cottage opposite him. Tottering on spindly heels she began to pick her way daintily through the overgrown wilderness that was once a kitchen garden.

Must be a townie, he found himself thinking as he gave up all pretence of sketching for a moment. No country person would traipse around in these conditions in a billowing skirt and wearing such inappropriate footwear. Nor were they likely to put their hair up in an elegant chignon. All right, so her hairstyle looked a little blown about, a few stray tendrils escaping from the pins, but she still looked far too chic to be tramping about in the middle of nowhere.

Making a snap judgement, which was typical of him, Chas decided that her slightly dishevelled air just added to her overall charm. To him she looked like a nineteenth-century milkmaid in twenty-first-century clothing. Now there was a thought, he mused with a smile. Time to unearth his half-forgotten collection of buxom wench fantasies.

Whereas Chas had already woven Sophie into a series of interesting erotic scenarios, she hadn't even noticed him. She was too busy concentrating on where she trod. How had the garden become this overgrown in such a short space of time? It could only have been three, no four – oh, hell – now she came to think about it, a good five months must have elapsed since she and Piers had visited the old place. That had been back in the summer when they had played at happy families with his two young nephews.

Phew, what an exhausting time that had been, she remembered with a wry grin. No wonder she didn't feel ready for motherhood just yet. Borrowing a four-year-old and a six-year-old for a week was the ideal antidote to the urge to procreate, no matter how overwhelming.

Weaving carefully around some rather dangerous-looking shrubs, she arrived at the back gate, opened it and took a couple of steps up the garden path. For a moment she paused, gazing up at the wisteria-clad cottage, appreciating the comforting feeling its slightly crumbling walls offered her. Then she took a step forward and found the whole world turning.

'Ouch— ooh, shit!'

Wincing, she tried to move and found she couldn't. Her behind seemed to be stuck to the ground and there was a sharp pain at the base of her spine which seemed to be trying to compete with the darts of agony shooting up her left leg. She was just wondering what to do and if she was going to be forced to spend the whole Christmas sitting outside the back door when, to her surprise, a pair of strong male arms reached down, grasped her under the armpits and hauled her to her feet. It was good to be upright again but before she had even managed to turn to thank whoever it was, her left ankle gave way and she cursed again.

'Bugger, bugger, shit, shit, bugger!'

'I'll pretend I didn't hear that.'

The friendly, slightly mocking tone caressed her right ear and she whirled her head around. Her heartbeat stepped up a gear when her eyes and brain rapidly reached the conclusion that turning her head had been worth the effort.

A pair of brilliant blue eyes met hers and crinkled at the corners into an endearing smile which suffused the rest of the finely chiselled face below. Flicking her eyes rapidly over the rest of her saviour she fleetingly noted the long, dark, wavy hair, battered brown leather jacket and faded blue denims. While her mind told her that he looked like a dubious character and shouldn't be holding her quite as firmly as he was, something primeval inside her screamed with desire.

No! She almost gasped the word aloud and stared wide-eyed at the man who showed no indication that he was about to let her go. She had Piers. She believed in monogamy. Other men didn't even exist for her outside her private fantasies.

'Thank you, I can manage now,' she said firmly, removing herself from his grasp. Her ankle flamed as she put her weight on it and she felt the slipperiness of the icy path beneath her feet. 'Oh, sod it. No I can't.' Gazing helplessly at him, she allowed the stranger to take control of her body again.

Supporting her with one arm, he took the key from her and made to open the kitchen door which swung back as soon as he touched it.

They exchanged surprised glances, then he took charge again.

'It looks as though you might have had visitors,' he said, 'brace yourself.' As he stepped forward over the threshold he took her with him and felt her body tense in horror as they gazed around the ransacked interior of the cottage.

Unintelligible words left Sophie's mouth on a long exhalation of breath. She couldn't believe her eyes and, more to the point, didn't want to believe them. Her cottage had been burgled. Burgled and vandalised. Every drawer had been turned out, every piece of furniture tipped over, every valuable item removed. The TV, the video recorder, the CD player. Oh, God – even the kettle!

Irrationally, she suddenly yearned for a cup of tea.

The stranger frowned and seemed to come to a decision. 'Wait here,' he ordered briskly, 'I'll go and check upstairs.'

Before he left he helped her to a plain wooden chair. Sitting down heavily, she gave him a vague smile of thanks and simply stared around in silence. For the moment she was prepared to let someone else take over. She couldn't bear to try and think. If she did she would probably burst into tears and where would that get her? Consumed by a sudden burst of anger she thumped her fist on the kitchen table. Why the hell wasn't Piers here to deal with all this?

When the stranger reappeared he was shaking his head in disbelief.

'It's the same story upstairs, I'm afraid,' he said, his compassionate expression contradicting his brisk tone, 'and they've yanked the basin away from the wall in the bathroom. That's why all the floors are soaking wet and probably the reason for such a lot of ice on the path. There's still some water trickling from the fractured pipe even now.'

Feeling defeated by events beyond her control, Sophie

sighed heavily and pointed to a cupboard in the corner of the kitchen.

'The stopcock is in there,' she said dully. Although it was painful she glanced around again, and it was then she noticed that the telephone cord had been ripped out of the wall. 'Look what else they've done, the bastards!' she wailed, pointing to the disconnected phone. 'Now I can't even call the police. Or the insurance company. Oh, God, Oh, God!' Breaking off, she put her head in her hands and burst into tears.

At once the stranger was beside her again, squatting at the side of her chair, his capable hands smoothing her hair and her shoulders. As he stroked her shuddering body he spoke softly to her, calming her as though she were a distressed animal.

'It's all right. Don't worry. We'll get it sorted out in no time.'

The words filtered through and gradually Sophie felt her sobs subsiding. Then she began to feel stupid. How must she look now, she wondered, with bloodshot eyes and a big red nose?

'Do you have a spare tissue or something?' she mumbled into her hands, feeling embarrassed.

A moment later she felt the soft caress of a cotton handkerchief against her cheek and without looking up, she grasped it between her fingers and surreptitiously blew her nose. Daring to take her hands away from her face at long last she noticed the stranger was gazing at her with an expression she could not fathom. Was it kindness – empathy – compassion? Whatever it was it made her feel nice and warm and tingly inside. Feeling as though she were about to cross an invisible line she held out a trembling hand and attempted a smile.

'Hi, I'm Sophie,' she said huskily. She paused to clear her throat, willing her heart to stop hammering at her ribs as her whole body went into overdrive. 'Believe me, I'm very pleased to meet you.'

Chapter Two

Time seemed to move in slow motion as the stranger glanced down at Sophie's hand and then back to her face. Reaching out, he trapped her hand with his and held it tightly while his eyes executed a similar mechanism with her gaze.

Staring into those deep blue pools, she felt as though she were on the brink of something momentous. Something that would change her life for ever. It was almost like peering into the depths of an active volcano, knowing that she could be blown to smithereens at any moment but taking the chance anyway. It was scary and exciting all at the same time and yet she still kept looking and still kept holding his hand.

'I'm pleased to meet you, Sophie,' he said with mock formality. 'My name is Charles although all my friends call me Chas.'

'Chas,' she repeated softly, wanting desperately to be his friend.

Glancing down to where their hands were still clasping each other, she noticed how tanned his skin was for the time of year. His fingers were long and looked dextrous – a fact which sent a tiny thrill rippling through her – the short oval nails neither bitten, nor ingrained with dirt. And his palms were sightly calloused but not really those of a manual worker. Like the man himself, Chas' hands were a total enigma.

'Do you work on one of the local farms— or own one of them?' she asked, knowing that employment options in the area were limited to say the least.

Although he looked quite young, the light feathering of

17

laughter lines at the outer edges of his eyes told her he was probably in his thirties. To her surprise he shook his head and let go of her hand, pushing his hands into the front pockets of his jeans instead.

'No, I'm not a farmer,' he said without bothering to offer her an alternative.

Distancing himself from her, he reclined casually against the kitchen wall, his shoulders touching the rough, whitewashed plaster, his hips jutting forward and legs crossed at the ankles. In that position the leather jacket was allowed to fall open, revealing a plain white T-shirt underneath, through which she could just make out the definition of his musculature. His body was lean but firm, his stomach as flat as a board and his shoulders broad. If he had been just a little taller he would have been her ideal man, she realised. As it was he topped her by barely half an inch, and she was only wearing three inch heels. In her new gold stiletto sandals she would be taller than him.

Her concern about his height made her laugh inwardly. Anyone would think she was planning to see a lot of him, when in reality all he had done was help her up when she had slipped over, and turned off the stopcock. It was hardly grounds for a relationship.

Chas couldn't take his eyes off the young damsel who now looked less in distress and much more in control of herself. He wasn't sure which version he preferred. The weeping, helpless Sophie. Or the calm, confident one whose generous mouth now curved into a slight smile.

Despite the bitterly cold weather her hand had felt nice and warm, he recalled, and her cheeks were flushed as though she had exerted herself in some way, or was sitting next to a fire. Neither of these were the case, so he wondered what had put the rosiness there and added a sparkle to her eyes.

Even from where he stood he was still able to see right into those eyes. And when he did he imagined he could see shoals of fish swimming in their green depths. Inwardly chastising himself for being so fanciful he realised the shimmering, darting things in her irises were actually little flecks of colour: hazel, blue and grey. They were lovely eyes in a lovely face that was not quite beautiful yet definitely attractive. Her bone structure was well defined but there were no harsh angles to her features. Everything about her was soft and rounded.

His glance dipped lower, following the graceful length of her throat to the point of the slight vee where the upper edges of her red duffle coat met. All the toggles were fastened and the coat was fairly shapeless, disguising the contours of the body beneath. Yet he had a good imagination – more active than most, as Charlotte was wont to point out in that dry, slightly mocking way of hers. And right now he could envision his fingers working the toggles from their loops and easing the coat over her shoulders, allowing it to drop to the floor.

In his fantasy she was completely naked underneath, her stomach gently curved and slightly tanned, her breasts full and firm with creamy smooth skin. He could even picture her areolae. A pinkish brown, he fancied, given her colouring, and tipped with prominent red nipples as hard and as sweet and juicy as winegums.

Unconsciously, he licked his lips. Winegums were his favourite indulgence and he always kept a tube of them about his person as well as a packet or two in the house. Now he imagined the twin pleasures of sucking this young women's nipples and tasting the unique flavour of her flesh.

'Why are you staring at me like that?'

Her question jolted him from his reverie. It was delivered quite flatly, with just the slightest tinge of interest but no irritation. He guessed that secretly she was enjoying the attention and hoped she found him as interesting as he found her. There he interrupted his own thoughts realising that, for once, his interest in a woman was not based solely on physical appearance and sexual desire. For some reason she was different to all the rest and affected him differently. This one he wanted to get to know properly. Her likes and dislikes. Her hopes and dreams. What made her tick.

It surprised him because he had long ceased to find other people fascinating. Almost fifteen years of relentless socialising had left him feeling jaded, as though he had seen it all and done everything. In his eyes most people were grey – grey and boring. Yet just occasionally along came someone with a little more colour than the rest. If he was really lucky a peacock of a person would strut across his path. But those times were rare and usually short-lived.

In comparison to all the other women he had met, this young woman was a bird of paradise.

'You haven't stopped doing it,' Sophie said, interrupting the meandering trail of his thoughts again, 'and you haven't answered my question either.'

A slow smile crossed Chas' face as he realised that, despite the distance he had deliberately put between them, he still held her spellbound.

He adopted his deepest, most charming tone. 'I can't help admiring beautiful things and you are very beautiful.'

It clearly wasn't the answer she was expecting and she immediately went into a blushing flurry of hair preening and skirt straightening. Then she tried to cross her legs and winced.

'Ouch! I shouldn't have done that,' she said with a pained expression.

'We're going to have to get the doctor to have a look at that ankle,' Chas asserted, taking charge again.

Straightening up, he crossed the room and bent forward. Carefully, as though she were a china doll, he slid one arm around her waist and the other under her thighs, lifting her easily.

'Wha— what are you doing?' Sophie protested. 'Put me down.'

Chas continued to smile and started walking towards the back door which was still wide open.

'Don't be silly. You need help and I'm here to help you.

Now, if I can get you back to my place you can call the police and insurance company from there. Plus, I'll give Doctor Jakes a call. He'll make a home visit, I'm sure.'

Realising that to resist would be pointless, not to mention downright stupid, Sophie glanced to her left side.

'My car keys are in my coat pocket,' she said.

He laughed. 'I don't drive and you can't put any pressure on that foot, so neither can you at the moment.'

Sophie looked amazed. 'You don't drive?' she said. 'I've never met a man who didn't think he was another Nigel Mansell. How the hell are we going to get anywhere? You can't possibly carry me.' She knew there were no other houses within a mile or so of the cottage.

'We'll take Rachel,' Chas said as he manoeuvred them both through the doorway. 'She's my horse. You might have noticed her outside in the garden keeping your lawn down.'

Sophie shook her head. 'No, I didn't notice anything when I arrived. I was too busy watching where I put my feet.' She grinned ruefully. 'Fat lot of good that did me.'

They were outside again at long last and she couldn't help noticing instantly how much of a relief it was to be in the crisp, fresh air and away from the depressing reality of the ransacked cottage. Glancing around she saw that the frost had all but melted and now everything seemed more springlike than wintry. Even the trees that bordered the lane still bore a few leaves on their branches and there were masses of evergreens, variegated shrubs and yellow-leaved hedges which lent bright splashes of colour to a stark canvas of ploughed fields and muddy footpaths.

Ignoring Sophie's feeble protests, Chas carried her over to Rachel and dumped her rather unceremoniously on the horse's back. Even to an experienced rider like Sophie, the prospect of riding a strange horse bareback was a daunting one and she tried to persuade Chas to leave her at the cottage and go in search of a taxi instead. To her dismay he would have none of it, ignoring her protests with a careless shrug of his shoulders.

Swinging himself up in front of her, he instructed Sophie to hold on tight to him.

'Rachel knows to take it steady,' he said, 'and I promise I won't let you fall. Just put your arms around me and relax.'

Sophie sighed. *Just put your arms around me and relax.* Oh, God, how blissful it was to hear a man say that. Tentatively, she reached around him and laced her fingers together so that her arms encircled him.

'Tighter,' he insisted and waited until she was holding him properly before he dug his heels into the horse's belly and made a clicking sound with his tongue against the roof of his mouth.

Rachel responded immediately, the sudden rolling movement forcing Sophie to cling even tighter to Chas than before. With the side of her face pressed against his back all she could think of was the smell of polished leather filling her nostrils and the warmth and hardness of his body.

She didn't think she had ever felt such an instant attraction for a man before, not even at parties when a few drinks made everyone look good to everyone else. Mind you, she wasn't that experienced really. Before Piers she'd only had two serious boyfriends and even the thought of *that* much sexual knowledge made her blush.

Picking her way daintily through the wilderness garden, Rachel had made her way to the lane. It was totally deserted and looked to lead off into infinity in either direction. Turning left, the horse began to clip-clop along the concrete part of the lane until the manmade road surface petered out and became a mud bath. Now Rachel's hooves made a sucking, squelching sound which, in Sophie's over-imaginative state, reminded her of sex.

Glancing down she watched the sticky, oozing mud pass by beneath them and wondered what it would be like to roll around naked in it. She imagined herself and Chas riding Rachel, all three of them bareback and barearsed – she paused to giggle inwardly – then she and Chas sliding slowly down.

Down, down. Letting go of Rachel and sinking into the mud.

A shudder ran through her as she almost felt the wet ooze slip between her fingers and toes. Their hair would become heavy with it, the gooey ends marking trails across each others' bodies as they rolled over and over. She envisioned muddy handprints on her creamy skin, one covering each breast, another on her stomach, more on her thighs.

Snuggling closer to Chas, she imagined his eyes fastening on hers as their limbs locked, his hard cock gliding into her with ease. In her mind her hips rocked, her vaginal muscles tightening, pulling him deeper and deeper inside her. Beneath her buttocks she could feel the warm, undulating movement of the horse and allowed her body free rein to enjoy the stimulation.

Ripples of pleasure ran up and down her inner thighs as she gripped harder, imagining she was riding Chas and not a horse. Within moments her sex began to respond. First a slight tingling which quickly grew to a dull pulse that flamed her body and consumed her mind. It was unbearably sweet torture to be fully clothed, her arms fastened around a complete stranger, as her body cantered irrevocably towards orgasm.

Her tights rasped on the silky hair covering Rachel's back and in response she flexed her thigh muscles. The inner ones screamed as she spread her legs wider, desperately trying to rub the throbbing bud of her clitoris against the horse's spine. Yes, yes, she'd succeeded – at long last! Feeling the canter of her arousal pick up speed until it turned into a full gallop she squeezed her eyes tightly shut and concentrated on hurtling pell mell into the dark abyss of gratification.

Her strangled cry roused Chas from a similarly erotic daydream and he turned his head to glance at her.

'Are you okay – is it your ankle?' he asked solicitously.

His expression was full of concern for Sophie as he reluctantly let go of the image of a helpless damsel who, in his imagination, had been facing him on Rachel's back and writhing feverishly against his body. Both of them had been completely naked, their bodies chilled by the sharpness of the air yet aroused to boiling point by the heat of their passion.

Blushing wildly, Sophie shook her head in answer to his question, not trusting herself to speak. Finally she managed a hoarse gasp.

'No, really. I—'

She broke off hastily. What could she tell him? *I'm fine, I just had the most monumental orgasm of all time, that's all.* Not very likely, she thought with a wry inner smile. Casting around wildly in her mind for something else to say, she suddenly remembered that she had left her handbag in the car. Genuinely concerned, she used that as her excuse.

'Don't worry,' he said. 'When we get to my place I'll arrange for someone to go and pick up your car. It'll be quite safe,' he added reassuringly, 'no one ever comes down the lane.'

Sophie had to battle with herself not to laugh aloud. Want a bet?

The splendour of Chas' home took Sophie completely by surprise. Although he explained that he only occupied one wing, the seventeenth century, traditional Cotswold style house was the stuff dreams were made of. Built in a 'U' shape, the classic, golden stone building with its pointed gables and leaded windows was unbearably picturesque.

As Chas helped her to dismount, Sophie couldn't help exclaiming on the beauty of the house.

He smiled at her enthusiasm and explained that Bickley Manor, as it was called, was usually a busy conference and hospitality centre.

'Of course, it's closed for Christmas right now,' he said. 'But I still need to be around to keep an eye on things.'

By that she assumed he was an estate manager of some kind and immediately thoughts of *Lady Chatterley's Lover* skittered through her head, inciting a fresh, feverish wave of erotic thoughts. Glancing up, she noticed that he was studying her carefully and thanked her lucky stars that he couldn't read her mind.

Pausing only to unlock a stable-type door around the side of the ivy-clad west wing, Chas helped her along a narrow timbered passageway and into a warm, welcoming kitchen. Once there he immediately settled her in an overstuffed wing chair in front of a red enamelled Aga before lifting her injured leg carefully and slipping a chintz-covered footstool underneath it.

Feeling immediately relaxed by her hospitable surroundings, Sophie's eyes followed him as he moved about the room. He filled and plugged in the kettle, opened several oak cupboards and drawers and took out a squat brown teapot, matching mugs and a couple of spoons which he assembled on the sturdy oak refectory table that dominated the kitchen. Then he picked up a cordless phone and handed it to her along with a black address book.

'Look in there under "B" for bobby,' he instructed. 'That's the number for the village constable. Then I'll call the doctor for you.'

'I suppose his number is under "Q" for quack,' Sophie responded with a smile.

Ignoring his raised eyebrows she flicked through the pages of the book, found the number and began to tap out the digits. On the third ring a gruff voice answered and demanded to know her business. In a halting voice, she explained about the break-in at the cottage and asked how quickly someone could get there. For a moment there was silence, although she was sure she could hear someone taking a deep breath.

'Well, now, that would be telling,' the constable said cryptically. 'There's only me, you see, and I'm expected down at the primary school to watch their Christmas concert.'

Sophie fumed. Surely her burglary was more important than a carol concert? Speaking tersely, she pointed this out and immediately wished she hadn't.

'You town people have no soul,' the constable said. 'All I

get from your sort is me, me, me. It makes my blood boil. Too right it does.'

'I am merely concerned about my property,' Sophie said, refusing to be drawn into an argument with someone she didn't even know. Good God, her taxes paid his wages!

The constable relented. 'OK, I'll take a look in at your cottage on my way to the school,' he offered magnanimously. 'But I can't vouch for the CID. They could take ages to get around to it.'

'Well, whatever.' Sophie sighed. 'Just have a look. Do what you have to do. Then let me know how soon I can go back and put things straight.' She didn't hold out much hope of her property ever being recovered, or the thieves caught.

Glancing up, she noticed that Chas was standing right in front of her holding out one of the glazed earthenware mugs. A plume of steam rose from it, instantly reminding Sophie of a charmed cobra rising from its basket.

Handing the mug to her, Chas retrieved the phone and the address book.

'Don't mind old Jack. He's a bit of a misery but he does a good job.'

'You could have fooled me,' Sophie muttered. 'He made me feel as though I had just turned his whole day on its head.'

Chas laughed. 'You probably did. We don't get that much crime around here. I shouldn't think he has had to deal with a burglary in years. Everyone here is into Neighbourhood Watch, either officially or unofficially, and anything unusual is immediately pinpointed and investigated. It's a pity your cottage is so remote. If it had been in the village the break-in would never have been allowed to happen.'

Sophie held the mug to her lips and sipped tentatively at the steaming tea. 'This would have to happen today of all days. Now, if my boyfriend Piers had been here—'

'Oh, your *boyfriend*.' Chas cursed himself inwardly for interrupting her and for his ironic tone.

Sophie gave him a sideways glance. 'Why did you say it like that?'

'Like what?' Chas tried to make his expression inscrutable as he tapped out the doctor's number on the keypad of the telephone and then lifted the ivory plastic to his ear.

'In a derisory way,' Sophie said. 'Do you know Piers?'

He shook his head. 'No, I don't think so.' He broke off and glanced away. Someone had answered his call at long last. It was Dr Jakes' housekeeper. Briefly, he explained the problem and asked if the doctor could make a house call. A moment later he nodded, said, 'Thank you. Much appreciated,' and pushed down the aerial on the phone. 'All sorted,' he said, smiling at Sophie.

Her tea was drinking-temperature by now and she sipped it gratefully. As it marked a warming trail down her throat and into her stomach she realised there was more than just tea in her tea.

'I laced it with a medicinal brandy,' Chas explained when she asked. 'What with the shock and the pain and everything, I thought you could do with it.'

Yet again she was touched by his thoughtfulness and her tense expression softened. 'Thank you,' she said gently.

Chas shrugged, suddenly looking embarrassed.

'How is your ankle feeling?' he asked after a moment's silence. Without waiting for her reply he knelt down beside the footstool and began to run his hands lightly over her lower leg.

A small sigh escaped Sophie's lips: his touch was so light, so gentle it was almost unbearably nice.

'I think it is probably sprained,' she said faintly.

Chas nodded. 'I think you're right. It looks quite swollen now.' He paused and prodded the soft flesh, noticing how puffy it looked in comparison to the slenderness of her other ankle. 'Don't think I'm being funny,' he said, glancing up at her, 'but would you mind taking your tights off? I'd like to get an icepack on that.'

Pursing her lips, Sophie looked steadily at him for a moment. His expression, she noticed, was guileless and he really did seem concerned about her ankle. Also, she couldn't think of anything more soothing than an icepack.

'If you think it will help,' she said doubtfully. Reaching under her skirt, she hooked her fingers around the waistband of her tights, lifting her bottom slightly off the seat so that she could pull them down. It was a difficult feat to remove them and preserve her modesty at the same time. She wasn't in the habit of undressing in front of complete strangers – unless they were medically trained – and he wasn't helping the situation by staring at her in that disconcerting way of his. By the time her tights had reached her knees, she was red-faced.

'Allow me,' he murmured as she struggled to lean forward and push them lower. She wanted to kick them off but her injured leg hurt too much to move even slightly and so she had no option but to let him help. As he drew the pale grey gauze down her legs and away from her feet, she felt a sudden rush of desire, as though he had just stripped her completely naked in one fell swoop.

With a mixture of relief and disappointment she watched as he got up and walked over to the fridge. Taking out a couple of trays of ice, he banged them on the table and then emptied the contents into the middle of a clean tea towel. Folding it carefully, he placed it in a plastic bag and draped it over her damaged ankle.

The shocking sensation of the cold ice on her warm skin nearly made her leap out of her chair. Then she relaxed and allowed the feeling to soothe her, imagining she could feel the swelling steadily going down as the minutes ticked by, each division of time marked by the hands on the huge brass clock which hung on the opposite wall.

Chas didn't touch her ankle again but paused to simply stroke a thoughtful hand along her shin. Sophie watched him, assuring him that yes, the ice pack did seem to be making a difference. She held her breath. His hand was poised upon her knee and indecision seemed to flicker across his face. It was as though he had reached a crossroads and couldn't decide which way to go, down again, or up further.

All at once she was tempted to wriggle slightly by way of encouragement and the wanton thought shocked her. All her life she was used to playing it safe with men. Now she felt decidedly unsafe and it was not due to *his* lack of integrity. It was her own latent sense of sexual daring that worried her. She was scared of the outrageous things she might feel tempted to do. While she was growing up her mother had often referred to her impulsive nature, saying if Sophie were a lemming she would jump off the first cliff she came to without hesitation.

While she battled against herself and the erotic thoughts that skittered through her mind, Chas reached his own decision.

Burying an exclamation of frustration, she watched his hand leave her knee, almost in slow motion. Then he glanced back at her ankle, gave a satisfied nod and walked resolutely away.

He made her a second cup of 'medicinal' tea before excusing himself, explaining that he had a couple of urgent chores to take care of. Sophie smiled and assured him that she would be perfectly content where she was. It was true. The floral chintz-covered chair was very comfortable and the heat from the Aga was incredibly soothing. In no time at all she fell into a light doze.

This time her fantasies came to her as a dream. Chas was the hero, naturally, not Piers. If Sophie had been awake she would have realised that Piers never usually featured in her fantasies anyway. There was nothing there to inspire her. Nothing in him to elevate him to hero status. Certainly nothing about him that boasted of sexual prowess and the ability to pleasure her in the ways she longed for.

In her dream she was Lady Chatterley and Chas was Mellors. Stripped to the waist he toiled away outside the woodshed attacking a huge log with an axe, his torso darkly tanned and rippling under a thin film of perspiration. Pausing just a little distance from him she allowed herself to dwell on the beauty of his appearance and appreciate the sights and sensations of summer in full bloom: the lush green grass beneath her feet, the heady scent of roses and hogweed, the urgent clamour of grasshoppers and the sweet melody of bird calls. The best, most erotic, sensation of all was the warmth of the sun as it caressed the bare skin of her arms and shoulders.

The ankle-length cotton skirt she wore in her fantasy did not impede her movements at all but it still felt heavy and cumbersome. Like the seaweed which wrapped itself around her legs the one time she had dared to swim out of her depth in the sea, the skirt clung irritatingly to her, increasing her desire to be utterly naked.

Her dream self stripped where she stood, dropping her clothing to form a little pile on the grass before stepping forward and into *his* line of vision. There he had spotted her. His feet planted firmly astride the upended log, axe poised in midair, he glanced up and saw her, a look of recognition then a knowing smile suffusing his handsome face.

A sudden rush of her own juices trickled down her inner thighs as she stood there as nature intended and felt the full impact of his gaze. Even from a distance she could see how passionately the desire burned in his eyes. It warmed and then inflamed her, turning her insides to molten lava. Fighting the threat of her knees buckling under her, she began to walk slowly, ever so slowly towards him . . .

'I say, young lady. Are you going to wake up, or am I going to be forced to tap you on the head with my reflex hammer?'

Startled by the strange voice intruding on her dream, Sophie's eyes flew open. Above her hovered the kindly, smiling face of an oldish man who she presumed, as she came quickly to her senses, to be the village doctor.

'I— I'm sorry,' she began but the doctor held up his hand to silence her.

'At least I know you are not concussed,' he said, feeling

her head for telltale lumps and bumps.

'No, I didn't bang my head,' she said as she glanced down at her propped-up leg.

The doctor immediately squatted down and moved his hands to her ankle, ignoring her occasional wince of pain as he felt all around the swollen flesh. Glancing back at her he pronounced a mild strain and said that he would bandage it straight away.

Just at that moment the door behind her opened and Chas reappeared. Sitting down at the kitchen table, he listened as the doctor repeated his diagnosis.

'She'll have to stay off it,' he said to Chas, as though Sophie were invisible. 'At least twenty-four hours rest.'

Sophie looked aghast. 'I can't,' she wailed, 'I have to see to the cottage and then there's Christmas. I must go home.'

To her consternation the doctor shook his head. 'No chance,' he said flatly. 'If you try and put any weight on that ankle you'll just do it more harm. Cottages and trips home can wait.'

'But Christmas can't,' she mumbled before adding in a louder voice, 'What the hell am I going to do?' For the second time that day she felt overwhelmed by a situation beyond her control and tears began to prick her eyelids.

Quickly, Chas intervened. He noticed her expression and realised how distressed she must be feeling.

'Don't worry,' he said soothingly. 'You can stay here tonight. I'll make up a bed for you, there's plenty of room. Let's face it, you'll have to stick around for the CID.'

As appalled as she felt at the idea of accepting his offer and sleeping under the same roof as a complete stranger, she could see the sense in what he said. Even so, she began to shake her head doubtfully.

Chas glanced at the doctor and then at Sophie.

'Look,' he said, 'I'm no rapist, or mad axe murderer. Doctor Jakes here will vouch for that.' He paused as the doctor shook his head vigorously and made reassuring noises. 'But if it makes you feel better we can try and find you a room in the village. I know the Country Lodge Hotel is fully booked but perhaps one of the inns will have a spare room.'

Without waiting for her reply, he picked up the phone and began to make a few calls. Finally, he put the phone down, the expression on his face telling the whole story.

'I checked the Country Lodge but I was right, they are packed to the rafters, and everywhere else is closed for the holiday.'

Sophie still looked doubtful about the alternative but realised she had little option.

'Well— I suppose I could,' she began, 'if you're sure you don't mind. I won't be any bother. I'll just go to bed early and be out of your hair as soon as possible tomorrow.'

Chas grinned. 'Things can get trapped in this hair,' he said, plucking at a single, silky strand and rubbing it between finger and thumb.

The idea that his unruly but obviously well groomed hair might be harbouring all sorts of obscure things made her laugh aloud.

'Okay,' she sighed, 'and thanks.'

Picking up her hand Chas held it to his lips. 'Think nothing of it, madam,' he said, depositing a light and yet sensuous kiss on the back of her hand. The involuntary shiver he sensed run through her made him smile inside.

Dr Jakes' discreet cough shattered the moment. Chas immediately placed Sophie's hand back on the arm of the chair and moved towards the kitchen door. The doctor followed and stopped at the door to turn and bid her goodbye. Chas followed the doctor outside and for a few moments Sophie strained her ears to hear what they were saying. They were talking about her, she was certain of that, and she wondered if she had done the right thing by accepting Chas' offer. How ever well intentioned it might have been, she couldn't help speculating whether he really could keep himself to himself for the next twenty-four hours.

Chapter Three

Holding onto Chas' arm for support, Sophie allowed him to lead her up a wide oak staircase to the second floor. Two doors along the dark-boarded landing, which had a broad strip of rose-patterned carpet running along the centre of it, he stopped.

'This is your room.' He paused to turn the brass doorknob and flung the door open.

It opened inwards and unable to help herself, Sophie peered curiously around him. Her first impression of the bedroom was that it reminded her of a lush variegated meadow. Decorated in various shades of green, the room featured two high, leaded windows on the opposite wall. To the right there was a huge stone fireplace and on the hearth a stack of freshly hewn logs nestled in a cast iron basket.

'Oh, a real fire, how wonderful.' Ignoring the pain in her foot, Sophie hobbled eagerly into the room and gazed around, enraptured.

'If you just let me help you over there, I'll light the fire for you,' Chas said, nodding towards a deeply padded and buttoned chaise longue which was upholstered in dark green velvet. The mahogany edges and bowed legs of the chaise gleamed in the wintry sunlight that bathed the room as if they had just been polished.

'Is this all real?' Sophie asked, her gaze as he helped her across the room taking in the wide four-poster bed draped with eau de nil silk to her left, and an ornately carved mahogany dressing table with matching stool.

'Of course it's real.' Chas grinned. 'What were you expecting from a seventeenth-century manor house, Ikea meets MFI?'

'No, of course not.' Sophie chuckled, then winced as she tried to make herself comfortable on the chaise. Wriggling into a better position she reclined against the luxurious velvet and casually draped her left arm along the sofa's undulating side. The mahogany felt warm to the touch and she sighed with pleasure. 'Now I really feel like the lady of the manor,' she said, deliberately assuming a haughty pose.

Chas smiled and left her to enjoy her new role while he knelt in front of the fire and began to scrunch up sheets of newspaper and arrange them with the logs so that the whole thing would catch light easily. Taking a Zippo lighter from the pocket of his jeans he flicked the cap and lit a taper. In moments the fire crackled into life.

As the orange flames began to lick higher and higher, the room quickly warmed. Unfastening the toggles on her coat, Sophie shrugged it from her shoulders and folded it carefully, using the makeshift pillow to prop up her injured foot.

Chas stood up and dusted flakes of bark from his hands into the fireplace. As he turned he felt his breath catch. Staring idly out of the window to her left, Sophie looked totally at ease in her surroundings. Having dispensed with her coat she revealed a torso that, even under its covering of pale pink wool, looked slender and yet enticingly curvaceous. Few women could look quite so voluptuous and yet innocent all at the same time, Chas realised, feeling his stomach clench tightly. Desperately, he willed his stirring cock to behave itself, for once cursing the fact that he wore tight jeans.

Sophie glanced around and immediately noticed him staring at her.

'Isn't the view marvellous?' she said, trying not to blush under the intensity of his gaze. She was sure her cheeks were as pink as her jumper.

Deliberately, she turned her head again and forced herself to concentrate on the landscape of barren, ploughed fields, their deep furrows glistening under a thin film of frost. The patchwork of fields were bounded by a variety of trees: tall plane trees – their branches bare and spindly like old men's arms – wide, spreading oaks, ethereal clumps of silver birch and the odd prickly green fir tree. In her mind she could picture the fir trees after a heavy fall of snow and suddenly felt overwhelmed by the spirit of the season.

'I hope I can go back to the cottage for Christmas,' she murmured, almost to herself, 'it would be a shame to spend the holiday in London when this place is so beautiful.'

'Even if your cottage is habitable, you could always stay on here for Christmas,' Chas blurted out, surprising himself. 'I— I mean, my step-sister and her husband will be arriving tomorrow evening with another couple, family friends. You're quite welcome to join us as another houseguest. The more the merrier,' he added quickly when he noticed her look of astonishment.

'Well, I— er— that's very kind of you to offer,' Sophie said cautiously. 'But I think I should push off tomorrow regardless.' She glanced down at her bandaged ankle. 'I could always get the train back to London if I'm still not fit to drive.'

'Oh, yes, that reminds me.' Chas slapped his forehead with the palm of his hand. 'I was going to get someone to fetch your car. Just hold on here a minute and I'll go downstairs and give old Ted a call.'

Leaning forward Sophie fumbled about in her coat pocket for her keys. She handed them to him with a smile. Just hold on here, he'd said, as though she were going to climb out of the window and scale down the ivy-clad wall the minute he left, and in her predicament too.

As if he could read her mind, he laughed. 'I know. Idiotic of me to say that, wasn't it?' He sat down at the foot of the chaise and stroked her ankle. 'How is it feeling now?'

Sophie trembled. Even through the bandages and the swollen flesh, she fancied she could feel the warmth of his touch.

'Uh, not too bad. Thank goodness for Doctor Jakes, eh?'

'Yes.' He smiled and stood up. 'I won't be a tick.' He nodded in the direction of a closed door next to the fireplace. 'The bathroom's in there if you need it.'

'Thanks,' she said, resting her head against the curved back of the chaise longue, 'but I think I'll just have a little nap. I've been up since the crack of dawn.'

To be honest, the warmth from the fire combined with the effects of the brandy that had laced her tea were starting to make her feel extremely drowsy.

'OK.' Chas jangled her car keys in his hand. 'I'll see you in a little while.'

As soon as Chas had left, Sophie quickly fell into a light doze that deepened into sleep. Gradually her conscious-self dissipated and in the darkest recesses of her mind her subconscious stirred. She snored gently as she dreamed. She was no longer a nineteen-nineties woman but a seventeenth-century heroine.

Having despatched Ted to collect Sophie's car, Chas made another pot of tea and a plate of cheese and chutney sandwiches. It was what he usually had for lunch and he hoped his unexpected guest would be too hungry to feel disappointed by such basic fare.

Carrying the heavily laden tray upstairs he paused in the open doorway to the green room and simply stared. Sophie was obviously sleeping, her right arm dangling so that her fingertips idly trailed the forest green carpet. She looked even more beautiful in repose, he thought, as soft and vulnerable as a kitten. Feeling a familiar stirring in his jeans, he hoped that beneath the kittenish exterior lurked the savage passion of a tiger.

She had long nails, unpainted but well manicured and he imagined them raking down his back and gripping his buttocks as he thrust urgently inside her. Her soft rosy lips would be stretched wide as she screamed her desire into the echoing stillness of the house, and her generous hips would thrust madly against his, meeting him stroke for stroke.

Shaking his head to clear the image he hastened across the room, pausing only to put the tray down on the dressing table before going to kneel beside her. Almost involuntarily, his hand reached out and stroked her hair for a moment before moving down to trace the fine contours of her face. Gently, his fingertips circled her rounded cheeks, outlined her generous lips and stroked the smooth sweep of her jaw and throat. It surprised him that his caresses didn't waken her but he supposed she was exhausted, glad to sleep off the unexpected trauma of her day.

Lady Sophie reclined on the chaise longue in her boudoir and welcomed the arrival of her lover, the erstwhile Baron De Winter. The temperature in the room was warm enough for her to have dispensed with her cumbersome dress and stays. Now she posed shamelessly, clad only in a thin chemise trimmed with the finest Nottingham lace, as the darkly-handsome Baron raked her feverish body with his wicked eyes.

He crossed the room briskly, his buckled leather shoes making no sound on the carpet, and fell to one knee beside her. Taking up the hand that she languidly offered him, he kissed the back of it, then turned it over and deposited a lingering kiss on the palm. Mumbling a stream of barely discernible words, mostly praising her great beauty, he laid a trail of soft kisses up her inner arm. He paused momentarily to press his lips into the scented flesh of her armpit before capturing her waiting mouth for a deep, probing kiss.

A small sigh escaped Lady Sophie's lips as the Baron moved his lips down her throat to linger on the upper swell of her lush bosom. Feeling his tongue dart out to investigate the enticing valley of her cleavage, she almost swooned with desire.

'Yes, my darling, yes,' she urged breathlessly as his hands cupped her breasts over the thin cotton of her chemise and his fingers began to toy with the hard, swollen tips ...

* * *

Chas gazed at the sleeping young woman with a mixture of surprise and wonder. He had no doubt that she was still sleeping and yet she welcomed his daring caresses with an eagerness that amazed him. Encouraged by her responses, he dared to allow his hand to drift lower, over the delicious curves of her breasts and torso, his fingertips lightly tracing the 'V' of her pubis over the thin cotton skirt she wore.

At that point Sophie muttered something and he snatched his hand away. Then he distinctly heard her say, 'Yes. Yes, darling. Oh, yes, please touch me there.'

He paused. Hovering between desire and indecision. Should he? Tentatively, he reached down and carried the hem of her skirt up to her hips, revealing a small triangle of white lace at the apex of her thighs. Peeping provocatively around the edges of her lace knickers were tiny golden curls. Hardly daring to breathe, he gently pulled the delicate material aside and allowed his eyes to feast on her naked sex.

'Mmm, oh, yes.' Lady Sophie writhed with unashamed delight as she felt the Baron's fingertips skimming her pubis. They combed delicately through her light covering of golden fluff and traced the line that bisected her labia.

Adoring his caresses she wriggled, parting her legs a little so that he could investigate further if he so chose. With a groan of arousal, she noticed that he did indeed choose. Gently parting her feminine lips, he reverently stroked the soft folds of her most secret flesh.

She knew she was already moist, his tantalising kisses and soft caresses having already awakened her greedy body to the prospect of the delights to come. Now she felt his fingertips seeking out the core of her desire, rubbing and circling the hard little bud until she moaned aloud and began to rotate her hips encouragingly.

Gracious, the room was warm, she thought, feeling the delicious sensations in her lower body mount gradually towards the inevitable explosion of pleasure. Spreading her legs still further, she allowed his fingers to delve into the moist entrance to her body, stroking the velvety walls and probing deep into her womb as she ground herself wantonly against his hands.

'Oh, yes, it's happening. The pleasure is upon me again!' she cried out, only half aware of her animal groans echoing around the hushed chamber.

Waves of lust and desire racked her willing body then slowly ebbed away. As they did so she sensed the Baron receding, his fingers sliding out of her body, his solid presence dissipating gradually into thin air. For a while she felt overcome by a heavy languor and allowed herself to sleep. Then she awoke.

Chas sensed that she was coming out of the dream she had obviously been enjoying. Fearful of discovery, he reluctantly released her body and rearranged her clothing so that when she finally came to she would be none the wiser – totally ignorant of his physical explorations.

In many ways he felt annoyed and disgusted with himself for taking such blatant advantage of her and yet, even in the depths of her slumber, she had seemed to enjoy it, her groans of pleasure encouraging him to go much further than he had intended. He couldn't deny that her body had responded eagerly, culminating in an unmistakable climax. He had felt the telltale clenching of her internal muscles around his fingers and watched the way her body had writhed with passion.

Standing up he walked briskly across the room to the dressing table, picked up the tray and retraced his steps, placing it on the floor beside the chaise longue. Reclining casually on the carpet beside the tray he smiled up at her stunned face.

'Hi, did you have a good sleep? I made us something to eat.'

Sophie eyed him quizzically. There was something odd that she couldn't quite put her finger on. Thinking of fingers immediately reminded her of her dream and she blushed at the recollection. God, she hoped she hadn't spoken in her sleep, or done anything embarrassing. Glancing hastily down the length of her body she could see nothing amiss. Thank goodness the dull pulsing between her thighs was not visible to the naked eye.

'I— er— yes. I must have been more exhausted than I thought,' she mumbled, struggling into a more upright position. She eyed the plate of sandwiches hungrily. Sex always gave her an appetite. 'Could I have one of those, please, I'm starving?'

Chas gave an inward sigh of relief. Thank Christ she obviously hadn't realised how badly he had conducted himself. Now he felt full of remorse, cursing himself inside for his lack of restraint. She was so innocent and so vulnerable, more or less at his mercy, and what had he done? Taken full advantage of the situation in a way that was both reprehensible and uncharacteristic.

'Yes, sure, help yourself.' Chas lifted the plate and watched as she helped herself to a sandwich, her nails digging slightly into the soft wholemeal bread. 'I'm sorry I can't offer you anything more exotic. The grocer won't be delivering my Christmas order until tomorrow morning, I'm afraid.'

'Oh, no, this is just great.' Sophie spoke with her mouth full, watching him as he raised a sandwich to his own mouth.

Just as Chas was about to take a bite of his sandwich his nostrils picked up the delicate, unmistakably feminine scent of Sophie on his fingers. Steeling himself, he put down the sandwich again.

'Must just pop to the loo first,' he said, beating a hasty retreat.

If Sophie had expected Chas to suddenly leap on her during the course of the evening, she was to be sadly disappointed. Having wheeled a portable TV set into her room, he settled down on the floor beside her and they watched an inane game show, *Coronation Street*, and then a rather good film, a thriller, that she'd never seen before.

Although they didn't say all that much to each other, the silence was convivial. In some ways it felt to Sophie as though she and Chas were old friends, or brother and sister. All right, she amended as she gave him a surreptitious glance, perhaps not brother and sister but there was certainly no sexual tension between them. No indication that he was secretly boiling over with lust and could ravish her at any moment.

As the evening wore on, she found herself cursing his lack of interest in her. The dream she had enjoyed earlier had been vivid, the realistic sensations she had experienced still lingering. During the game show he had gone off and returned with a plate of scrambled eggs and grilled bacon for each of them. Instead of tea, he brought a bottle of claret which he poured into delicate crystal goblets.

Sophie twirled the glass between her fingers, admiring the delicate stem through which threads of milky glass were entwined.

'Is this old?' she asked, holding the glass in front of her and admiring the way the ruby wine reflected the pool of light cast from the table lamp positioned behind her. Apart from the flickering glow of the fire, it was the only source of lighting in the room.

'Mid-eighteenth century,' Chas said, in an offhand manner. 'Nearly everything in this house has been in my family for generations.'

The shock of his casual disclosure registered on Sophie's face.

'Oh, so this is your house?'

He smiled. 'Well, mine and Charlotte's. She's my step-sister. The one who will be arriving tomorrow.'

'Do you have any other brothers or sisters?' Sophie sipped her wine, her eyes questioning him over the rim of her glass.

'No, just Charlotte, thank God.' He reclined on his elbows and stretched his legs out in front of him, crossing them at the ankles. 'She's enough to be going on with. Ever since Mother and Father died she has taken it upon herself to try and rule my life. Just because she is two years older than me. I try and make allowances for her by reminding myself that her real mother died during childbirth.'

Sophie pulled a sympathetic face and chuckled. 'I know what it's like, I've got two elder sisters and a brother who's younger than me: Patty, Joanna and Jimmy.'

'Are your parents both still alive?'

'Yes, thank goodness.'

She couldn't help noticing he looked a little sorrowful.

'I envy you that,' he said. 'Unfortunately, my father died fairly young, of a heart attack. A year or so later my mother joined him. Everyone said it was grief that killed her.'

'Oh, that's awful.' Without thinking Sophie reached out a consoling hand and placed it on his shoulder.

Her touch was electric, he noticed, with a jolt of arousal. Even though talking about his late parents invariably filled him with sadness, he couldn't help acknowledging how Sophie's presence seemed to take the edge off it. It was the first time he had been able to talk about his mother and father without getting a lump in his throat.

'It was, but it happened quite a long time ago – almost eight years,' he said.

Sophie squeezed his shoulder in what she hoped he would interpret as a friendly gesture.

'Time is a great healer,' she said solemnly.

To her surprise, Chas burst out laughing. Reaching up he caught her hand between his own, turned it over and kissed her palm.

'God, Sophie. You're priceless.'

She pursed her lips, unsure how to deal with his comment and his surprising action which had a strange ring of familiarity about it. Deep inside her she felt something move, like the gentle shifting of sand.

'Actually, I'm feeling a bit tired,' she said, gently disengaging her hand from his loose grip. 'If you don't mind, I'd like to go to bed.'

Mind? Chas thought, his stomach doing a somersault before he realised she meant she wanted to go to bed alone.

'Er, no, of course not.' He released her hand and rose to his feet with exaggerated stiffness. 'Do you have everything you need?'

Sophie glanced at her suitcase, which he had brought upstairs and placed next to the dressing table.

'Yes, I think so,' she said.

'Well, if you do need me in the night, that door over there connects with my room. Don't worry, you can lock it,' he added hastily, seeing the frown that momentarily ruffled her brow.

'Oh, right.' Sophie glanced at the door which was some three feet away from the head of the ornate four poster. 'I'm sure I'll be okay though.' She paused. 'I just want to— er— thank you for everything. You've been really brilliant, you know.'

He shrugged. 'Don't thank me. It's been a pleasure. I don't get that much company.'

Sophie laughed. 'Oh, well, by this time tomorrow you'll have a houseful.' She couldn't help noticing how he seemed less than excited by the prospect. 'Aren't you looking forward to seeing your sister and your friends?'

'Yes, of course.' Chas sighed. 'It's just that, as I said, Charlotte can come on a bit strong. I daresay I'll feel like throttling her before Boxing Day.'

She didn't have an answer to that one. Family get-togethers could be hell on earth, she knew that as well as anyone. It was why she had been so overjoyed at the prospect of spending the holiday alone with Piers. Suddenly remembering him, she realised he would have no way of contacting her. With the phone ripped out at the cottage he might have already been trying unsuccessfully to call her. Oh, well, first thing tomorrow Florida time she would give him a ring and let him know what had happened. Or, perhaps she wouldn't, perhaps she would pretend everything was OK until he got home. He didn't need any unnecessary worries to cloud his judgement. According to Piers, certain promotion was riding on the outcome of this trip.

'I'll see you in the morning then,' she said over her shoulder, suddenly remembering that Chas was still there.

'Yeah, sure,' he murmured softly. Opening the interconnecting door, he stepped through it. Then he paused and glanced back at her. 'Oh, Sophie, just one more thing.'

She whirled her head around. 'Yes?'

'Sweet dreams.'

Giving her a distinctly cheeky wink, he closed the door behind him, leaving her to wonder exactly why she felt so embarrassed.

Sophie awoke the next morning to be greeted by the sight of a changed world. Outside the window, she could see the now familiar landscape but now it was covered with a thin layer of snow.

Snuggling back into the comforting warmth of the wide four poster bed, she gazed up at the canopy of green silk above her. This was the life, she thought happily, forgetting for a moment that her visit would be short-lived. As soon as she could, she would have to get onto the village bobby again to find out what was happening as far as the break-in was concerned.

With a heavy heart, she realised that there was no way she would be able to stay at the cottage over Christmas after all. The damage done by the flooding was bad enough in itself and she didn't fancy the prospect of trying to cope without a kettle or TV. Sitting alone, surrounded by the debris of the break-in, was no way to spend the happy holidays.

All at once, Chas' offer flickered tantalisingly through her mind. No, she shook her head, trying to rid herself of the notion that she might actually accept. Almost immediately she countered her blanket refusal with the realisation that she had no justifiable reason to go back to London. Her parents weren't expecting her. Her friends all had their own lives to lead. No one would miss her if she wasn't there. They had no reason to. Oh, well, she decided, stretching luxuriously under the light-as-a-goosefeather duvet which was covered in eau-de-nil silk to match the bed hangings, perhaps I'll just see how things go.

Having indulged herself in the deep, claw-footed bath, and dressed with more than usual care in a long, cream wool wrap-around skirt and matching cashmere jumper, Sophie wandered downstairs. She found Chas in the kitchen jiggling a cast iron frying pan on top of the Aga.

He glanced up as she entered. 'Good morning, lazybones. Fancy some eggs?'

Lazybones? She flushed as she looked at the clock on the wall. It was almost eleven o'clock.

'Yes, please. I'm sorry about sleeping so late.'

She sat down at the kitchen table and played idly with a fork. The plain, stainless steel utensil was definitely not an antique, she concluded as she twirled the handle between her fingers.

'Don't apologise. I was only joking,' Chas said.

She watched as he slid a couple of eggs onto a blue and white china plate. Right on cue, a couple of slices of toast popped up from the toaster. Placing the eggs and toast in front of her, he pointed in turn to several pots that stood in the centre of the table.

'Butter, strawberry jam, honey,' he said.

Sophie nodded her thanks and reached for the butter. It was thick and creamy, she noticed, literally slathering her toast. Sod the calories, this was the real McCoy. For a few minutes she ate in silence then, when Chas sat down opposite her and began to tuck into his own brunch, she put down her knife and fork and glanced up.

'You— er— you know your offer yesterday?'

Chas looked at her. 'Offer?'

'Yes, you know, about staying here for Christmas?' Now she felt uncomfortable and wished she hadn't mentioned it after all.

'Oh, yeah.' He leaned forward, an encouraging expression

on his face. 'Have you changed your mind? I hope so.'

Sophie gave a sigh of relief. 'Well, I have as a matter of fact. If you're sure you don't mind. And provided your sister won't be put out by sharing her Christmas with a stranger.'

'I don't give a fu— er— I mean, I don't give a damn if she is. Which she won't,' he added hastily. 'For all her faults, she's quite a sociable person. It's only me she doesn't approve of.'

Sophie laughed. 'What's wrong with you – is there something I should know?'

Chas grinned endearingly and pulled at a tendril of his hair. 'This, for a start. She thinks I'm too old to wear my hair long. And she hates my choice of music. She'd rather I listened to Pavarotti than Pearl Jam.'

'Boring!' Sophie pulled a face. 'Pavarotti, I mean. I love all types of music but rock, funk and Latin American are definitely my favourites. Opera is out.'

'Join the club.' He reached across the table and squeezed her hand impulsively. 'Perhaps later you'd like to have a look at my collection of CDs?'

'I'd love to.' She smiled across the table, feeling her heart miss a beat as she found herself drowning in his deep blue gaze once again. 'But first I'm going to finish this.' She forced herself to tear her eyes away from his and glance down at her half-eaten plate of eggs. 'Then I need to contact the police, my insurance company and, if you don't mind, my boyfriend who's spending Christmas in America.'

Chas felt his stomach turn to water at the mention of her boyfriend. Then his spirits lifted almost immediately. What kind of wanker could he be, to choose to spend the holiday on the other side of the Atlantic when he could be snuggled up in front of a roaring log fire with someone as delicious as Sophie?

'No problem.' He shrugged carelessly. 'The phone's there on the dresser. Anytime you want to use it, help yourself.'

An hour later, Sophie had managed to get all her calls out of the way, except the one to Piers. She would wait a little while longer before she made that one. She didn't want to wake him too early, otherwise he would only be annoyed with her and she didn't fancy having to deal with his wrath.

As it turned out, both the village constable and the CID had visited her cottage the previous day and made a note of the break-in.

'Someone from CID will need to take a statement from both you and Mr Carruthers,' the constable said.

'Mr Carruthers?'

'Yes, the gentleman who helped you out yesterday. I understand from Doctor Jakes that you're staying at the manor house.'

Sophie stifled a giggle. So Chas' surname was Carruthers, was it?

'Er— yes. I'll be here all over Christmas,' she said, trying not to grin as she imagined him thinking the worst. Villagers were like that, she'd discovered quite early on. With little else to occupy them, they loved nothing better than to speculate and gossip about the other residents.

Chas had disappeared somewhere – to do some work, he'd said – so she got up, washed up the plates and mugs that still littered the kitchen table and then decided to hobble off for a look around. He had explained to her that the main part of the house was mainly used as a conference centre and so was not strictly habitable but she found the west wing was much larger than she had first realised.

On the ground floor were several sitting rooms, one with a large-screen TV and quite modern furnishings, the others more in keeping with the age of the house. Another room, which was obviously the dining room, contained a long mahogany table around which were grouped a dozen chairs with red brocade seats, and along one wall was a huge matching sideboard. All the wood gleamed and smelt ever so slightly of polish, telling her that someone had been busy that morning.

Just as she reached the conclusion that either Chas had

done it all himself, or else the house was haunted by a housework-mad ghost, she bumped into a stout, middle-aged woman.

Giving Sophie what could only be described as 'the once over', the woman pursed her lips and demanded to know who she was and what she was doing in Mr Charles' residence.

Sophie pulled herself up to her full height of five feet three. 'I'm here for Christmas actually, as a houseguest.'

The woman made a clicking noise with her tongue against the roof of her mouth. 'I don't know what the mistress Charlotte will be saying about that. Does she know all about you?'

'No.' Sophie shook her head, unwilling to expand on her reasons for being there in the first place. 'Chas, er, I mean, Mr Carruthers invited me to stay. I understand his step-sister will be arriving this evening.'

'Yes, well, that's as maybe.' The woman eyed her carefully and transferred the duster and tin of polish she was holding in her left hand to the right. 'But it doesn't do to go snooping around.'

'I wasn't snooping. I—' She was interrupted by the welcome arrival of Chas.

'Mrs Lavender, you old busybody, you're not giving Sophie here the third degree are you?' His eyes twinkled merrily but there was a slight note of warning in his tone.

'No, of course not, Mr Charles. Just goin' about my business as usual.' The woman puffed out her ample bosom. 'If you'll both excuse me, I must get on. There's still the bedrooms.'

Chas nodded and she bustled off down the hallway, turning left to go up the stairs. As soon as she was out of earshot Chas turned to Sophie and smiled.

'Sorry about that. She's very protective of me. Used to work for my mother before she died.'

Sophie shrugged. 'She didn't bother me. I've got used to dealing with all types. You wouldn't believe some of the people who come into the shop.'

'What shop?'

As they talked Chas led Sophie into the sitting room with the TV.

'I work in a small secondhand bookshop,' she explained. 'Most of the books are paperbacks but I still dream of handling a first edition.'

She paused to glance around the room as she sat down at one end of a peach, brushed cotton sofa. It was soft and squashy and she found herself sinking into it. There was an identical sofa opposite, with a small pine table separating the two. The walls were pine panelled and painted in an unusual aqua shade. Two huge abstract paintings hung on the wall to her right, separated by a large open fireplace. Aside from a few pine side tables dotted about the room and a huge floor-to-ceiling shelf unit that took up most of one wall, the room was starkly modern.

'This is a bit of a contrast to the rest of the house,' she said.

'Well, this is the real me,' Chas responded, walking over to the wall unit. 'I can't really stand all that antique stuff.' He picked up a stack of CDs and started to rifle through them. He held up two. 'What do you fancy, Lenny Kravitz or Madonna?'

'Either, I don't mind.' Sophie reclined in the sofa and crossed her legs. 'Actually,' she said, 'I think I'm in a Madonna mood.'

Chas glanced at her and grinned. 'Feel like a virgin, do we?' He couldn't help noticing the way her cheeks flushed pinkly.

'Oh, no, I never feel like that,' she said, with a daring chuckle. Unable to meet Chas' interested gaze, she concentrated on the paintings instead. One was of an adult and a child, their seated forms picked out in grey and white squiggles against a plain black background. The other painting was similarly executed but this time it was just a single triangle surrounded by black which faded to grey and finally white around the border.

'Those are interesting.' She nodded towards the paintings.

The unmistakable strains of one of Madonna's gentler ballads flooded the room as Chas turned around and smiled.

'They are mine,' he said. 'I mean, I painted them.'

'Really?' Sophie was amazed, she'd never met a real artist before. She leaned forward encouragingly. 'Have you done any more?'

'Yes, but not any that are as good as those.' He eyed her thoughtfully. 'I don't normally do portraits but I wouldn't mind having a bash at painting you. You have very interesting features.'

Taken aback, Sophie blinked. 'Do I?'

She tried not to shrink back into the depths of the sofa as Chas suddenly crossed the room in a couple of strides and hovered over her. His hand reached out and cupped her chin, tilting and turning her head this way and that.

'Wonderful bone structure,' he breathed softly. 'Quite, quite beautiful.'

Chapter Four

Sophie sensed that Chas was about to kiss her before he actually did so. Part of her tried to fight the rising sensation of desire and yet she sensed, deep down, that she was incapable of resisting him. The moment his lips touched hers she knew she had lost the battle.

His mouth was soft, as lush and as moist as a ripe fruit and seemed to fit perfectly with hers. Closing her eyes, she concentrated on the warmth of his arms as they encircled her, the sweet-sour aroma of his aftershave and the sensation of his lips pressing more urgently against hers. Her mouth opened willingly, allowing his tongue to probe gently, capturing her own tongue in an erotic embrace.

Reaching up she stroked his hair, her fingers entwining with the soft waves, bunching them in her hand as she caressed the back of his head. With her other hand she investigated the hard, muscular line of his shoulder and upper arm, sliding her palm up under the sleeve of his T-shirt to caress his bare flesh. It felt smooth and hairless, the muscles bunching under the satin covering of his skin as he gripped her harder, his hands roaming her back.

Deep inside she felt the familiar stirring of passion, a liquid, melting sensation that made her feel limp and helpless in his arms, overlaid with a burning urgency to take control. More than anything she wanted to hasten the languid pace of their kiss, to throw him to the floor and grind her body against his. He was squatting before her and it would be easy to make him lose his balance. Just as she felt herself inexorably drawn to following the urgent call of her desire Sophie heard the door open. A slight creaking sound of floorboards followed, then a discreet cough.

Jumping apart, she and Chas both glanced up to see Mrs Lavender standing just inside the doorway. She was wearing a coat in place of her overall and carried a large brown leather shopping bag.

'I'll be off then, Mr Charles,' she said, narrowing her eyes as she glanced momentarily at an embarrassed Sophie. 'The upstairs is done. I've put all the things from the green room outside on the landing. As you know, Miss Charlotte prefers to stay in that room.'

'Oh, Christ, I forgot!' Chas stood up and ran his fingers distractedly through his hair. He nodded in Mrs Lavender's direction. 'Yes. OK. That's fine. I'll put Miss— er— Miss—?' He turned to look inquiringly at Sophie.

'Wilde,' she supplied for him.

'Right, er, I'll put Miss Wilde in one of the other rooms.' He paused to reach into the back pocket of his jeans and pulled out a slightly crumpled brown envelope. 'Here you go, Mrs Lavender. Can I still count on you for Christmas lunch?'

'Of course.' The woman opened her shopping bag and dropped the envelope inside without checking the contents. 'I'll come over tomorrow evening and do all the vegetables. If you could just heat up the Aga and pop the turkey in by nine at the latest on Christmas morning, I'll do the rest when I get here.'

Chas smiled. 'Thanks, Mrs L, you're a treasure.'

'Humph!' The woman tried to dismiss his flattery but looked pleased all the same.

After she had gone, closing the door carefully behind her, Chas turned to look at Sophie and they both burst out laughing.

'Oh, God, it's going to be all over the village now,' he said, wiping a stray tear from the corner of his eye.

'What is?' Sophie sat back again and tried to look composed.

The memory of his kiss still lingered on her lips. She touched them thoughtfully with her fingertip, noticing that they felt slightly swollen.

'Us, of course.' He sat down beside her and reclined, his hands cupping the back of his head. 'You wait and see. The villagers will have us walking down the aisle together before you can say "tinsel".'

Sophie grinned but inside felt a tingle of anticipation. He didn't seem all that perturbed by the possibility. Or was that just her overactive imagination at work again?

'I'm sorry about you having to move rooms,' he added. 'I don't know why I wasn't thinking straight when I put you in the green room.' Suddenly, he turned to look at her, his expression quizzical, as though he had just remembered something. 'By the way, I hope you didn't mind me kissing you earlier. It just seemed like a natural thing to do at the time.'

Sophie smiled. 'Yes, it did and no, I didn't mind. Not in the least.'

'In that case' – Chas edged a little closer to her, – 'do you think we could carry on where we left off? I was rather enjoying it.'

Sinking into the inviting circle of his arms, Sophie turned her face up to his, an expectant expression on her face.

'Do you know something?' she said softly, her fingertip tracing the generous contours of his mouth. 'I thought you'd never ask.'

It seemed their kisses were never destined to last very long, Chas thought ruefully as he disengaged himself from Sophie's warm embrace to answer the telephone. He had just reached the point where he dared to caress the luscious mounds of her breasts over her jumper, when the insistent ringing broke through his lascivious thoughts.

The call turned out to be from one of the estate workers. Apparently a careless rambler had left one of the field gates open and right at that precise moment a herd of Friesian cattle were trampling Bickley Manor's famous rose garden.

'I'll be right there,' Chas said briskly. 'Just try and contain those bloody animals until I get there.'

Putting the phone down he thanked his lucky stars that at this time of year the garden was virtually barren. Although no doubt some of the hibernating flora would be damaged beyond recovery. Fucking typical, he mused, more irritated than angry, now I'll have to go and see Ralph Purvis and ask if he'll meet me halfway with the expense. Ralph Purvis owned the neighbouring farm from which the cows had escaped and could usually be relied upon to show some give and take.

Irked that his slow seduction of Sophie had been interrupted yet again, Chas marched back down the hallway and popped his head around the door to the TV room. Sophie glanced up.

'Sorry about this but there's a bit of a crisis that I've got to go and sort out,' he said. 'Please feel free to watch TV, or put on another CD or something while I'm gone. I shouldn't be more than an hour top whack.'

Sophie felt her earlier arousal trickle away to be replaced by a twinge of disappointment.

'Don't worry about me, I'll be fine.' Kicking off her shoes and stretching her legs out on the sofa, she smiled up at him.

As soon as Chas had left, Sophie settled back against the deeply padded arm of the sofa, closed her eyes and tried to sleep. The house was so warm and comfortable that it was very conducive to taking short cat-naps. However, this time, sleep eluded her. Her mind kept straying to the image of Chas cupping her chin and staring deep into her eyes. Almost as if he were still there, she felt his searching hands roaming her back and shoulders, the pressure of his lips on hers.

She could feel the heat flooding her womb as she concentrated on the image of him. Gradually, her feminine flesh began to tingle, the tingle turning to a dull pulse and then an insistent throb. She could feel her juices mounting, slowly seeping out of her body into the crotch of her knickers. Ooh, ouch! The scant material had worked its way somehow into the slit between her labia and was chafing the delicate folds. I'll have to adjust that, Sophie thought, reaching under the edge of her skirt where it wrapped over itself and delving between her thighs.

As her fingertips brushed her mound she felt a jolt of arousal which she tried desperately to ignore as she worked the damp material from between the outer lips of her slightly swollen sex. Having achieved her aim, she patted herself lightly, immediately feeling the residual tremors in her soft flesh. She repeated her action, noting how her clitoris seemed to have emerged from its secret hiding place and was now a hard little bud beneath her middle fingertip. Mm, that felt good. Using her fingertip she patted her clitoris again and again . . .

Penny Driver rang the front doorbell of Bickley Manor for the fourth time and then took a step back. Gazing up at the front of the house she turned to her husband.

'It doesn't look as though Chas has opened up the whole house this year, Tim, it seems deserted,' she said.

'Well, we'd better walk round to the west wing. He's bound to be there.' Tim juggled the suitcases in his hands. 'I certainly don't want to stand around here much longer. These cases are outrageously heavy and it's bloody freezing out here.'

Penny nodded and tucked a strand of her bobbed auburn hair under her beret.

'OK. Come on then.' Quickly descending the wide stone steps that led up to the front door, she reached down and picked up her Louis Vuitton vanity case.

'I'll take this, darling. We don't want you straining yourself do we?' She winked at Tim who sighed with exasperation.

That was bloody typical of Penny, he thought, grinding his teeth with frustration. She'd quite happily leave him to struggle along with three huge suitcases – two of which were hers –

while she made a great show of carrying a piddly little vanity case.

He watched her tottering a couple of feet ahead of him along the gravel path that ran right the way around the house. Trust her to wear something totally inappropriate. He would have thought three consecutive Christmases at Bickley Manor and a job as assistant fashion editor for a leading woman's magazine would have taught her something. As it was, her fake leopardskin leggings and perilously high-heeled ankle boots were not proper countryside attire.

Penny waited by the kitchen door until Tim caught up with her. She couldn't help noticing the way his dark, beetle-brows were scrunched up in a frown.

'Darling, don't look like that, what will Chas think?' she complained, reaching up to smooth the lines from his face.

'Chas will think I'm getting a bloody hernia from lugging this lot around.' Feeling thoroughly disgruntled, Tim dropped the suitcases on the gravel and inclined his head in the direction of the closed door. 'Have you rung the bell?'

Penny nodded. 'Yes, of course I have. Still no reply though.'

'Well, Rachel's not out in the paddock. Perhaps he's out. What time did you say we would be arriving?'

'Oh, about five*ish*,' Penny said airily.

Tim looked at his watch. 'It's only half-past three. Oh, Christ, Penny! I told you we had plenty of time to stop off at that pub. Now we're going to have to sit around in the bloody cold until he gets back.'

'Not necessarily. Mrs Lavender might be around, or old Ted.'

Leaving the vanity case on the doorstep, Penny set off around the house, stopping to peer through each window she passed. Suddenly she stopped, peered more closely through the window, then turned and waved urgently.

'Tim, quick, come and look at this,' she hissed loudly.

Shrugging, Tim wandered up to her to see what all the fuss was about.

'Look, there. I don't know who she is, do you?'

Tim followed the line of Penny's finger as she pointed excitedly through the window. His breath caught suddenly as he realised what had caught his wife's attention. Just a few feet away from them, on the other side of the glass, a young blonde-haired woman lay on the sofa idly masturbating.

'Christ almighty!' Tim turned away for a moment to gaze at Penny in amazement. 'I've never seen her before, although I must say, she certainly looks interesting from this angle.' The young woman had now pulled the lacy crotch of her knickers to one side and was urgently rubbing a single finger up and down the slit between her labia.

'She's a natural blonde then,' Penny said tersely. She pulled at the sleeve of his tweed overcoat. 'Tim, come away. It's not decent.'

'No, bugger off, Penny. I want to see what she does next.' He glanced sideways at his wife. 'Do you remember how you used to do that in front of me? How come it's all stopped? I used to love it.'

Penny glared at him. 'That's not the only thing that has stopped, if you recall. What was the latest in your catalogue of excuses, a strained tendon from playing squash? My God! I bet you're cursing yourself for not being born a woman, otherwise you could add "the time of the month" to your list.'

'That's not fair, Pen,' Tim retorted, frowning, 'you know I'm under a lot of pressure at work.'

With a sigh, Penny turned away from him and the disturbing sight of the mysterious young woman with her hands between her legs. She leaned against the cold wall and crossed her arms in a half-angry, half-protective gesture. In all honesty, she sympathised with Tim and had been hoping that this break would provide a much-needed revival to their flagging sex life. Well, if nothing else, it had certainly got off to an interesting start.

'Tim, darling, is it making you feel randy watching her?' She turned back to him and glanced through the window again. Now the girl was fingering herself feverishly, obviously only moments away from orgasm.

He nodded dumbly as Penny's fingers plucked at the sleeve of his coat.

'Well, why don't we go and do something about it?' she crooned. 'The car will be much warmer and it'll be *so* comfortable in there if we recline the seats.'

Hardly able to tear his gaze away from the window, Tim followed Penny across the lawn to the place where they had parked their car. As he watched her tight, leopardskin-covered bottom wiggling provocatively in front of him as she picked her way carefully across the frost-tinged grass, he felt his spirits – and something else much more substantial – rise to the occasion.

As soon as they got to the car, a pale blue BMW, Penny flung open the passenger door and reclined the passenger seat. Turning to face Tim she unbuttoned her short fake-fur jacket, flung it inside the car and then proceeded to inch her tight leggings down to the top of her boots. She was grateful that her earlier concerns about visible panty line had encouraged her not to wear any knickers. Sinking her bare bottom onto the passenger seat, she lay back and allowed her thighs to drop wide open.

'Oh, Christ, Penny!'

Tim looked down at her, his eyes fixed to the inviting pouch of her sex which was partially obscured by a silky thatch of auburn hair. Through the hair, pink folds glistened invitingly. Struggling with his clothing, he managed to ditch his coat and unzip the fly on his dark brown cords. He noticed how her eyes, and her legs, widened as the hungry length of his cock sprang free.

'Wow, darling! What a wonderful early Christmas present,' Penny said, her eyes gleaming wickedly. 'Come here and let me have all of it. Every last inch.'

As he manoeuvred himself into the footwell between Penny's legs, she reached out and grasped his cock, her cold

58

fingers almost having a negative effect on him until they began squeezing and rubbing enthusiastically. Right in front of his very eyes, he watched her sex blossom, the pink folds gradually unfurling. Blowing on his fingers first to warm them, Tim reached out and stroked her sex, opening her out even more until the hard bud of her clitoris was completely exposed.

Penny shuddered as a cold blast of air snaked across her hot flesh. It seemed to circle her clitoris and tug at it before skimming the moist outer edges of her pouting vagina.

'Oh, help, oh, God! Please give it to me,' she cried, gripping Tim's cock and guiding it towards her desperate body.

She arched her back, urging her pelvis upwards as he plunged forward, filling her body with the delicious hardness of his erection. Tim's cock was not all that long but it was wonderfully thick and she felt stretched to capacity as he began to slide slowly in and out of her vagina, his thrusts gradually increasing in tempo. Penny felt her clitoris rubbing against his belly, the wiry curls of his pubic hair tantalising the core of her desire until she felt her passion soar.

Sliding his hands under Penny's buttocks, Tim pulled her closer to him, desperate to get as deep inside her as possible. He could feel the lush, cushioned walls of her vagina gripping him as he pushed deeper, and the soft cheeks of her bottom brushing against his thighs. The image of the young woman on the sofa in Chas' house suddenly flashed into his mind. She had looked so wanton, so totally absorbed in her self-pleasuring.

'Aagh, oh, God!'

All at once his balls tightened and he felt the blood engorging his cock, forcing him to peak before he was certain that Penny was ready. He kept on thrusting manfully, riding the waves of pleasure that racked his mind and body until he felt the unmistakable spasming of Penny's vagina that signalled her climax. He watched her face contort in the agony of ecstasy, her mouth opening wide in a silent scream. Then she went limp and moments later he eased himself gently from her, reaching to the centre console for a couple of tissues as he did so.

He wadded up the tissues and began to stroke them over her sodden vulva, wiping her clean in a solicitous, almost reverent way. For some reason he felt profoundly grateful to his wife for having had the inspiration to suggest such an immediate and hugely gratifying fuck. Later, he vowed silently to himself, when they were nestled in the comforting warmth of a four-poster, he would make love to her properly. It was the least she deserved.

The sound of hooves on the gravel drive roused Tim and Penny from their euphoria.

'Quick,' Penny said, hastily dragging her trousers up her legs, 'that must be Chas coming back.'

A moment later Chas' familiar figure rounded the drive, riding bareback on Rachel. When he saw Penny sitting in the car he waved cheerfully.

'Now we get to find out who our mystery woman is,' Tim murmured as he deftly tucked his limp cock back in his trousers and zipped up his fly. Climbing awkwardly from the car, he stood up and stretched.

If Chas was surprised to see both Tim and Penny emerge from the passenger side of their car, he didn't show it. Instead, he jumped down from Rachel's back and, leading the horse by her rein, walked briskly over to them, his face all smiles.

'You're early,' he said. 'We weren't expecting you until teatime. Well, come on, don't let's stand about in the cold.' Clasping his arm around Penny's shoulders, he led them both up to the house.

Sophie was awakened from a light doze by the sound of voices. She could hear Chas speaking and then another man's voice, followed by that of a woman. Hastily rearranging her dishevelled clothing and hair, she sat up straight on the sofa. Her earlier orgasm had been so all-consuming that she'd simply drifted off to sleep straight afterwards. Thank goodness Chas hadn't turned up and found her with her skirt bunched up and her knickers all askew.

A moment later Chas entered the room followed by a man and a woman. Sophie glanced up. The man was quite tall, about five feet ten, with short, dark brown hair combed back from his brow, his handsome face dominated by a pair of thick, silky eyebrows. The woman, in contrast was quite petite, with auburn hair cut in a chin length, unstructured bob. Her features were quite regular, there was nothing particularly outstanding about her although her clothes were another story entirely.

'Sophie,' Chas said, the three of them walking over to her, 'I'd like you to meet my oldest and dearest friends, Tim and Penny Driver. They used to live in the village but now they prefer the hustle and bustle of the big city.'

'Oh, Chas, honestly, I'd hardly call Oxford the big city.' Penny laughed and held out a slim, nicely-manicured hand. 'Pleased to meet you, er, Sophie.'

Sophie smiled and shook the young woman's hand, then Tim leaned forward and took Sophie's hand instead. He glanced down, noticing her fingers grasped lightly by his own and was suddenly assailed by the recollection of those very same fingers burrowing into her sex.

Dropping her hand hastily he tried to banish the disturbing thought from his mind.

'Are we in our usual room, Chas?' Tim said. 'The one overlooking the deer park?'

Chas smiled. 'Absolutely, wouldn't put you anywhere else, old mate. Why, do you want to go and freshen up?'

Tim glanced inquiringly at Penny who nodded enthusiastically. Between her thighs she felt all sticky and was dying to have a proper wash. Or better still, a shower.

The moment Tim and Penny were gone, Sophie glanced at Chas who sat down on the sofa beside her.

'I bet they think I'm your girlfriend,' she said. 'Or did you tell them the real reason why I'm here?'

'No, I didn't actually.' Chas grinned and gave her an appraising glance. 'Now you come to mention it, it wouldn't be so bad if they did think you and I had something going together.'

'Oh, why is that?'

To her surprise Chas pursed his lips and his wide brow creased into a frown.

'Penny mainly,' he said. Lowering his voice a fraction he added, 'She's always had a bit of a thing for me. We used to date when we were teenagers, then she met Tim. I always thought they were love's young dream but last Christmas she could hardly keep her hands off me. It became very embarrassing. Tim's my best friend, has been since primary school.'

Sophie felt a dart of sympathy for Penny. No wonder she couldn't keep her hands off Chas. What sane, healthy, heterosexual woman could?

'I see,' she said solemnly. 'So, what are you suggesting, that we play-act at being lovers or something?' The very idea sent a shiver of desire running through her. Of course, it would just be pretend, she reassured herself. After all, she still had Piers to consider.

Chas felt taken aback by her suggestion. Lovers? Now there was a thought.

'Well, it's up to you, of course. I certainly don't mind pretending to be your lover, or boyfriend, or whatever. And it would have the dual benefit of keeping Charlotte off my back as well. She's always nagging me to find someone "suitable"' – he crooked his fingers – 'and settle down.'

Forcing herself not to look as elated at the prospect as she felt, Sophie gave a careless shrug.

'OK. I'm game.' She grinned. 'It might be fun.'

A little while later, Chas went off to make some sandwiches and as soon as he'd gone, Sophie reached for the phone. It was the ideal time to ring Piers. After a certain amount of hassle with the receptionist who insisted that Piers had left strict instructions not to be disturbed, her call was put through to his room.

'Yes, what?' Piers' familiar voice snapped.

'Darling, it's me, Sophie.'

'Oh, er, yes, Sophie, how are you?'

Sophie frowned, Piers was acting as though he hardly knew who she was.

'I'm fine. Well, no, I'm not fine actually,' she amended quickly, 'I sprained my ankle yesterday.'

'Oh, really?' Piers sounded less than interested.

'Yes, really!' Sophie snapped. 'And it bloody well hurts.' She bit her lip, knowing it was not strictly true. Her ankle had ceased to hurt hours ago. In fact, she was positive that the swelling had gone down completely.

'Well, was that all you called to tell me?'

Piers seemed irritated and a moment later Sophie heard the distinct tinkle of female laughter.

'No, that wasn't all,' she said crossly. 'Who is that laughing in the background?'

'Oh, er, just someone the hotel sent up to carry out some secretarial duties for me.'

Sophie fumed. Piers sounded distinctly evasive now, not to mention hostile.

'And I suppose she's got a mane of hair and legs that go all the way up to her bum,' she said.

'No, er, well, yes. How did you know?'

'I've seen *Baywatch*,' Sophie snapped. 'Well, I hope you're having a good time because I'm having a bloody awful one. Someone's broken into the cottage and everything that hasn't been stolen is ruined.'

'Oh, God, Sophie, that's terrible.'

'Yes, isn't it?' She felt like putting her head in her hands and crying, Piers sounded such a long way away. 'I miss you, darling. I wish you were here.'

Piers cleared his throat. 'Yes, er, well, er, same here.'

'I love you, Piers.'

'Hmm, yes, absolutely.'

'Oh, come on, darling, you can do a bit better than that.' Panic started to hammer behind Sophie's ribs as she realised that for some reason, no doubt the 'secretary' in his room, he didn't want to return the sentiment in so many words. 'Tell me you love me, Piers,' she crooned. 'I want to hear you say it.'

'For Christ's sake, Sophie! Stop playing silly games. I've got a meeting in five minutes.'

'Tell me, Piers.' She spoke through gritted teeth.

'The same goes for me, Sophie, you know it does. Now, just let me get on, will you.'

'Right, fine, I'll let you get on, Piers.' Sophie found she was trembling as she gripped the receiver. In the background she heard the woman speak. It sounded distinctly as though she said, 'Come back to bed, honey.' The bastard! The complete and utter bastard.

'Are you in bed with that woman, Piers?'

'No, I, er, of course not.'

'Liar,' she hissed. 'I heard what she said.'

'No, Sophie, you must have misunderstood. I—'

Sophie shook her head from side to side, trying desperately to rid herself of the sick feeling that assailed her.

'Goodbye, Piers,' she said tersely. 'In fact, if you love fucking other women so much you can fuck off! Fuck off and don't ever come back!'

Flinging down the receiver she burst into tears.

When he returned to the TV room with a tray of sandwiches and a bottle of claret, Chas was surprised to find Sophie in floods of tears. Putting the tray down hastily on the coffee table, he rushed to sit beside her.

'Hey, what's all this, what's going on?' Gently he pulled her head away from her hands and cupping her chin, turned her face so that he could look at her. Her eyes were red and swollen and thick lines of black mascara had formed rivulets down her cheeks. 'Looks pretty bad, whatever it is,' he added softly.

'Oh, God!' Sophie's lower lip trembled as she gazed at him. 'I just rang my boyfriend and we had a row.'

'Is that all? I'm sure it will blow over,' he said reassuringly.

She glanced down, unable to meet his eye. 'No, it won't,' she mumbled. Looking up at him, she gazed beseechingly. 'He had another woman with him. In his room. He tried to deny that there was anything to it but there was. I know there was. And, anyway, to cut a long story short I told him to eff off and never come back.'

'Really, did you?' Chas forced himself not to smile. He couldn't imagine her saying the F-word.

'Yes,' she said in a small voice. She shrugged her shoulders and gave a huge sigh. 'I suppose it's been on the cards for ages. Everyone's been telling me what a two-timing bastard he is and I've just laughed them off. Well, I know now, don't I?'

'Are you sure you weren't mistaken?' Chas asked gently. 'I mean, he is a long way away. How can you tell over the phone?'

'I heard her,' Sophie said miserably. 'I heard her giggling and asking him to come back to bed.'

'Oh, I see. That does seem pretty conclusive, doesn't it?' Chas gazed at her, watching her nod. The light had died in her eyes, he noticed, feeling a pang of regret which turned to anger as he wondered how anyone could treat such a lovely young woman so badly. He reached forward and poured out a glass of wine. 'Here, drink this,' he said, handing it to her.

Sophie took the glass from him and gulped at the wine gratefully. She sniffed loudly and searched the sleeve of her jumper for a tissue.

'Use this,' Chas said, fishing a clean handkerchief out of his pocket.

Smiling wanly at him, Sophie licked the corner of the handkerchief and then began to scrub at the black lines on her face.

'Hang on, you keep missing a bit.' Chas took the

handkerchief from her and dabbed delicately at a stray smudge of mascara.

'Thanks.' She sniffed again and then took another large gulp of the wine. 'That's better.' She let out a long sigh and to his relief, gave him a proper smile. For a while she remained silent, lost in her own thoughts, then she turned to him again and fixed him with a resolute gaze. 'You know what we were talking about earlier,' she said.

'Er, yes. Do you mean the boyfriend and girlfriend scam?' He laughed and felt relieved when she joined in his laughter.

'Yes, that. Do you still want to go on with it?'

'I do if you do.'

'Oh, I do.' Sophie reclined her head against the back of the sofa and looked at him from under her lashes. 'Now I really want to.'

What she didn't bother to add was that this time, she wasn't contemplating merely acting the part of his lover. Now she had no reason to hold back any more she would go for it, no holds barred.

Chapter Five

Penny and Tim walked into the TV room just as Chas was about to pull Sophie into his arms and pick up where they had left off earlier. He sensed the change in her demeanour and was not surprised. Obviously, the row with her boyfriend had been serious enough for her to consider their relationship well and truly over. Which left the way wide open for him to fill the breach.

It wouldn't be difficult, he thought. Although he had only known her for a little over a day he couldn't fail to be bowled over by her charm and the understated serenity of her beauty. The prospect of spending the next week or so in her company and being able to get to know her properly, delighted him. And she would certainly provide a little light relief from Charlotte's constant harping, not to mention Penny's determination to ensnare him in some way.

'Well, well, this is a cosy scene,' Penny said tersely, 'I hope we haven't interrupted anything.' She flopped down onto the sofa opposite looking anything but contrite.

Ignoring her sarcasm, Chas straightened up and waved his hand at the plate of sandwiches.

'Are you two hungry?' he asked, 'Or thirsty?' He picked up the open bottle of claret and waved it in the air. 'There's plenty more where this came from.'

Feeling slightly mollified by Chas' typical bonhomie, Penny nodded and picked up an empty glass.

'Just a drop then,' she said.

Chas exchanged a knowing look with Tim. Just a drop didn't

exist in Penny's world. Just a bottle or two, more like.

'Did you have a good drive down?' Chas asked.

'Up, old man, up,' Tim corrected. 'Yes, we did as a matter of fact. The roads were practically empty.'

'What time are Charlie and Robert coming?' Penny interrupted, helping herself to a sandwich.

Chas glanced at his watch. 'Any time now, I imagine. She said about six but you know Charlie, ever the eager beaver.'

'Yes, isn't she just?' Penny flashed Tim a glance. Even though Charlotte was her best friend and had a gorgeous husband of her own, it seemed she always had difficulty keeping her hands off other men.

Tim flushed uncomfortably. The previous Christmas, Charlotte had made a point of flirting with him. Just the recollection made him shiver. Penny hadn't spoken to him for three days and Chas had looked like thunder most of the time. In fact, he mused, Chas was so possessive as far as his step-sister was concerned that he couldn't help suspecting there was something more to their relationship than simply the fact that they had shared the same father.

Right on cue, it seemed, they heard the sound of a door opening and closing and the clatter of heels on the tiled floor of the entrance lobby. Then a sharp voice spoke.

'Robert, for goodness sake, move that case. I nearly fell over it.'

Chas raised his eyes to the ceiling then grinned at Sophie. 'I hope you're feeling stronger emotionally by now,' he said, 'because my darling sister is about to make one of her entrances.'

He was as good as his word. Moments later the door to the TV room was flung open and a tall, willowy brunette strode into the room, her fur coat and long, rippling hair billowing out behind her.

'Darling!' Charlotte advanced into the room and flung herself onto Chas' lap, covering his face with kisses.

Sophie witnessed the scene with a blatant look of amazement.

'Don't mind our Charlie, dear,' Penny said, winking at Sophie conspiratorially, 'she's a total exhibitionist, aren't you Charlie, darling?'

Whirling around, her arm still encircling Chas' shoulders, Charlotte smiled at her friend.

'Penny, sweetie, how wonderful to see you.' She switched her gaze deftly to Tim. 'And you, Tim. You're looking as gorgeous as ever. Penny, how ever do you keep him under control? He looks so good, the entire female population of Oxford must be creaming their Janet Regers.'

Penny forced a smile and patted Tim's knee. 'Oh, well, you know me, Charlie. I have my wicked ways.' She winked broadly and grinned, firstly at Chas and then at a startled Robert. That'll serve her right, the bitch, Penny thought savagely. If she thinks she can get her claws into my husband there's no harm in letting her think I've got similar designs on Robbo.

'Oh, God, Penny, you're priceless,' Charlotte said. Disengaging herself from Chas, she stood up and shrugged her fur from her shoulders. Underneath she was wearing a tight, very short, red wool dress that left very little to the imagination.

Oh, heavens, she's beautiful, Sophie mused, eyeing the fine bone structure, the silky waves of hair and the endless legs. However can I compete with that? Suddenly, her thoughts brought her up short. What would she be competing for, exactly? In the next second she realised the answer to her own question. Chas' attention, of course. Despite all he had said about his sister, it was obvious to anyone with half a brain that he was clearly besotted with her. The very idea made her feel uncomfortable.

'Robbo, come in and sit down,' Chas said, glancing over his shoulder at the young fair-haired man who still hovered in the doorway. 'I'd like you to meet Sophie.' He reached for

Sophie's hand and squeezed it before glancing at his sister. 'Charlotte, this is Sophie.'

Sophie shrank back into the sofa as Charlotte's thin, highly-arched brows dipped and her eyes narrowed for just an instant. Then the other woman's lips curved into a smile that didn't quite reach her eyes. She had a small purse of a mouth, Sophie noticed and slightly hollowed cheeks that made her look as though she were sucking on a slice of lemon.

'Darling, you didn't tell me you had a girlfriend.' Charlotte forced herself not to sound accusing as she glanced firstly at Chas, then at the young woman seated next to him. Hm, she mused, this one didn't look like his usual type. Not the slightest hint of horsiness about her, or inbreeding. In fact, she didn't look as though she possessed any breeding at all. 'Are you local?' she asked, directing her question at Sophie.

'Er, no, I come from London,' Sophie said, desperately trying to sound composed, 'although I do own the cottage at the top of the lane as well.'

'Oh, how sweet!' Charlotte perched on the arm of the sofa next to Penny. 'Haven't I always said how sweet that cottage is, Pen?'

'Oh, er, yes,' Penny lied. 'Absolutely.'

'So, Sophie,' Charlotte continued, 'who do you know?'

'I'm sorry?' Sophie gave Charlotte a quizzical look.

'Around here, who do you know?' Charlotte persisted. 'The Haughton-Bells, the Lascombe-Spindleys—'

'The what?' Sophie burst out laughing. 'The Lascombe-Spindleys, they sound like some terrible disease.'

Chas failed to stifle a grin. He could tell sister dear was going to have her work cut out trying to demoralise Sophie. The girl was a natural.

Thankfully Robert came to the rescue. Reclining gracefully on the carpet, he reached out and helped himself to a sandwich.

'Don't mind our Charlie,' he said to a grateful Sophie, 'she can be a real bitch but her snarl is worse than her—'

'OK, thank you very much, Robert,' Charlotte interrupted quickly. 'I'm sure Sophie didn't take offence.'

Smiling, Sophie shook her head. 'Of course not. Besides,' she added cheerfully, 'I don't let other people's remarks bother me. I'm too much of a happy person.'

Charlotte clenched her teeth. Too much of a happy person? God, the girl was sickening. Well, let's just see how long she can stay happy, she thought nastily. Penny was hell bent on getting her hands on Chas and Charlotte knew herself capable of assisting her friend in any way that she could.

Dinner was a haphazard affair. Mrs Lavender had already been pressganged into preparing most of the holiday fare so Chas hadn't felt justified in asking her to make something for that evening's meal. Instead he ordered a selection of dishes from the local Chinese takeaway and had them delivered to the house.

'Chas, darling, what is all this?' Charlotte raised the lids of several foil containers and sniffed the contents suspiciously. 'Why haven't we got any real food?'

'This is real food,' Chas mumbled, tipping each dish into a serving bowl and placing them on the dining table. 'Instead of complaining, why don't you sort out some plates and forks?' He stepped aside as Charlotte sighed and tried to open the door to the sideboard that was directly in front of him. 'Napkins are in that end drawer now,' he added.

'Mmm, this all looks wonderful,' Sophie enthused as she sat down where Chas had indicated – next to him and as far away from Charlotte as possible. Picking up a solid silver fork, she smiled across the table at Penny. 'This is all a bit swish, isn't it? I usually eat takeaway straight out of the foil dish.'

Chas noticed that Charlotte was about to say something and silenced her with a warning look. From the corner of his mouth he hissed, 'Leave her alone, for Christ's sake, or I swear I will throttle that swanlike neck of yours.'

Charlotte clapped her hand to her breast and raised her

eyebrows theatrically but Chas interrupted her yet again.

'Don't even try to act the innocent, Charlie, it doesn't become you as well you know.'

'Chas, darling, how could you? I promise I will be as nice as pie to your little friend.' As she took her place at the table, Charlotte missed her step-brother's look of blatant mistrust.

Despite the odd, veiled comments from Charlotte and Penny, Sophie found herself enjoying dinner immensely. Instead of claret, Chas had chosen a nice, crisp Chardonnay to go with the meal and she found herself accepting glass after glass to wash down the delicious assortment of Chinese dishes. Candle-lit plate warmers kept all the food hot and further candles set in ornate silver candelabra cast a convivial glow over the elegant room.

Cognac accompanied the dessert course of lychees and fried bananas in syrup, its comforting warmth making her feel extremely contented. She caught Chas' eye as she failed to stifle a yawn.

'Would you like to call it a night?' he asked solicitously.

Penny, who by this time had consumed more than her fair share of wine and was now on her third cognac, smirked knowingly.

'I bet she does. Probably can't wait to get you alone, Chas, and who can blame her. Oh, stop glaring at me like that, Tim,' she added when she noticed her husband's warning look, 'they're young and in love. Probably can't wait for dinner to be over so they can fuck the arse off each other.'

Chas coughed and Sophie went pink with embarrassment.

Leaning sideways, Sophie whispered in Chas' ear. 'Where am I sleeping, by the way?'

He glanced uncomprehendingly at her for a moment, then remembered that she no longer occupied the green room. 'Shit, I forgot all about that. I don't know which room to put you in. The others will just assume that you're sharing my room.'

Feeling flustered, Sophie concentrated on the blue and

white pattern on the edge of her plate. Suddenly, she felt a hand gripping her elbow.

'I'm, er, just going to see Sophie up,' Chas said, rising to his feet and pulling Sophie up with him, 'if you'll just excuse us for a moment.'

Penny gave a dirty laugh. 'Oh, don't mind us, darling. You take your time.' She paused and glanced at her husband. 'Tim and I are just about ready for bed ourselves, aren't we, darling?'

Looking nonplussed, Tim nodded. Earlier he had planned all sorts of erotic things when bedtime came around. Now though, with his stomach heavy with food and his brain numbed by alcohol, all he felt like doing was going straight to sleep.

Unexpectedly, Charlotte stood up as well. 'In that case, shall we all call it a night? It's been a long day. We can leave this lot until tomorrow.' She waved her hand dismissively at the dirty plates and cutlery that littered the damask tablecloth.

All at once, everyone was on their feet, Tim and Penny leaning across the table to blow out the candles. They all trooped up the stairs together and, at the door to Chas' room, seemed to hover expectantly.

Chas reached down and picked up Sophie's suitcase and handbag which stood accusingly on the landing, reminding him that Mrs Lavender had turned Sophie out of her room to make way for Charlotte.

'OK, right,' he said, reaching for the brass knob on his bedroom door, 'we'll see you in the morning.' Putting his arm around a startled Sophie, he opened the door and ushered her into his room.

As soon as he closed the door behind them Sophie turned to glare accusingly at him. 'What are you playing at? I can't share your room. I hardly know you.'

'It's just for appearances' sake,' he said consolingly, 'I promise I'll sort something else out tomorrow. We can pretend we've had a row or something.'

'Oh, that will be absolutely great, won't it?' Sophie walked across the room, hardly noticing the glorious antiques that decorated it and sat down heavily on the edge of his ornately carved oak four-poster. It was hung with thick red brocade drapes and covered with a matching bedspread. Slowly, she ran her palm over the luxurious fabric. She glanced up again, noticing that Chas was still standing by the doorway, looking totally confused. 'What I mean is,' she said in a deliberately patient tone, 'is that your sister and her friend will have an absolute field day if they think we've fallen out already.'

Chas nodded. She had a point. And a very good one at that.

'So, what else can we do?' he asked. Walking across the room he sat down beside Sophie and reached for her hand. Gazing at it he added, 'Our only other option is to share this room for the entire holiday.' He glanced over his shoulder at the rest of the bed. 'Do you think you could bear to sleep in the same bed as me? We wouldn't have to do anything. I promise I'll behave like an absolute gentleman.'

Sophie forced herself to look at him. His gaze was open, totally without guile, leaving her in no doubt that he meant every word. The trouble is, she thought, although I believe I can trust him, I'm just as certain I can't trust myself. Taking a deep breath she considered her options before coming to a decision.

'OK. I can go along with that,' she said, watching with interest as Chas seemed to visibly relax, 'we'll give it a go for tonight and see how things pan out.'

'All right, that's my girl.' Chas smiled and gave her a chaste kiss on the cheek. 'You can use the bathroom first if you want to.'

Chas' bathroom was very similar to the one she had used before, she noticed. The old-fashioned white porcelain fittings would have made the room seem very cold and austere were it not for the thick pile carpet, maroon in this case, and the tongue and groove panelled walls which were stained a warm honey colour.

Stripping off her clothes, she quickly used the lavatory, then stepped into the bathtub and pulled the cord that operated the shower. Immediately, warm jets of water cascaded down on her and she had to incline her head to avoid getting her hair wet. Having soaped and rinsed herself thoroughly she turned off the shower, stepped out of the bath and wrapped herself in one of the thick maroon towels that hung on a heated towel rail.

The warmth of the towel seemed to seep into her body as she enveloped herself in it, securing it around her bust. Using a second towel she blotted the water droplets on her legs, arms and shoulders, then she walked back into the bedroom and stopped dead in her tracks. Naked apart from his jeans, Chas was in the process of uncorking a bottle of champagne.

'I thought you might enjoy a little nightcap,' he said airily. He poured the fizzing liquid into a couple of tall flutes, waiting until the froth died down before topping them up. Picking up the glasses he crossed the room, handed one to a startled Sophie and touched the rim of her glass with his own. 'Salut,' he said softly, 'or should I say chin-chin.'

'Tim would say that.' Sophie laughed softly. 'He's terribly English, isn't he?'

'Oh, terribly,' Chas agreed. 'He's so English it's almost painful.' He gave her a slow, easy smile and sipped his champagne before putting the glass down on a small round oak table. He tried not to look too hard at Sophie who looked achingly desirable clad only in a towel. 'I'd, er, better use the bathroom myself now.'

As the bathroom door closed behind him, Sophie put down her own glass and crossed the room to open her suitcase. As she rifled through its contents she remembered, with a pang of dismay, that the only night-time attire she had bothered to bring with her were a pair of very old, very unsexy, brushed cotton pyjamas. Knowing how cold her cottage could become at night and not expecting any romantic encounters, she had opted for comfort rather than desirability.

Considering the pyjamas thoughtfully, she quickly rejected any notion of actually wearing them. If she did, she certainly wouldn't have any problem keeping Chas at arm's length. She chuckled softly to herself. His thoughts toward her may be entirely chivalrous but hers bordered more on the lascivious. Briefly, she recalled the image of Chas as he had been moments before. Clad only in his jeans, his tanned, hairless, nicely muscular torso rippling as he moved, he had looked far more sexually provocative than if he had been completely naked.

All at once her inquisitive fingers came into contact with something satin. Pulling at the cream-coloured garment she realised it was one of her underslips. Short, strappy and ever so slightly transparent it would make an ideal substitute for a nightdress. Dropping the towel, she stepped into the slip and pulled it up her naked body.

Carefully folding the towel she draped it over the back of a chair, retrieved her glass of champagne and hopped quickly into bed. Moments later the bathroom door opened and Chas appeared.

All the time Chas had been in the bathroom he had been conducting an inner battle. He had given Sophie his word that he wouldn't try anything and yet he was aching to hold her and touch her. He was dying to explore every inch of her delicious body. She seemed so enticing in clothes, what must she look like without them?

Stepping back into the bedroom, he felt his gaze immediately drawn to her. Oh, God, she was in his bed – actually *in* his bed! And she looked absolutely gorgeous, her long, honey blonde hair falling over her shoulders which were bare save for a couple of very thin straps. Through the thin material of her nightgown he could clearly see the outline of her breasts, the darker circles of her areolae and the tantalising prominence of her nipples. Under the towel that he wore wrapped around his waist, he felt his cock stir. Oh, no, he prayed silently, please don't.

'This champagne is lovely,' Sophie said brightly, her eyes sparkling at him over the rim of her glass. She gulped down the last drop then held her glass out to him. 'Please, sir, can I have some more?'

He grinned at her parody of the famous Dickens character. Crossing the room to pick up the champagne bottle he sat down on the bed beside her and poured out another glassful. Her words were the only similarity between her and the young Oliver Twist, she certainly didn't look like a boy, or smell like one. Inwardly cursing his own weakness, he leaned forward impulsively and dropped a light kiss on her lips.

Hastily, Sophie put down her glass on the bedside table and wrapped her arms tightly around him. She returned his kiss with fervour, her satin-covered breasts pressing into his bare chest. She could feel her nipples harden immediately as a fierce flame of desire suddenly ignited and flared inside her. Her body seemed to melt under the heat, her lips and sex moistening as she engulfed him in the most passionate kiss she had ever experienced.

'Oh, God! I'm so sorry.' She broke away, looking anything but contrite. 'I didn't mean to get you all aroused.'

'How do you—' Chas broke off as he watched her mouth curve into a cheeky smile. Following the line of her gaze he saw that the tip of his erection peeped out endearingly from the gap where his towel had fallen open. 'Whoops!' He tried to cover himself but Sophie's hand stopped him.

'No, don't,' she said, 'I feel very flattered.'

Before Chas could even think of protesting, she insinuated her fingers under the towel and gripped his shaft. After a moment her grasp slackened and she began to rub rhythmically instead. As she bent forward, her hair tumbling around her face, one of her shoulder straps inadvertently slipped down her arm, baring one breast.

Chas felt his gaze riveted by the sight of her naked breast. It looked lush and ripe, the creamy smooth flesh tipped by a hard rosy bud, her nipple framed by a circle of blush-pink puckered skin. With tentative fingers he reached forward and stroked her exposed flesh, delighting in the way the nipple hardened even more as his fingertips brushed across it. A soft moan escaped Sophie's lips.

Bending his head, he caught her nipple between his lips and began to suck gently. This was where his imagination collided with reality, he thought, as he tasted the ripe sweetness of her flesh. His fingers kneaded her breast gently as he sucked, his free hand urgently questing under the thin satin to capture and hold her other breast. He felt faint with pleasure. Her breasts were generously proportioned in comparison to the slenderness of her torso and seemed to spill over his palms as he cupped them.

He moved his mouth to her other breast, capturing the nipple between his lips, suckling gently, then more insistently, pulling her ripe teat right into his mouth and rolling her nipple around on his tongue.

Throwing her head back, Sophie whimpered with pleasure and thrust herself urgently forward. Take me, take all of me, her body language seemed to cry out. Releasing his cock, she allowed her hands to roam feverishly over his torso, her fingertips pinching and rolling his nipples before travelling over his chest and down his sides, then around to skim the damp skin on his back.

She kicked wildly at the sheet and duvet, trying desperately to free her lower body. Sitting back a little, Chas helped her, pulling the bedclothes away from her wriggling body and pushing the meagre scrap of satin up her thighs to expose a delicate triangle of blonde curls. The pink lips of her sex were clearly visible through the fine hairs, a soft, intriguing purse that cried out to be prised open and investigated thoroughly.

Reclining against the pile of pillows behind her, Sophie allowed the hem of her nightgown to travel over her hips, up to her waist. She felt herself trembling with barely contained passion. He was looking at her body with such blatant desire that she felt weak. Too weak even to beg him to touch her where she burned for him the most.

With relief, Sophie realised that her inability to voice her wants didn't matter at all. He could read her mind, interpreting her needs in a way that was both gratifying and deliciously thrilling. No man had ever succeeded in touching her quite the way she wanted him to yet here was Chas, his fingers gently stroking her mound, gradually easing the lips of her sex apart as she allowed her thighs to spread open wider and wider upon the cool linen sheet.

Even through the thick walls of the old house Charlotte could hear the unmistakable sounds of Sophie's pleasure. As her ears encompassed the harsh, then soft groans coming from the room next door she felt herself begin to burn inside. Envy battled with desire as she forced herself to concentrate on her interpretation of the scene currently unfolding.

'Those two certainly sound as though they're having a good time,' Robert said, inclining his head towards the wall that divided their room from Chas'.

Charlotte forced herself to toss her dark head airily. 'They certainly do. Good for them.' The words were like acid on her tongue.

'So, how about us joining in?' he suggested, 'I fancy a bit of a shag, don't you, old girl?'

'Robert, for Christ's sake!'

She hated the way he spoke sometimes. Particularly the way he had taken to calling her 'old girl', as if he was anxious to remind her of their difference in ages. Sitting down in front of the dressing table mirror, Charlotte brushed her hair with brisk, angry strokes, at the same time regarding his reflection dispassionately. He was what her mother and father would have described as a pretty boy.

At twenty-four he was handsome in the classical sense, with a strong, square face featuring a pair of wide-set hazel eyes with finely arched brows, a straight patrician nose and a full, petulant mouth. Unlike his ex-Eton contemporaries, his chin was not a bit weak and bore a vague cleft. His hair was literally his crowning glory: thick, wavy and collar-length it was originally mid-brown but now, thanks to the renowned skills of Nikki Clarke, expertly streaked with various shades of blonde.

As a successful male model, Robert spent more money on his hair and clothes than she did. And that was saying something. Her own career as joint-owner of a thriving art gallery in London's W1 meant she had to look good at all times.

'Are you coming to bed, Charlie, or what, I'm getting cold lounging around here like this.' His tone sounded as petulant as the mouth that uttered the words, she noticed.

'Well, get under the covers then, I'm not stopping you. And it's not as though I haven't seen you in all your glory before.'

Charlotte gave him a mock glare through the glass of the mirror. He was reclining on top of the bed, his long, lithe body totally naked. He looks like an advert for rent boys, she thought unkindly, eyeing his slim, slightly tanned behind as he knelt up on the bed to pull back the green silk bedspread and duvet. Silently she admonished herself. Despite his effeminate, slightly ethereal looks there was certainly nothing homosexual about his behaviour. Between the sheets he was all man. The recollection made her tingle, her sex moistening instantly, soaking the crotch of her pale blue silk-and-lace teddy.

Putting down the brush, she crossed the room in a couple of lithe strides and flung herself energetically on to the bed, straddling him as she landed.

'Take me from behind,' she hissed urgently. 'Do it to me like an animal.'

He grinned, flinging her off him and throwing her onto her stomach. Raising her hips he spent a moment or two smoothing his palms over her buttocks, taking his hands up the length of her spine and then down again, following the curves of her waist and hips.

'You're disgustingly wet, Charlie,' he murmured, parting her labia and sinking two fingers deep inside her. 'Have you been having wicked thoughts? Has Daddy got to smack you for being a naughty girl?'

Waves of hot lust rippled through Charlotte's body. Even though he was younger than her, Robert had the uncanny knack of making her feel as though she were about sixteen years old. Sixteen . . . Trying not to allow her mind to dwell on the significance of that period in her life, she arched her back and thrust her bottom at him urgently.

'Daddy must do whatever he thinks best,' she whispered, deliberately assuming a lisp. ''Cos I've been a very bad girl.'

When the distinctive sound of the first series of smacks echoed through the wall, Sophie stilled Chas with a hand on his shoulder. 'What on earth is going on next door?' she said in a stage whisper. 'It sounds as though Robert's hitting your sister. Or vice versa,' she added, not wishing to sound sexist.

To her surprise Chas raised his head from her breast and gave her a wolfish grin. 'He probably is, Charlie's into that sort of thing.'

'What, physical abuse? She should tell him to sling his hook.' Sophie couldn't help sounding as outraged as she felt.

'Don't look like that,' Chas said, 'she likes it.'

For a moment or two Sophie allowed his words to sink in, then the light of understanding came on her head. 'Oh, I see. They're like that, are they?'

'Like what?'

'You know? Kinky.'

He laughed aloud at her remark. She looked so horrified he couldn't help himself. 'Oh, Sophie. You are wonderful!'

'Am I?' She gazed innocently up at him from under her long fair lashes. Without makeup she looked younger than ever, barely in her mid-teens let alone her twenties.

'Yes, you are.' Chas allowed his hands to travel down the length of her torso, skimming her breasts, stomach and belly. He slid his palms under her buttocks, squeezing and separating them. 'Turn over,' he said huskily.

As Charlotte felt Robert's hard cock driving into her, she allowed her mind to wander of its own accord. Unlike many women, she didn't need fantasies to fuel her arousal. Reality was enough. Half a lifetime ago she had enjoyed her first sexual experience. It was a memory that had stayed with her ever since, the sensations so strong in her mind that she could instantly retrace her steps back in time. Back to the grounds of this very house where, on his sixteenth birthday, Chas had pitched his tent and changed her life forever.

Chapter Six

The two-man tent had been Chas' main birthday present from their parents or, rather, their father and his mother. He had been overjoyed when he opened the huge box. One of his main passions at the time was hiking around Bickley Manor's surrounding countryside and he had often bemoaned the fact that he couldn't go too far afield because he had to get home before darkness fell. The tent would change all that, give him a taste of freedom that was hitherto unknown.

He had immediately erected it in the paddock. His mother had refused to entertain the idea of tent pegs making holes in the carefully tended lawns. Charlotte remembered her brother announcing that he intended to spend that very night in it, sleeping under the stars and she had begged to be allowed to share the experience.

Permission was duly granted and she and Chas had set about amassing all the things they would need to make their adventure a little more comfortable: camp beds and sleeping bags, sandwiches and a flask of hot chocolate, even a portable TV set that worked off a car battery. Their father had laughed at this, saying there was nothing like a bit of luxury when it came to 'roughing it'.

At first, she found the experience exciting but quickly became bored. The war film Chas had chosen to watch on TV was not her cup of tea at all and she bemoaned the fact that she had brought nothing along to read. The tent was lit on the inside by a couple of lanterns which hung from the ridge pole and she contemplated running back up to the house in her oversized, Snoopy T-shirt to get the teenage romance she had been reading.

Finally, sick of his sister's complaints, Chas reached into his pillowcase and drew out a slightly crumpled glossy magazine.

'Here, read this,' he said, throwing it casually on to her stomach.

It was a warm night and she had soon become too hot inside the sleeping bag. Unzipping it she had peeled back the top cover and lain on her back, the hem of her short nightie only just covering her decency. Picking up the magazine she gazed idly at it until she realised what it was, then her eyes widened and she began to flick through the pages with a mounting sense of horrified excitement.

It was a girlie mag. Or porn, as her father would have called it disdainfully. All the girls photographed inside were young and beautiful, with full, well-developed figures. Most of them started off wearing a little clothing but the last few photographs in each set were very explicit, the girls posing with their legs wide open, showing off everything they'd got.

'Chas, this is disgusting!' Charlotte said, pretending to be more outraged than she actually felt. If the truth be known, she was feeling more than a little warm from looking at the photographs. She also felt a bit worried. Did the fact that she liked looking at these pictures of naked women mean that she was a lesbian? 'Chas, did you hear what I said? What are you doing with a magazine like this?'

'Oh, I've got stacks of them,' he said airily, hardly glancing at her. 'This is just my latest.'

Charlotte opened the magazine again and began to turn the pages more slowly. She paused to read some of the reader's letters. True accounts, they claimed, but she had difficulty believing that sensible adults could possibly get up to such things. It was disgusting. Perverted. Slowly, without meaning to, she allowed her left hand to drift to her thighs, her fingertips inching up under the hem of her nightdress until they brushed the tightly compressed lips of her sex.

Every now and again she glanced at Chas. His eyes were glued to the TV screen, watching enthralled as soldiers clad in jungle greens yelled at each other and shot wildly at the Vietcong. Carefully, she pushed her fingers between her fleshy lips and began to stimulate the hard little bud underneath.

Her breathing grew shallower as her excitement mounted. She had never actually allowed anyone else to do this to her. In fact, she had only discovered this particular pleasure by accident a couple of years earlier. Now it had become part of her bedtime ritual, a way of giving herself comfort and enjoyment that worked better than ten cups of cocoa at making her feel sleepy.

'Charlie?'

Through the haze of lust that enveloped her, Charlotte heard Chas speaking her name. Blushing furiously, she whipped her hand out from under her nightie. With her heart hammering behind her ribs she concentrated on staring at the canvas ceiling.

'What?'

She heard Chas switch off the TV set and sensed him moving. Finally, turning her head on the pillow, she noticed he was sitting upright on the edge of his camp bed staring at her in amazement.

'You were doing it, weren't you?' he said, still staring. 'You were touching yourself up.'

'Don't, that's a disgusting thing to say.' She made to pull the top of her sleeping bag over her but Chas' hand stopped her.

'Stay like that,' he murmured huskily. 'Let me watch you doing it.'

'No!' She struggled to sit up, her dark hair tumbling around her face and shoulders. Annoyed, she flicked her hair out of the way. As she moved her breasts jiggled under the thin T-shirt material and she watched as his eyes moved to her chest. 'Why are you looking at me like that?' she demanded, feeling the hateful warmth of another blush stealing over her. Clasping her hand to her burning throat, she tried to glare at him. 'Don't do it. I don't like it.'

'Yes, you do,' Chas said thickly. 'You love it. All you girls do.'

'And I supposed you know, Mr Casanova?'

He assumed a supercilious expression that annoyed her. 'I do, as a matter of fact.' He laughed. 'Christ, Charlie. You don't think I'm still a virgin, do you?'

Charlie gazed at him wide-eyed. She didn't know what to think. She supposed she had assumed . . . Well, it wasn't the sort of thing one went around boasting about. Come to think of it, that was exactly what boys did, boast about their conquests, either real or fictional.

'Don't give me that crap,' she said crossly. 'Who'd look at you?'

He chuckled softly, annoying her even more. 'Your friend Penny for one.'

'Oh, come on, Penny?' She started to laugh. Now he really had stretched the bounds of credibility too far. Penny was her best friend. They shared everything and yet she had never breathed a word about any sexual encounters with Chas. Surely, if it were true, Penny would have been unable to keep it to herself?

Despite his sister's blatant look of disbelief he nodded. 'Yes, Penny, several times. And others. Linda Penhaligon, Zoe Lampton, Susie Barclay . . .'

'Oh, well, Sinful Susie,' Charlotte scoffed. Suddenly it occurred to her that he was telling the truth.

'What, er, what's it like then, sex?' she mumbled. Unable to meet his gaze, she turned her head and stared back at the canvas ceiling.

'You mean you really don't know?' His voice was soft and questioning, with no hint of derision. Slowly, she shook her head from side to side. 'Do you want to find out?'

His tone of voice offered an inducement that she felt

powerless to resist. Moments later, a couple of fingertips skimmed the tops of her thighs and she gave an involuntary shiver. She didn't trust herself to speak. Her body was already betraying her, her nipples hardening under her nightie, her vagina moistening as she felt his fingers creep up her leg, describing small circles on her goosepimple-covered skin as they moved inexorably towards their goal. She wanted to tell him to stop. That what he was doing was wrong. But she couldn't. She couldn't because her curiosity was aroused even more than her body.

Still staring at the tented roof above her she felt a cool draught as his hands lifted her nightie up to her waist, then higher, until her breasts were uncovered as well. She shivered then shook her head when Chas asked her if she was cold.

'Not cold, scared,' she said hoarsely. 'We shouldn't be doing this.'

'Do you want me to stop?' Chas' hands stroked her breasts, his fingers grasping her nipples and pinching them lightly.

Feeling a sharp dart of arousal travel from each nipple to pierce her womb Charlotte let out a long moan, 'Nooo . . . !'

She felt a certain detachment as she watched his hands release her breasts to travel the length of her torso. He paused at her thighs, gradually inching them apart. Charlotte bit her bottom lip. Now she imagined she looked like one of those girls in the photos, her legs spread wide, her private parts revealed to his interested gaze. Oh, God. She moaned again as a trickle of moisture seeped from her exposed sex.

'You have a lovely body,' Chas murmured as he gently parted her outer labia, 'so slim, so feminine.'

She shuddered as she felt his warm breath caress her inner flesh. Then his finger touched her *there*, on her secret pleasure bud and she jumped, as though she had been stung.

'Nice, isn't it?' he said, in a way that made her wonder if he could feel the warm ripples of pleasure coursing through her.

Slowly, he started to stroke her, his fingertips travelling up and down the groove between her labia, pausing every now and then to brush the core of her arousal. Her throat was too dry, too closed up to speak and so she nodded, watching with heavy-lidded eyes as he caught her bud with his fingertips and began rolling it between them. He tugged it gently, coaxing it from its hood. She knew all about her clitoris. Knew how it was formed and how it responded to different types of stimuli. With the help of her makeup mirror she had often studied her own body in all its magnified glory.

To her surprise, Chas took his hand away abruptly and moved to the front of the tent. Reaching through the closed flaps he plucked a blade of couch grass and held it above her with a wickedly triumphant expression on his face.

'Remember how you used to always tease me when we were children?' he said, spreading her labia wide apart with the fingers of one hand. 'Well, now it's my turn to tease you.' Deftly he flicked the tip of the blade of grass over her clitoris.

'Ah, oh no!' Charlotte struggled to sit up. Reclining on her forearms, she watched as he tantalised her swollen bud with the soft, seeded end of the grass. 'Oh, God, yes!'

She sank back down again, feeling the distinctive warmth of arousal creeping over her. It started in the tiny place where he teased her and rippled outwards, spreading throughout her whole body like a forest fire before converging back into that same spot. Moments later she felt her desire explode. It was the most powerful sensation she had ever experienced and for that reason she felt profoundly grateful to him.

As her climax started to recede she felt his fingers exploring inside her, stroking the velvety walls of her vagina – yes, she knew how she felt there too – inciting another strange feeling. His knowing fingertips had found something she hadn't, another secret pleasure button just behind her pubic bone. To her amazement, she felt her arousal mounting again.

'Please, oh, please.' She tossed her head from side to side on the pillow, feeling her body melt from the inside, dissolving over his fingers. She ground her pelvis urgently, suddenly feeling overwhelmed by the desire to feel something more substantial inside her.

'I'm not going to fuck you, it wouldn't be right.' His voice sounded muted, as though it came from somewhere far off in the distance.

She was disappointed and yet relieved all at the same time. Much later she would wonder at his strange set of morals. Ones which allowed him to think it was perfectly all right to caress his step-sister intimately yet not take the next logical step.

Remembering how it had felt to have Chas' fingers probing inside her that night brought Charlotte back to the present with an erotic jolt. Robert was still thrusting manfully, totally oblivious to the fact that her mind had been somewhere else.

That was why she preferred to be taken from behind. It meant that he couldn't see her face. For some wicked reason not even clear to herself, she didn't like him to watch her enjoying herself. Didn't want him to see the way he made her face contort with pleasure as she came. He was already too cocky by far and so she denied him the satisfaction of watching the results of his efforts. It gave her some vestige of authority over him, kept him wondering, never quite sure how much she really cared for him. If he knew the truth, how much she really desired him, she would never, ever be able to call the shots again.

Chas heard Charlotte cry out. It did strange things to him, hearing that scream of pleasure. Jolted his memory banks back to the one night of his life that he didn't care to dwell upon if he could help it. He glanced down at Sophie.

Eyes closed, mouth wide open in a silent scream of her own, she seemed oblivious to the goings on in the bedroom next door. Her legs were wrapped tightly around his waist, her strong internal muscles pulling him deeper inside her. He revelled in the feel of her body, the wide-open wetness of her vagina, the methodic rasping of her hard clitoris against his pubic bone, the soft lushness of her breasts which were now flushed with the rising heat of her desire.

On her part, Sophie felt as though she had died and gone to heaven. Chas' lovemaking was so sure, so skilled that she couldn't deny the pleasure he gave her for a moment. His beautiful cock filled her up and touched her inside in a way that she had never been touched before. It was more than merely a physical thing. It felt spiritual, as though his mind caressed hers as surely as his body tantalised her and drove her right to the outer limits of her endurance.

Their coupling felt both erotic and esoteric. A coming together of minds and bodies. Inside her lust-laden mind, she almost giggled. They had managed to come together twice already.

She awoke the next morning surprised to discover that she and Chas had actually slept at all. Their lovemaking seemed to have gone on all night, a blissful, wonderful period of eternity, when time seemed to stand still. As far as she was concerned, nothing else had existed outside the draped sanctuary of Chas' sumptuous bed.

The bed was exquisite but thankfully sturdy, she mused to herself, recalling how vigorously they had fucked at times. Loving caresses interspersed with wild, almost bestial lust. Feeling the lure of Chas' divine body overwhelm her again she reached out to him, only to discover that his side of the wide four-poster was empty.

With a sense of profound regret, she lay back and allowed her hands to investigate the swollen folds of her sex instead. Perhaps it was just as well Chas was not within ravishing distance, she felt distinctly tender down there. The flesh still puffy and sensitive to the touch. Oh, well, in a moment she would get up and go in search of some breakfast. For some reason she felt extremely ravenous.

She found everyone waiting for her in the dining room. Or at least, she sensed they were waiting for her. Covered silver dishes formed a serried rank down the centre of the table yet in front of each of them sat an empty plate.

'Sorry, am I late?' she said brightly, taking the vacant seat next to Chas.

He reached for her hand and squeezed it. 'It doesn't matter, although we were just about to start without you.'

Across the table, Penny leaned sideways and whispered something to Charlotte who was seated beside her.

'Come on, Penny, play fair,' Chas said, 'no secrets please.'

Penny pouted at him as Charlotte glanced up.

'She just said WATS, that's all.' His sister betrayed her friend with a smirk, pronouncing the acronym as a whole word.

Sophie looked at Chas in confusion as he burst out laughing. 'What does WATS mean?'

Charlotte sighed. 'It means Well And Truly Shagged, darling.'

It took a moment for her words to sink in, then Sophie blushed. 'Actually,' she managed to retort, 'right now I think it means Well And Truly Starving.' She was gratified that this time Robert and Tim both laughed as well as Chas.

'Well, that told you, didn't it, old girl,' Robert said, winking broadly at Charlotte who glared back him.

'Less of the *old*, Robert if you don't mind.'

He grinned. 'Oh, I don't, but you obviously do.' He was seated on the other side of Sophie and now he murmured conspiratorially. 'My lovely wife hates to be reminded that she's ten years older than me.'

As Charlotte's glare intensified, Sophie gazed at him in amazement. 'Really? That makes you two years younger than me. I could have sworn you and Charlotte were the same age.'

Little did she know, her candid response succeeded in instantly thawing out Charlotte's previous hostility towards her.

'Well, thank you, Sophie dear,' Charlotte said. Her lips

formed the first genuine smile Sophie had seen her make. 'It's nice to meet someone with proper manners.' She leaned across the table. 'Penny and I were thinking of going into town to do some last minute prezzie buying, would you like to come with us?'

'Yes, thanks, I'd love to.' Sophie felt amazed and not a little honoured by Charlotte's unexpected gesture of kindness. She glanced at Chas. 'Do you mind, er, darling, if I go with them?'

He smiled. 'No, of course not, you're here to enjoy yourself remember.'

Sophie didn't know if it was her imagination but his expression seemed to be trying to convey something meaningful. She blushed again, remembering how much enjoyment she'd experienced the night before.

'Oh, I am,' she whispered softly, so that only he could catch her words. 'And I plan to enjoy myself a whole lot more.'

His answering squeeze on her thigh was all the confirmation she needed that he felt exactly the same way.

To Sophie's surprise, accompanying Penny and Charlotte on a shopping trip was not nearly as horrendous as she'd imagined. In fact, she had quite good fun choosing small but appropriate gifts for her new companions. She bought several things for Chas: a couple of books on art, some liqueur chocolates, a pure silk tie – although she wasn't sure that he actually owned a proper shirt – and a black lacy basque and stockings. Of course, she didn't expect him to actually put them on himself but she had a strong suspicion that he might appreciate it if she wore them for him on Christmas night.

Being Christmas Eve the small market town was packed with shoppers and so, by mutual consent, the three women decided not to linger once they'd got what they came for. Back at Bickley Manor they found the double doors of the front entrance wide open and just inside they could make out the decorated branches of a huge Christmas tree.

Charlotte immediately bounded up the front steps with

uncharacteristic enthusiasm, while Sophie and Penny lagged behind as they each juggled numerous carrier bags.

As she stepped through the doorway Sophie stopped and stared around in awe. The huge marble-floored entrance hall was magnificent. Facing her was a wide oak staircase that ended at a galleried landing and hanging on all four pale lemon walls were dozens of huge paintings. To her inexperienced eye they looked like priceless old masters. Some of them were portraits, the subjects wearing clothing that dated back several centuries and others were of horses and farm animals: huge, bloated pigs, shaggy, horned sheep and well-muscled cattle.

'Like it?' Chas startled Sophie by coming up behind her and grabbing her waist.

'I love it,' she enthused, her gaze now taking in the huge Scots pine that glistened and sparkled with hundreds of white fairy lights and yards of silver tinsel and streamers. 'It all looks magnificent.'

Chas smiled. 'Magnificent, now there's a word. Do you hear that, chaps?' he called out to Robert and Tim who appeared from behind the Christmas tree. 'Sophie thinks our efforts are magnificent.'

'And so they are,' Tim said, taking a step back to admire their handiwork. 'So magnificent that I think they call for champagne.' Walking over to a long side table, he produced, with a theatrical flourish, a bottle that had been nestling in an ice bucket. Also arranged on the table were six crystal flutes. Topping up all the glasses, Tim walked over to Sophie and Chas and handed them each a glass, while Penny, Charlotte and Robert all helped themselves.

'OK, here's the toast,' Chas said, raising his glass in the air and winking at Sophie. 'To Christmas. Goodwill to all men, especially our lovely ladies.'

'I'll drink to that,' Robert said. 'Bottoms up.'

To everyone's surprise, Charlotte blushed.

After they had drained their glasses, Chas took Sophie's hand. 'Dump those bags,' he said softly, 'I want to take you outside and show you something.'

Sophie felt her heartbeat quicken as she allowed him to lead her out of the front entrance and around the east side of the house. There she found herself confronted by a long stable block. She could see Rachel's familiar face peering over one of the doors and in the stall next door a very pretty looking grey popped her head out and whickered softly.

'This is Annabelle,' Chas said, reaching up to stroke the grey. 'I bought her for you this morning.'

'For me?' Sophie looked at him in astonishment. 'How can you just go out and buy me a horse, I'm only going to be here for a week?'

He glanced at her. 'Maybe,' he said, 'I'm not exactly planning to throw you out in the New Year. Anyway,' he added briskly, 'what I mean is, she's yours whenever you want to ride her. She can stay here and whenever you come up to the cottage you can take her out and give her some exercise.'

Sophie felt overwhelmed by his generosity. 'That's, er, quite a gift.' She reached up and patted Annabelle's forehead, then combed her fingers through the soft white mane between the horse's ears. 'She is absolutely lovely. Can we go out for a ride now?'

'I don't see why not. You're dressed for it.' Chas glanced at the beige jodhpur-style leggings that she was wearing along with a thick cream jumper, dark brown leather jacket and matching ankle boots. 'I'll just get you a hard hat.'

A tack room was built on to the stable block and he emerged moments later carrying two hard hats and a saddle and bridle for Annabelle.

'I prefer to ride Rachel bareback,' he said, opening the stable door and proceeding to equip the mare in the manner to which she was accustomed. 'Although, as I recall, you already know that.'

Sophie smiled at him, remembering her ride from the cottage to Bickley Manor. Was it really only two days ago? It seemed like light years. Another lifetime. With a little help from Chas, she swung herself up into the saddle and slipped her feet into the stirrups, heels down, back straight. Picking up the rein, she looped it and held it lightly in her hands. It seemed ages since she last rode a horse all by herself.

Looping a bridle around Rachel's head, Chas led her out from the stable to stand beside a mounting block. Within moments he too was seated and ready to go. Turning his head to grin at Sophie, he led the way around to the front of the house and up the gravel drive to the lane. Instead of continuing as far as Sophie's cottage, he veered off to the left, following a bridle path that seemed to go on and on forever into the misty distance.

They trotted along in silence for a while, then on an unspoken signal began to canter. After a couple of miles, Chas called something over his shoulder. His words were whipped away by the cold wind but Sophie followed his pointing finger. The track he chose led off to the right, towards a small copse. When they reached the outer trees, Chas stopped and dismounted. Sophie followed suit, tethering Annabelle's rein to a low branch.

'I thought we could look for some holly,' Chas said, nodding in the direction of the gloomy cavern of trees. 'Are you game?'

'Of course I am.'

Sophie strode up to him and took his proffered hand. It felt warm and natural, as comforting as a glove. All at once the recollection of the same hand touching her naked body the night before whispered through her mind, inciting a shudder of anticipation. Tonight was Christmas Eve, a special night by anyone's estimation. This year though, nestled in Chas' bed with his hard, virile body pressed against hers, it would be the best Christmas Eve she'd ever had.

Although it was winter, the floor of the copse was obscured here and there by a thick, thigh-high carpet of ferns. Littering the hard, muddy patches in between the ferns were discarded acorns and their caps and small twigs which snapped under their trampling feet. The sounds echoed eerily around the dense thatch of trees which was shrouded in mist and a strange half-light.

Sophie watched her breath emerge from her mouth in small puffs as she picked her way delicately through the undergrowth, mindful of the fact that her ankle had only just recovered from its sprain.

'Do you mind if we stop a moment?' she asked after a while, 'These boots weren't really made for walking.'

'Oh, God, Sophie, I'm sorry,' Chas said. 'I forgot about your leg and everything. Do you want to go back?'

Sophie laughed, pausing for a moment to hear the distinctive sound echo away to nothing. 'Not at all. And don't worry about my leg. It's fine now. I'm just a little footsore from tramping around the shops with your sister and Penny.'

'Were they OK?' Chas eyed her carefully as he guided her to a fallen tree. It was just the right height for sitting on. 'They didn't say anything to upset you?'

'No, of course not, why should they?' Sophie shook her head and gazed up at the canopy of bare, silvery branches above them.

Chas thought the other two women had plenty of reasons and certainly enough ammunition to make Sophie doubt her burgeoning relationship with him, but he kept his thoughts to himself. Instead, he pulled Sophie into his arms and began to kiss her.

She returned his kiss with all the fervour she could muster. It felt good to be sitting beside him in the mystical silence of the copse. Beneath her, the fallen tree felt broad and sturdy, certainly broad enough to lie upon. To Chas' obvious surprise she disengaged herself from his embrace, leaned forward and began to unlace her boots. Kicking them off, she stood up and began to pull down her leggings.

'What are you doing?' Chas stared at her in amazement as he watched the familiar, creamy flesh of her buttocks appear, then the soft, slightly reddened pouch of her sex as she bent forward from the waist and pulled her leggings right off.

Underneath she wore no underwear.

Ignoring him, Sophie folded her trousers to make a pillow for her head, then lay down full length on the fallen tree. With little regard for modesty she allowed her legs to fall open and dangle either side of the silvery wood.

'I'm being inventive,' she said. She smiled up at him. 'Hurry up, it's freezing.'

Chas didn't need any further encouragement. The blatant offering of her body draped over the tree, was too much for him to ignore. Unzipping his fly he was pleased to discover that just the sight of her half-naked body had made him go hard. Straddling the tree, he raised her hips onto his thighs and probed the moist entrance to her body with the tip of his cock.

'Oh, God. Oh, yes please,' Sophie cried. She urged her pelvis towards him, flexing her hips so that her thighs spread even wider apart.

Just for a moment he delighted in the sight of her sex blossoming before his very eyes, the soft rosy flesh of her outer labia slowly opening outwards to reveal the juicy inner folds and the creamy offering of her vagina. Taking a deep breath, he grasped her hips and thrust inside her.

Mindful of the cold and the urgency of her cries, he didn't attempt to delay his orgasm. Letting go of one of her hips, he spread his fingers across her sex, opening her out even more and gently stroking her clitoris. The contrast between the softness of her flesh beneath his fingertips and the rough texture of the bark rubbing his inner thighs was so acute he thought it was an experience he would never forget.

In all the years he had lived in the country he had never taken a woman in this way. In the open air, in lush green fields and on riverbanks yes, but never in a situation such as this. It seemed so earthy, primeval somehow, as if he and Sophie were really communing with nature as they fucked. Gradually, he sensed her pleasure rising, watched her face contort with ecstasy as she peaked and felt the rhythmic contractions of her vaginal muscles drawing the very life out of him it seemed.

His cries echoed into the still wintry air as he came, the harsh, unleashed sound bouncing off the trees and startling hidden flocks of birds. A couple of wild fallow deer skittered across the clearing beside them, their mottled rumps disappearing into a thicket of ferns. He sighed with pleasure, feeling the intensity of his orgasm leave him as quickly as it arrived. It wasn't just his imagination. Fucking Sophie was the most natural thing in the world to do.

They returned to the house looking a little sheepish. Sophie's hair was dishevelled, with bits of bark still falling out of it as they rounded the drive and trotted sedately up to the stable block.

'Go in and have a hot bath,' Chas ordered, taking Annabelle's rein as Sophie dismounted. 'I'll just see to the horses then come and join you.'

His offer seemed too good to refuse. Walking into Chas' room, Sophie was relieved to see that someone had been kind enough to bring her carrier bags upstairs and dump them on his bed. Stowing them quickly away in an empty drawer, she made a mental note to find half an hour of seclusion so that she could wrap all her gifts without anyone seeing them.

Turning on the huge gold-plated taps, she watched the deep tub fill up with steaming water. Then she quickly stripped off her clothes and climbed into the bath, immersing herself in the soothing water. Mindful that Chas might join her, she didn't bother to add any perfumed bubble bath and instead allowed clouds of steam to envelop and soothe her aching body. Tomorrow, she would pay for her ride on Annabelle, she thought, idly splashing the water over her breasts. No doubt she had used muscles which had long since forgotten the rigours of horse riding.

Chas turned up about fifteen minutes later, carrying two steaming mugs of tea. 'I thought you might appreciate this more than a glass of wine,' he said, sitting down on the rolled edge of the bath.

She took one of the mugs from him and sipped the tea gratefully. 'You were right. Now I feel warm right through again.'

'How warm?' He gave her a meaningful wink.

'Very warm.' Spreading her legs as far as the wide tub would allow, she caressed herself. 'Why don't you join me?'

Chas smiled and stood up. 'In my experience baths are not the best places for making love. I've got a better idea. You'll find me in the bedroom when you're ready.'

Sophie assumed that he would be in bed waiting for her when she emerged from the bathroom. Forcing herself to wait ten whole minutes before climbing out of the tub and wrapping herself in a towel as she had done the night before, she opened the door and hovered for a moment on the threshold, her eyes taking in the scene that confronted her. Once again, Chas had succeeded in surprising her.

Chapter Seven

Almost identical to the green bedroom, Chas' room also featured a large open fireplace. In the grate a stack of logs crackled and glowed red and orange, sending sparks shooting up the wide stone chimney. On the floor in front of the fireplace was a thick antique rug, patterned in shades of red, brown and cream and it was here that Chas now lay, his body as naked as the day he had been born.

Sophie chuckled. He lay on his stomach, his legs bent at the knees, feet kicking idly in the air in the classic 'naked on a bearskin rug' pose.

'That looks wonderful,' she said, dropping the towel instantly, 'mind if I join you?'

She knelt beside him, feeling the warmth from the fire caress her naked body. Arching her back she felt the damp ends of her hair tickling the upper swell of her buttocks and she sighed with undisguised pleasure as Chas' hand stroked idly across her stomach and over her hip. His palm slid around and grasped her bottom, suddenly pulling her towards him and making her lose her balance. She fell across him in an ungainly sprawl as he rolled over onto his back and lay still for a moment, gasping with laughter. Her face was pressed into his right shoulder and now she began to kiss it, her lips and tongue following the line of his collarbone.

Squirming, she lay full length on top of him, lips pressed into the dip at the base of his throat as their toes teased each other. Her breasts were squashed into his chest and as she raised herself up onto her elbows, she moved slightly from side to side so that her breasts swung like pendulums, her nipples brushing his warm skin. He was covered with a thin sheen of perspiration, the faint, musky scent tantalising her nostrils, sending an urgent primeval message down to her womb.

Like a cat she licked him, laving his body with the flat of her tongue, taking long, sweeping strokes and every so often smacking her lips theatrically as she licked the salt from them.

'Mm, you taste so good,' she murmured as she worked her way lower down his body. 'I want to taste all of you.'

At his navel she paused to flick the pointed end of her tongue around and around the outer edge before plunging her tongue into the shallow depression. Lower still she pressed her face into his belly, nuzzling him for a moment before allowing her lips to follow the faint line of hairs that arrowed down to his groin.

His cock nudged her chin. Half awake it lay, slightly curved, upon its nest of dark silky hair.

'I think you've killed it,' Chas murmured wryly. 'It's not used to so much exertion.'

Scrambling between his slightly spread thighs, Sophie smiled knowingly up at him. 'Where there's life there's hope. I do believe Nurse Sophie can do something with that.' Kneeling up, she used her finger and thumb to raise his stiffening member and move it from side to side, regarding it thoughtfully as though it were a medical specimen. 'Yes,' she added. 'Just as I thought. Plenty of scope there.'

Placing one palm flat down by the side of his hip to steady herself, Sophie suddenly gripped his cock around the shaft and squeezed gently. With indecent haste it sprang into life. Throwing Chas a cheeky grin she lowered her head and engulfed him completely with her mouth, sliding her lips up and down the shaft and pausing every now and then to flick her tongue around his swollen glans.

Cupping the back of his head in his hands, Chas tilted his chin and gazed down the length of his body. His senses were instantly stirred by the sensation of Sophie's mouth enticing his cock into full erectness and the sight of her lush breasts swinging tantalisingly over his upper thighs.

Her hair swept delicately over his stomach as she moved her head, and every so often a nipple brushed the sensitive flesh of his inner thighs, causing him to draw in his breath sharply. Desire coursed through him and seemed to gather in his groin. He felt his balls tighten as his arousal mounted and he sensed the blood engorging his cock, pushing it towards explosion point.

With perfect timing, Sophie released his cock from her mouth, straddled his hips and guided his throbbing member inside the hot channel of her vagina instead. It was a different sensation but every bit as pleasurable, and Chas groaned deeply as he felt her velvety walls engulf him. Slowly, she began to move her hips, rocking and rotating rhythmically, her movements becoming faster and faster as her own passion mounted.

As she leaned forward to rest her weight on her palms he reached up and cupped her breasts, squeezing them gently in time to her movements. She was grinding herself against him, rubbing her clitoris against his pubic bone. Small whimpers issued from between her slightly parted lips as she concentrated on smiling hazily into his eyes.

Although his eyelids felt heavy he refused to give into the urge to close them. He wanted to see her come, to witness her taking her pleasure. His fingertips sought her nipples and pinched them gently. The simple act seemed to be Sophie's undoing. Suddenly, she bucked wildly on top of him and screamed, her face and body frozen in a rictus of ecstasy until she suddenly became limp. It was as though her orgasm had drained the life out of her and she had nothing left to give him. Rolling Sophie over on to her back Chas thrust urgently inside her, giving in to his own pleasure now that she had taken hers.

For a long time they lay together in front of the fire, their bodies entwined. Gradually their breathing slowed and each felt the beguiling tug of languor. They were awoken by a sharp rap on the bedroom door and Penny's strident tones announcing that supper was about to be served.

Grumbling slightly, they both disentangled themselves, allowing a moment for a deep passionate kiss before rising stiffly to their feet. Sophie stretched, her fingertips reaching to the ceiling, her back arching.

'God, you're gorgeous,' Chas said with a lazy smile. 'I can't get enough of you.'

'Same goes for me.' She paused to run her hands thoughtfully over the smooth curves of her torso, her hands lingering at her breasts to cup them. 'I feel as though I've just come alive. Woken up from half a lifetime of slumber like Sleeping Beauty.'

'And am I the handsome prince who woke you, Sleeping Beauty?' Chas asked, giving her a wolfish grin.

She shivered, feeling the full impact of his blatantly lascivious gaze. 'Ooh, yes! What do you think?'

Reaching into her open suitcase, she pulled out a long-sleeved, ankle-length dress in dark blue jersey. The dress buttoned all the way down the front and had a scooped neckline that just showed off the slightest hint of cleavage when she put it on.

'You'll notice that I'm not bothering with any underwear,' she said nonchalantly.

'Oh, bloody hell, how am I supposed to concentrate on food and small talk when I know your body is lurking with delicious availability under that meagre covering?' Chas rolled his eyes theatrically and laughed along with Sophie's soft chuckle.

Stooping to slip a pair of navy court shoes on her bare feet, she glanced provocatively over her shoulder. 'Provided you don't let the others see you, you can touch me wherever and whenever you like.' Picking up her hairbrush she winked at Chas' reflection in the mirror.

Predictably, Sophie thought, Chas opted to wear a clean pair of jeans which he teamed with an emerald green brushed cotton shirt that seemed to make his eyes sparkle an even deeper blue. Pulling on a pair of socks and cowboy boots, he straightened up again and held out his hand.

'Come on, Sleeping Beauty, your courtiers await you.'

Once again, everyone was seated around the dining table. This time the damask-covered table was laid with the finest plain white porcelain edged in gold leaf, and silver cutlery that gleamed richly in the candle light. Red and green candles had been chosen to add a festive air now that Christmas was officially upon them and generous swags of greenery – spruce, berry-laden holly and variegated ivy – decorated the wide stone mantle over the fireplace and the sills of each of the two huge windows that occupied the far wall. The *pièce de résistance* was another fir tree, smaller than the one in the main hall but every bit as decorative.

'Oh, this all looks so lovely, who did it?' Sophie gazed around the large room with undisguised delight. Her nostrils quivered to the sweet scent of fresh pine.

Tim smiled. 'It was a joint effort. We all took a hand in it.'

Seeing the holly reminded Chas that he and Sophie hadn't actually got around to picking any as he'd originally intended when they stopped at the small copse. With an inner smile he recalled the events that had distracted them.

'Sorry about not being around this afternoon,' he said, taking his place at the table. 'Sophie and I went for a ride and got so frozen through that we had to warm ourselves up with hot baths and things.'

Penny smirked. 'I don't have to stretch my imagination too much to guess what the *things* were. We heard you two moaning and groaning like Marley's ghost.'

Oh, God! Sophie went bright red and busied herself with unfolding her napkin and smoothing it across her lap. When she finally dared to glance up she realised that the others were unconcernedly helping themselves to supper.

Unlike their makeshift meal of the evening before, this evening's spread was definitely home cooked. Mrs Lavender had thoughtfully brought across a huge beef casserole from her cottage on the Bickley Manor estate. And to go with it were light-as-a-feather dumplings, crispy potatoes gratin and several kinds of vegetables, all cooked to perfection.

'I always said Mrs L was a treasure,' Charlotte said, helping herself to a child-sized portion of the food.

'Is that all you're going to eat?' Robert asked her. 'It's hardly enough to keep a fly alive.'

'Watching my figure, darling,' she responded, patting her flat stomach indulgently.

'You know what Ma would have said if she were still alive, don't you, Charlie?' Chas glanced across the table at his sister who raised a quizzical eyebrow. 'Time you were eating for two.'

Penny snorted into her claret.

'Oh, balls to all that, little brother,' Charlotte said dismissively. 'Robert and I don't want babies cluttering up the place. We're blissfully happy as we are, aren't we, darling?'

Looking anything but blissfully happy, Robert managed a nod.

Charlotte reached up and ruffled his hair. 'Don't mind him, he's just got the sulks because I didn't want to play doctors and nurses this afternoon.'

'Oh, Charlotte, for Christ's sake!' Robert brushed her hand away angrily. 'Do you have to tell everyone our private business?'

Sophie couldn't help noticing that Chas' sister looked totally unconcerned by her husband's behaviour.

'You should know as well as I do by now' – Charlotte paused to pick up her wine glass and take a sip from it – 'that nothing remains secret in this house for very long. Isn't that so, Chas?'

Chas coughed and mumbled something unintelligible. Glancing at him, her expression curious, Sophie couldn't help noticing he seemed horribly embarrassed by whatever it was that Charlotte had intimated. They were all in on it, she thought, glancing from face to face. Penny, predictably, wore a knowing smirk, while Tim and Robert both looked distinctly uncomfortable.

'Care to enlighten me?' Sophie said airily.

Chas' expression darkened. 'Not really.' He reached forward and picked up the ladle that lay beside the huge casserole. 'We should get stuck into this before it all goes cold.'

Sophie helped herself to some of the stew but it seemed she ate almost mechanically. She felt unaccountably hurt by the knowledge that secrets – or *a* secret – were being kept from her and that Chas obviously didn't trust her enough to let her in on them so that she could make up her own mind. His cryptic behaviour seemed to clash with their previous intimacy and left her with a hollow sensation in her stomach that no amount of food or wine could eliminate.

Anxious to dispel the unwelcome feeling, she found herself drinking copious amounts of the rich red claret, then several glasses of sweeter white wine with dessert before finally rounding the meal off with a couple of cognacs. By the time she stood up to accompany the others into the TV room, her head was reeling.

Chas caught her by the arm as she swayed. Her legs felt insubstantial, her body weak.

'Hello, looks like someone's been hitting the bottle a bit too hard this evening,' he joked. Then he frowned as he caught Sophie's expression, unnervingly stony despite the fuzzy look in her eyes. 'What's up?' As the others filed out of the room he detained her, holding her arm lightly but firmly. 'I said, what's up, Sophie?' he repeated when she didn't answer.

'I don't like being the odd one out,' she mumbled, unable to meet his eye.

'Odd one out, what are you talking about?'

Suddenly, she glared at him. 'You know. All those little secrets that everyone except me seems to know about.' Her speech was slightly slurred, her lips numb as she forced herself to enunciate each word.

Chas laughed. 'Oh, come on, sweetheart, that was just friendly banter. There aren't any secrets.' He bit the inside of his bottom lip, knowing full well that he was lying. Ages ago Penny had let slip that Charlotte had confided in her about what had happened on Chas' sixteenth birthday.

'Oh, yeah?' Sophie retorted. She raised her free hand, holding her finger and thumb just a hair's breadth apart. 'Do you know how much I believe you? That much. And the little bit of doubt I do have is only because I've come to trust you implicitly over the past couple of days. I find it hard to believe, deep down, that you would lie to me.'

Taking a deep breath, Chas sat on the nearest dining chair and pulled Sophie down with him to sit on his knee.

'Look,' he said, gently stroking her hair. 'I'm not even one hundred percent sure what Charlotte was actually getting at, but I think it was something to do with the mirrors upstairs in the main house.' He surprised himself sometimes with his ability to improvise at the drop of a hat.

'Mirrors?' Sophie gazed at him in confusion.

Chas smiled. 'Some of the bedrooms in the main house have two-way mirrors. I'm not sure if my parents ever realised they existed. When I carried out the conversions to open up the conference centre the surveyor discovered that some of the walls in the bedrooms were actually false. When they were knocked down we discovered the mirrors behind them. Six bedrooms are now a foot wider than they were and of those, three of them allow their occupants to spy on the goings on in the adjoining bedrooms.'

'Ooh, how thrilling.' Sophie's eyes glittered with excitement. 'And I take it certain people have been caught out by these mirrors?'

'During the Bickley Manor's New Year's Eve parties mostly,' Chas said. Now that he was on solid ground again he found her response to his disclosure amusing. He grinned broadly.

'More than one over-amorous couple has been spied upon by Charlotte and Penny.' He gave a wry laugh. 'Over the past few years their annual foray into voyeurism has evolved from an accidental diversion into a preplanned art form.'

'How do you mean?' She was thoroughly intrigued now.

'Every year they target the couples they most want to watch and then deliberately direct them to the appropriate rooms. So far I've managed to draw the line at them using a video camera.'

'Shit!' She clapped her hand over her mouth in horror. 'Sorry. I mean, oh, dear, that's terrible . . . video cameras.' All at once she started to giggle.

Shaking with laughter himself, he watched as tears of mirth coursed down her face. 'Now, are you satisfied?' he said.

'Oh, yes.' She tried and failed to compose herself. 'I promise I won't let on that I know.' She paused. 'Provided you promise me something, that is.'

'Aha, and what's that?' Chas' fingers began to creep stealthily under the hem of her dress, seeking out the moist warmth of her naked sex.

'Mm, er, that you, ah, show me one of the mirrored rooms tomorrow.' Sophie sighed with pleasure and allowed her thighs to drift apart. 'And that you don't stop what you're doing until I come.'

Chas grinned, his fingers easing between the soft folds of her labia. 'Then it's a done deal.'

Having enjoyed a delicious, if hastily snatched orgasm, Sophie floated dreamily upstairs to wrap her presents. Chas had told her that everyone placed their gifts around the Christmas tree in the dining room last thing on Christmas Eve, to be opened just before lunch on Christmas Day.

He was surprised that she had any gifts to distribute but she reminded him of her shopping trip with Charlotte and Penny.

'Oh, yeah, right,' he said, glad that he had managed to slip out and buy a few things for her as well. 'Afterwards, if you want to, we can go down to the village church for Midnight Mass.'

'That would be lovely,' she enthused. Her eyes sparkled as she reached up to give him a light kiss on the lips. 'I won't be long.'

Sophie was no stranger to the tiny village church. During her stays at the cottage she had often wandered inside to look around and enjoyed spending an hour or so wandering around the graveyard, reading all the headstones. Even the vicar recognised her.

'Miss Wilde, how lovely to see you again, and Mr Carruthers.' Reverend Thompson's eyes widened with surprise. 'I didn't realise you two knew each other.'

'Oh, yes, we're very close friends,' Sophie said.

'Well, er, welcome, do take a pew.' The reverend took a couple of steps back to allow them to pass.

As soon as they were out of earshot, Sophie snorted with laughter. 'Take a pew,' she said to Chas, using her hand to disguise her mouth, 'can you believe he really said that?'

Chas smiled. 'Shut up or you'll get us thrown out of here. I should have made you drink a couple more cups of black coffee before we left.'

'Ugh!' Sophie pulled a face. 'I hate the stuff. It's OK, really, Chas, I'm not the least bit drunk any more.' All at once she paused and a strange expression stole over her face.

'What is it now?' Chas asked, pretending to sound cross with her.

'I've just realised something,' she whispered. 'I'm sitting in church with no knickers on. Do you suppose that's blasphemy or something?'

This time Chas couldn't help laughing aloud, his laughter abating a little as several interested parishioners turned their heads.

'No, I shouldn't think so. It's only blasphemous if you pull your dress up over your head and flash everyone. No, Sophie, don't!' he added quickly when she reached for her hem.

She sat back and grinned at him. 'Just teasing,' she said, 'you should see your face.'

The service itself was very moving. Sophie kept glancing at Chas as they sang the familiar carols, wondering what it would be like to stand next to him at the altar. Oh, get a grip, girl, she admonished herself, you've only known him a few days and you've already got him marching up the aisle. Still, it was a pleasant thought.

Back at Bickley Manor, Sophie, Chas, Charlotte, Robert, Penny and Tim all congregated around the Christmas tree, glasses of egg nog in hand to wish each other an official Merry Christmas and to offer up a toast of continuing good health and happiness. Afterwards, they trooped upstairs to their respective bedrooms.

'I feel shagged,' Penny said, throwing herself on the bed as soon as she and Tim were alone in their room. 'Doesn't that reverend go on?'

'I thought it was a nice service,' Tim countered. Pausing to pull off his shirt, jacket and tie in one go he added, 'Really traditional.'

'Oh, bollocks to traditional,' Penny scoffed, 'I would have preferred a party myself. Haven't been to a good one in ages.' Sitting up on the bed she hitched her short skirt up to her hips and spread her legs suggestively. 'Come on, Tim, come and give Mama a nice Christmas fuck.'

Draping his trousers neatly over the back of a chair, Tim turned around and gave her a wan smile. 'Do we have to, Pen? I'm—'

'Tired,' Penny cut in sarcastically. 'Yes I know, Tim. You're always tired. So what's new?'

'That's not fair.' Flinging back the duvet, he crawled into bed beside her. 'Tell you what, let me sleep tonight and I'll wake you up with a nice surprise in the morning.'

Jumping up, Penny stalked across the room and began dragging off her clothes. 'I'll believe that when I feel it,' she said crossly. 'What do I have to do, get sweet little Sophie to start playing with herself in front of you again?'

Tim stared at her, aghast. 'I thought we agreed we wouldn't mention that.'

'Only while I thought you were going to start showing some enthusiasm at long last,' she retorted. Totally naked, Penny slipped her petite, boyish body under the duvet beside him. 'What happened in the car was brilliant. Totally spontaneous and totally out of character for you. I couldn't believe my luck. And now, here you are again, having spent all day loafing around, complaining that you're still too tired to make love.'

Unable to argue that point with her, he sighed. 'I promise, I *will* make it up to you tomorrow.'

With an exaggerated shrug, Penny reached out and switched off the bedside lamp, throwing the room into complete blackness. 'Oh, you'd better,' she warned icily, 'otherwise Mama is going to have to start looking around for another little boy to play with.'

Tim wasn't the only one who felt exhausted. As soon as Sophie's head touched the pillow she fell into a deep sleep. Gazing tenderly down at her relaxed face and the pale, almost virginal innocence of her shoulder, Chas vowed to himself that he would do everything in his power not to let Charlotte, or any of the others, ruin Sophie's Christmas with their traditionally scandalous behaviour.

Penny had already made it abundantly clear that she expected something more from him for Christmas than a box of chocolates, and Charlotte, although much less obvious than her best friend, gave him the distinct impression that she had her eye on Tim. All things considered, it was going to take a lot of fast talking and clever footwork to avoid the total breakdown of harmony that he knew, with absolute conviction, was destined to follow.

* * *

Sophie awoke the following morning with a blinding headache and the realisation that she'd fallen asleep on Chas the night before. Rolling over to him, she nestled against him, her breasts pressing into his back as she curved her body around his. He awoke gradually to her kisses on his shoulder.

'Oh, good, you're awake,' she said brightly, 'I'm sorry about last night.'

Turning over onto his other side, Chas propped himself up on one elbow and smiled down into her face. 'Don't apologise,' he murmured, lightly encircling one of her nipples with the index finger of his free hand, 'we were both shattered.'

'I know.' Sophie gazed up at him, marvelling at his understanding. 'But I was drunk as well.'

To that, Chas laughed quietly. 'You can say that again. Do you remember exposing yourself to the vicar?'

'Oh, no, I didn't!' She stared at him in horror, her stomach clenching tightly until she realised that he was only teasing her.

'No, you didn't,' he confirmed with a grin. 'Although you were pretty out of it.'

'I'm sorry.' She would have hung her head if she hadn't been lying down.

'Don't be.' He smiled. 'I rather like you when you're squiffy.'

Sophie laughed. 'Squiffy! I haven't heard that word in ages. So' – she rolled over to face him – 'why do you like me when I'm squiffy?'

'Because I can do what I like to you. Touch you where I want to.' His fingers drifted down her torso, seeking out the warm thatch of curls at the apex of her thighs. 'How I want to.' His hand slid between her legs and he thrust a couple of fingers inside her. 'When I want to.'

She let out a long sigh of pleasure as she felt her body melting all over again. 'You can anyway. I couldn't deny you. Not ever.'

'Is that a promise?' Chas grinned wolfishly as he pushed

her onto her back and rolled on top of her. He worked her legs apart with his knees.

'Oh, absolutely.' Sophie wrapped her legs around his waist and pulled him tightly against her. Moments later she felt his hard cock slide into her eager body. 'You name it, I'll do it.'

Penny awoke to the sensation of something hard nudging the cleft between her sleepy buttocks. As though she were swatting a fly, she flapped her hand ineffectually behind her.

'Leave me alone, I'm still asleep.'

Tim grinned at her back. Typical Penny, he thought wryly, contrary to the end. Sliding his palm over her prominent hip bone his fingers spanned the concave depression of her belly.

'Wakey, wakey, rise and shine,' he murmured in her ear. 'Santa's got a special present for you.'

Pressing her face into the soft, goosedown pillow, Penny grinned wickedly. Oh, so he was ready to play now, was he? Quick as a flash she rolled over and grappled with his cock.

'And I've got a special present for you, but you're going to have to unwrap me slowly.' She lay back and bent her legs at the knees, allowed them to fall wide apart. At the same time she reached up and caressed the back of his head for a moment before applying a subtle, meaningful pressure.

'OK, OK, I give in.' He laughed softly, a throaty guttural sound that she had always loved but seldom heard these days. It sent a tiny thrill rippling through her, making her nipples harden and her vagina moisten.

Raising himself onto his hands and knees, he turned himself around so that his face hovered above her soft mound. Beneath the silky covering of auburn hair he could see the tantalising purse of her outer labia. They were slightly parted allowing him an intriguing glimpse of pink, slightly wrinkled folds of flesh. With the fingers of one hand he gently eased her outer lips apart, bending his head to suckle them for a moment before flicking his tongue over the newly exposed bud of her clitoris.

Penny sighed as she felt his breath caress her most intimate flesh. His mouth felt good. Too good, really. If it wasn't for this she might have given up on him long ago. Seven years of marriage had resulted in an increasingly annoying itch which she had so far managed to avoid scratching. Not that she was short of offers. Oh, no. A number of her male colleagues had expressed more than a passing interest in her. And one Italian photographer at the Milan fashion show last year had almost succeeded in breaking through her carefully erected defences.

But, at the end of the day, she was loyal. Loyal to her marriage vows to Tim and loyal to the memory of her previous relationship with Chas. She sighed again. Chas. Dark, inventive, sinfully sexy and a rebel like her. He was her first love and the only man who would ever induce her to leave Tim. Poor Tim, she thought regretfully, the only reason she was still married to him was because Chas had not yet crooked his finger and beckoned to her to leave.

In her own room, Charlotte was entertaining similar thoughts. It seemed the older he got, the more desirable her step-brother became. A wicked notion, yes, but wasn't she, Charlotte the harlot, prone to wicked thoughts?

She and Robert fucked mindlessly, more from a sense of physical need than of real passion. Even though they had been married for almost a year their relationship was like an endless one night stand, she thought regretfully, as she felt his hardness slide in and out of her moist vagina. He touched all the right buttons but never quite reached her soul. That was reserved for only one man.

She and Chas were twin flames. Soulmates. He knew her like no one else on this earth. For sixteen years she had let the memory of their unforgettable encounter lay fallow. But the time was fast approaching for the piece of no-man's-land that connected them to be ploughed. For the fresh, fertile earth to be turned over and a seed planted within its deep furrows. A child. She wanted a child. But it had to be the boy child who haunted her dreams; dark and Byronic with thick-lashed, shimmering blue eyes. The forbidden fruit of Chas' loins and the sole produce of her aching womb.

Chapter Eight

The exchange of gifts was a lighthearted affair. Delicious smells wafted down the hallway and into the dining room from the kitchen, accompanied by the high, slightly off-tune humming of Mrs Lavender who was putting the finishing touches to Christmas lunch.

'She sounds happy,' Penny remarked, inclining her head towards the open doorway.

'So she should be,' Chas said, with a grin, 'she's already downed a quarter of the bottle of Bristol Cream I gave her this morning.'

'Old soak.' Charlotte smiled. 'I hope you gave her something more than a bottle of sherry.'

Chas glanced at her, pleased to see his complex sister looking so relaxed for once.

'Of course I did, what do you take me for? I gave her the usual couple of hundred quid bonus and a hamper. Plus, do you remember how she has always admired that James Hadley porcelain cat in the morning room?' He paused as Charlotte nodded. 'Well, I found one just like it in an antique shop in Chipping Norton. She was thrilled to bits.'

'I'm not surprised,' Tim chipped in. 'That piece must be worth about a grand.'

'I paid seven hundred for it actually.' He shrugged when he saw his sister's shocked look. 'Oh, come on, sis. I can afford it. Business is booming and Mrs L has been good to me.'

'She's been good to all of us. Including Ma and Pa when they were still alive,' Charlotte conceded. 'Tell you what, little brother, let me go halves. Your business is not the only one that's booming.'

'Sure, if you really want to.' Chas gave his sister a warm smile.

Inside, Charlotte glowed. She could sense Robert's eyes digging into her, wanting to know what the hell she was playing at offering to shell out three hundred and fifty quid on a woman she hardly ever saw. But she could care less. Even though *he* might think the opposite, Chas' approval mattered to her more than he would probably ever know.

Sophie barely listened to the conversation taking place around her. She was too enthralled by the small stack of beautifully wrapped gifts that Chas had casually placed in front of her on the table.

'But how— when—' she had gasped, looking up at him in surprise.

In answer, Chas had merely given her a wink and tapped the side of his nose.

Excitedly, she tore the paper off the top package. It was small and slightly oblong, barely larger than a bar of soap. Perhaps it *was* a bar of soap. But, no, it was too flat. Stripping away the glossy red and silver striped paper she found a small white box. And inside the box, nestling on a bed of cotton wool was a fine thread of gold chain from which hung a tiny gold acorn.

'Just to remind you of our ride together yesterday.' Chas spoke softly as he took the vacant seat next to hers.

'But you must have bought this before then, surely?' Sophie said.

He nodded. 'I did. But I knew we would take that ride.'

Sophie blushed, wondering which ride he actually meant, the one on horseback, or the one across the fallen tree. At his indication she gathered up the back of her hair, holding it out of the way so that he could fasten the chain around her neck. Shivering to the touch of his fingers, she glanced down. The chain was quite long, allowing the acorn to nestle just inside her cleavage and absorb her body heat.

Although not as meaningful as the acorn, the rest of his gifts to her were delightful. The latest Madonna CD. A small bottle of perfume which smelled of fresh flowers and cut grass. 'A touch of spring to brighten your winter days,' he said. A lavish box of Belgian chocolates and a book about modern art.

She laughed when she opened this particular gift. It was exactly the same book she had bought for him. Smiling sheepishly, she handed him the gifts she had bought, urging him to open the book first.

He also laughed when he saw it. 'How did you know? I really wanted this book for myself and was hoping that you'd let me look at your copy.'

Opening the other gifts with all the excitement of a small boy, he claimed liqueurs were his favourite and said he was delighted with the tie.

'I wasn't sure if you actually wore proper shirts,' she admitted, eyeing the plain black T-shirt he had chosen to accompany his jeans that morning.

'Well, rest assured that I do own one or two,' he said. 'No doubt you'll find out how well I scrub up on New Year's Eve.'

She raised her eyebrows quizzically. 'What's happening on New Year's Eve?'

'The party, of course,' Chas said. '*The* event of the season.'

'Oh, of course.' Sophie remembered now and shivered with anticipation at the thought of Penny and Charlotte indulging in their taste for voyeurism. She eyed him carefully as he opened the last gift. The black basque and stockings.

'Do you know something about me that I don't?' Chas held the basque up and gave her a lopsided smile.

'Don't be silly.' She punched him lightly on the arm. 'I plan to wear them for you tonight.' With a sharp dart of desire she watched his eyes darken.

'I'll look forward to that.'

They were interrupted by the arrival of a flushed-faced

Mrs Lavender who had come to announce that lunch was all ready and she just needed a hand to set the table. Hasty hands cleared all the scraps of ribbon and wrapping paper from the festive red tablecloth and Charlotte announced that she would be happy to sort out the place settings if the men agreed to bring in the food. Penny and Sophie were detailed to light the candles and open the ubiquitous bottles of claret which stood to attention on top of the sideboard.

The meal was traditional and wholly delicious. Smoked salmon and cream cheese terrine was followed by roast turkey and all the trimmings. Then plum pudding and brandy sauce. They even had crackers. Sophie pulled hers with Chas and out fell a tiny porcelain miniature of a grey mare.

'To remind you of Annabelle when you're back in London,' he said.

It was a thoughtful gesture but Sophie felt a pang of disappointment at the fact that he obviously expected her to leave after the holiday as planned.

Then Charlotte leaned across the table and asked Chas if she could pull his cracker with him. They seemed to tug for ages on the thick gold paper, then the loud *snap* was accompanied by a shower of streamers. They lay on the table between them and, trying not to look too excited, Charlotte instructed Chas to look among them for his trinket.

Only half-interested, Sophie glanced at them from the corner of her eye. She was surprised to notice that Charlotte's eyes seemed to glitter with a strange excitement. Moments later Chas' fingers encountered something and he lifted it into the air. Immediately his expression became as dark as his sister's was bright. Between his fingertips, dangling from a tiny silver loop was a lucky charm. It's design was the number sixteen.

'Er, thank you, Charlotte,' Chas said as he hastily pocketed the charm.

Charlotte smiled sweetly. 'Think nothing of it, darling.'

Her curiosity aroused, Sophie watched the exchange with

interest. Seated beside her, Penny seemed to be trying, unsuccessfully, to catch Charlotte's eye. More secrets, Sophie thought, with a tremor of alarm that felt like a premonition. Somehow she doubted that Chas would be as forthcoming about this particular mystery as he had been about the two-way mirrors.

After lunch was cleared away they played charades for a little while, then Robert leaned across to Charlotte and whispered something in her ear. Looking slightly flushed she stood up and announced to all and sundry that she and Robert were going for a walk.

'A likely story,' Penny said, earning herself a glare of contempt from her best friend.

'Oh, get your mind out of your knickers, Pen, for Christ's sake.' Charlotte took her husband's hand. 'Robert and I just feel the need to work off some of the millions of calories we've just consumed.'

'That's what I mean.' Penny was clearly undaunted. 'What better way to do it than a good fu—'

'Yes, thank you, Penny. I think everyone's got the general idea,' Tim cut in. 'In fact that's not a bad idea, are you game?'

She stared at him in amazement. It wasn't like her husband to be so blatant in front of other people. No matter that they were close friends. And twice in one day, whatever next?

'OK, course I am,' she said, jumping up from her chair and grabbing his hand. She pulled him along with her and paused at the door to smile at Chas and Charlotte. 'See you later, folks.'

Charlotte and Robert went off for their walk a few minutes later, which left Chas and Sophie all alone.

'Then there were two,' he said softly, reclining in his chair and clasping his hands over his stomach.

'What do you want to do now?' Sophie asked. 'There's probably something on TV, or we could—'

'We could go for a tour of the main house, like I promised you yesterday,' Chas offered.

'Great, I'd love that.' She smiled, feeling only slightly disappointed that he hadn't suggested something a little more physical than merely accompanying him on a guided tour.

As soon as they reached the foot of the staircase Robert grabbed Charlotte by the wrist. 'Not up there,' he said urgently, 'this way.'

'But I need to get my coat if we're going out for a walk,' she protested. 'It's freezing outside. I wouldn't mind betting it snows tonight.'

'We're not going outside.' Still grasping her firmly, he led her along the hallway and stopped outside the closed wooden door right at the very end. Reaching out, he turned the brass doorknob.

'Why are we going into the main house?' Charlotte ducked under his arm as he ushered her through the doorway.

'It's an adventure,' he said. 'You like adventures, don't you, and mysteries?'

'Yes but—'

'No buts, just do as you're told.'

She thrilled to Robert's masterful tone. Usually quiet and fairly easy going, these unexpected changes in his demeanour always took her by surprise. Normally, he reserved such behaviour for the bedroom but today, it seemed, he had other plans.

As soon as he started to stride across the marble floor of the main hall she realised that he was heading for the staircase. And that could mean only one thing. Their final destination would be one of *the* bedrooms.

Chas had only converted the ground floor of the main house when he opened the conference centre. He had originally intended to use the rooms on the upper floors as well and indeed, a couple of lesser rooms had been cleared out to make way for office furniture, but he had decided that it was better for the conference centre to remain small and exclusive.

All those years ago, Charlotte had realised that his *volte face* had been prompted by a desire to keep the rooms which had belonged to her father and step-mother and their own suites as intact as possible. Despite his claims to the contrary, Chas was an incurable romantic and a traditionalist. Deep down, she knew, he didn't care all that much about making a fortune. As long as the conference centre earned enough to keep the estate going, that was good enough for him.

Personally, she had no desire to live permanently at Bickley Manor. The occasional long weekend and the Christmas break there were enough to remind her that she was really a city person at heart. Although her name was on the title deeds, the house and the surrounding countryside belonged to her step-brother. The only thing that would induce her to live there would be if she finally gave birth to her longed-for son.

She was brought out of her reverie by the realisation that Robert was standing outside one of the bedrooms, holding the door open so that she could enter. Dismissing all her thoughts about Chas and the house, she concentrated on the present. It was clear by the determined look on Robert's face that he had plans for the two of them. Plans that would give both of them a great deal of pleasure.

As soon as he had locked the bedroom door behind them, Robert ordered her to strip. She obeyed instantly, feeling a familiar surge of arousal course through her. Robert as her lord and master was Robert at his best.

While she undressed, he went around the room, stripping dustsheets from the four-poster bed and the rest of the antique furnishings. Then he lit a fire in the grate. Obviously, she thought, watching him set light to a stack of freshly-hewn logs with a taper, he had planned all this in advance. The knowledge thrilled her. Touched the very core of her where desire lurked, as ready to burst into flame as the handful of fragrant sandalwood chips that he now scattered over the logs.

'Lie on the bed.' He turned around suddenly, startling her for a moment. 'Flat on your back, arms above your head, legs apart.'

His orders were issued in a curt, almost emotionless tone. Although she could see by the way his pupils dilated, turning his hazel eyes to flint, that he was as excited as she by the prospect of what was to come.

He had hardly glanced at her nakedness but now, as he approached the bed, she saw him appraising her, his hard eyes taking in every minute portion of her bared flesh. Reaching into his pocket he pulled out a ball of red ribbon.

'What, what's that for?' Charlotte found she could hardly speak, her excitement was so intense. She forced herself to lie flat and motionless on the soft, midnight blue velvet counterpane as he approached the bed.

'Do you realise?' he said, moving closer to her, his hand reaching out to stroke her thigh. 'The most enticing Christmas presents are those which come gift-wrapped.'

She watched wide eyed as he unravelled the ball of ribbons. Instead of being a single continuous length, she noticed the ribbon had already been cut. Four short pieces and one very long one. Just before he reached for her wrist she realised his intention.

'Oh, no, oh, Robert, I don't think—'

'Shush, I don't want you to think. I just want you to enjoy.'

'But supposing someone—'

'No one will come in, I've locked the door, remember?'

He deftly tied both her wrists to the wooden posts either side of the bed, then did the same to her ankles until she was spreadeagled and totally at his mercy. Finally, he took the longest length of ribbon and began winding it around her torso, pulling the ribbon quite tightly so that it bit into her pale flesh. The two ends of the ribbon he passed between her legs and tied each around her upper thighs, making a visual feature of her vulva.

The scarlet ribbon edging her jet black pubic hair was a very pleasing contrast, he decided, satisfied with his efforts. Very pleasing indeed.

'What a pretty package you are,' he murmured as he stepped

back to admire the results. 'A trapped firebrand. That's what you are, isn't it, Charlotte, darling?' Noticing the flicker of alarm that crossed her face, he softened his tone. 'You can trust me. You know I would never do anything to really hurt you. This is just a game. Just pretend. Like you and Chas used to play when you were children.'

Charlotte felt her mouth go dry. Was that just an innocent remark, or was he aware of something else?

'Of— of course, I know that, darling.' She forced the words out, hoping they sounded as light and convincing as she intended.

'Good. That's OK, then.' Sitting down on the edge of the bed, he reached out and stroked his hand thoughtfully over her torso, his fingertips following the lines of ribbon that bisected her.

He was still fully dressed, in casual taupe trousers, teamed with a white round-necked T-shirt and a sage green linen jacket which had deep pockets. Charlotte eyed him warily as he reached into one of the pockets and pulled out a familiar item: her vibrator, thick, black and ridged. He held it over her face. She watched his fingers turn the base of the vibrator and heard it whir into life. Oh, God, she realised with a jolt of lust, he could spend as long as he wanted teasing her and she wouldn't be able to do a damn thing about it. She certainly wouldn't be able to hide her pleasure from him.

With an almost dismissive air, he allowed the tip of the vibrator to travel aimlessly over her torso, the vibrations touching her nerve endings and sending tiny thrills of delight coursing through her. He circled her breasts slowly, moving the vibrator in concentric circles so that she felt her mouth go dry as she waited for the inevitable moment when it would caress the oh-so-sensitive flesh of her areolae and nipples.

'Robert, Rob—'

She could hardly breathe let alone speak. The arousal she felt was intense, mind-blowing. And she could feel her sex tingling and moistening, her clitoris starting to pulse gently at first, then more insistently, anxious for gratification.

'You are a wanton woman, aren't you, Charlotte,' Robert said.

His fingertips played with one nipple as he tantalised the other with the vibrator. The more he touched her, the larger her ruby-tipped breasts swelled, the ivory skin flushed with desire.

Glancing down, she could see how huge her nipples became as he plucked at them. They seemed so long, a quarter of an inch maybe. Not really like her nipples at all. In fact her whole body felt as though it belonged to someone else. Unable to touch him, or herself, she was forced to allow Robert to dictate her arousal. It was incredible the way her body responded to the inanimate, plastic caresses of the vibrator.

The knowledge seemed deliciously lewd somehow, as though her capability for pleasure had been reduced to a mechanical response. Her mind, her wants, her conditional love for Robert were of no importance. As long as there was a human being present to direct it, a simple vibrating instrument could give her all the gratification her body required.

She found herself holding her breath, waiting for the moment when the black tip would burrow between her labia and tantalise the true core of her desire.

'Please,' she gasped, 'please make me come.' She began to pant with need as he skimmed the vibrator down her stomach and over her belly. He deliberately tormented her, avoiding her pubis and instead describing small circles on the sensitive flesh of her inner thighs. 'For God's sake, please!' She screamed, the sound echoing around the impersonal chamber of the unused room.

Sophie stopped Chas in his tracks. Having explored the ground floor of the main house they were now strolling along the broad, galleried landing of the first floor.

Chas hesitated. He thought the scream sounded as though it belonged to Charlotte but he couldn't be certain. As far as he knew, his sister and her husband were somewhere outside in the grounds, walking off their Christmas lunch.

They waited for a moment, frozen in time, surrounded by silence.

'Show me one of the special bedrooms,' Sophie urged, forgetting all about the scream. 'I want to see one of those mirrors you told me about.'

'OK, no problem.'

By this time Chas was convinced that the scream must have come from the TV downstairs. No doubt Penny and Tim had finished doing whatever had taken their fancy and had decided to watch one of the Christmas blockbusters. It didn't occur to him that they must have the sound turned up pretty loud for it to reach the main house.

He and Sophie were standing in one corner of the landing, next to a decorative eighteenth-century Royal Worcester jardinière containing an aspidistra which must have been alive almost as long as Sophie. He remembered it being there when he was a young child and now he reached out and rubbed one of the thick rubbery leaves between his thumb and forefinger. It felt strangely vibrant, as though the plant had managed to absorb impressions of all the events that had taken place in the house.

Sophie took his free hand and tugged at it impatiently. 'Come on, dreamer.' She laughed, gazing at the faraway look in his eyes. 'God, I thought I was bad. You're even more fanciful than me, aren't you?'

He glanced at her, without even seeing her for a moment, then he remembered her request. Letting go of the leaf, he began to lead her down the landing.

'We'll try this one,' he said, pausing by a door. 'I can't remember which rooms have the two-way mirror on their side.' He turned the doorknob and pushed the door open, ushering Sophie inside.

It was dark inside the room and they both blinked hard, trying to adjust their vision to the gloom. Chas crossed the room, feeling his way uncertainly until his fingers connected with the tasselled end of the curtain cord. As he pulled it, weak wintry daylight filtered into the room. The windows were grimy on the outside and he made a mental note to get one of the estate hands to clean them as soon as the holidays were over. Moving more swiftly now, he drew the curtains that obscured the other two windows.

There was not much to distinguish this room from all the other bedrooms, Sophie noticed. It was strange how quickly she had become accustomed to being surrounded by priceless antiques. Now she hardly noticed them. They were just items of furniture. Like the largely Habitat furnishings in her and Piers' London flat. *Her* flat, she corrected herself quickly. It was her name on the lease. Piers could pack his bags when he came back from Florida. Let him find another bedpost to carve notches in. Now she believed all the stories her well-meaning friends had tried to convince her about. Piers *was* a two-timing shit and good riddance to him.

The only thing that was different about this particular bedroom, she noticed, compared with the others in the west wing, was that the traditional four-poster was sited in a different place. Against the wall where the bed would have been standing, were the room the same as the others, was a long, low ottoman, its top deeply buttoned and padded, covered with rich red velvet. And above it hung a pair of matching curtains fringed with gold cords and tassels. The curtains occupied a space about four feet high by six feet, she estimated.

'The mirror is behind those curtains,' Chas said, breaking through her thoughts. So saying, he pulled the curtain cord and revealed a gold framed mirror that seemed more like a window. A window into the next room. 'Shit! I don't believe it.'

Sophie heard his gasp of surprise before she looked properly. Then she realised what had prompted his exclamation. On the other side of the mirror she could clearly see Charlotte, naked, bound in red ribbons and spreadeagled on a four-poster bed. Beside her sat Robert, fully dressed and holding something black between her legs. With a jolt of excitement she realised that the instrument Robert held was a vibrator.

She hardly glanced at Chas as she felt herself mesmerised by the scene taking place on the other side of the invisible screen. It was as though they stood in the same room, except Charlotte and her young husband were obviously oblivious to the fact that they were being watched.

Charlotte was writhing on the bed. Like a human marionette her body jerked and twitched as much as the ribbons restraining her would allow. She tossed her head from side to side and her mouth moved – in silence as far as Sophie and Chas were concerned, yet Sophie could easily imagine that the other woman was moaning and whimpering.

She felt herself grow warm as she watched. Charlotte was undeniably beautiful. Her body was slim. Slender bordering on thin. Perfect for showing off clothes to their best advantage but not quite so attractive when naked. Sophie could see the delineation of her ribs and the concave depression of her stomach, a hammock of ivory flesh suspended by her jutting hipbones. Her pubic hair was thick and black, curly like the hair on her head, the hair which now fanned across the blue velvet background. Sumptuous, Sophie thought. It was the only word which could adequately describe the silkiness of Charlotte's hair and the rich fabric on which it lay.

'Every other Christmas I've had to make do with watching the Bond film,' she joked nervously. 'Chas?' Blindly she reached for his hand, wondering what on earth *he* was thinking right at that moment.

Turning her head away from the scene with difficulty, she gazed at his profile. His expression was stony, a mixture of disbelief and something else she couldn't fathom. What *was* going through his mind? Robert and Charlotte weren't doing anything wrong. Their behaviour was a little kinky perhaps but nothing that two consenting adults should feel ashamed of. Perhaps it was the fact that Charlotte was his step-sister. Seeing her in such a lewd situation must have some affect on him. She knew she would feel a bit shocked if it were a member of her family lying there.

Chas could hardly bring himself to look at Sophie. He couldn't bear to wrench his gaze from the scene unfolding in front of them and he felt unwilling to meet her eyes in case she could detect something lurking within his own eyes. What would she see there: guilt, desire, or a painful, animal longing?

He couldn't deny his arousal at seeing Charlotte so wantonly displayed. The sight of the ribbons bisecting her delicate flesh excited him. It could have been any woman lying there and he would have felt almost as stirred. But it wasn't just any woman. It was Charlotte. And for that reason he experienced a yearning so strong that he felt as though it were eating him alive.

'Fuck you,' he said hoarsely, forcing himself to turn his head in Sophie's direction, 'I must fuck you.'

He took Sophie off-guard, grabbing her urgently and throwing her to the rich antique carpet. She was wearing a long, loose-fitting red wool dress and now he pushed it up to her waist, his fingers grappling urgently with the waistband of her sheer tights. As he dragged them over her hips, he ripped them.

'Chas!'

Sophie was startled by his behaviour. No, more than startled, shocked. And excited. She couldn't deny the exhilaration she felt. Even though she knew what had caused his unexpected behaviour she couldn't, for one minute, blame him. Playing the voyeur had aroused her beyond belief.

As soon as she said his name, Chas seemed to come to his senses.

'Sophie, I'm sorry, I don't—'

'No.' She reached up to him as he hovered over to her. 'Don't apologise and for pity's sake don't stop. I want you. I want you now. Here. All of you.' To prove it she kicked her shoes and the remains of her tights from her feet, then began to pull the filmy lace of her knickers down.

He responded then. Seeing the delightful triangle of golden curls emerging from their scant covering as Sophie struggled, he helped her, pulling her knickers down her thighs and over her feet. For just a brief moment he stroked her golden mound almost reverently, then began to grapple with his fly. He had to be inside her. He had to be inside her now.

Sophie tensed when she felt his cock-head nudge the rim of her vagina. She was ready for him, of course, she was always ready for him. Anytime. Anywhere. And yet she couldn't help feeling as though she hardly mattered to him right at that moment. She could have been anyone, any*body*, a vessel for his arousal. Deliberately tossing aside the thoughts that tried to crowd her mind she gave in to her basic instincts instead, spreading her thighs wide and welcoming his hardness inside her.

Propping himself on his elbows he thrust hard, his hands groping under her dress to feel for her breasts. She was wearing no bra and his fingers soon came into contact with the soft mounds of flesh, their tips already hardened into little bullets. In his head the image of Charlotte, naked and bound, taunted him. He could see her breasts, the tiny peaks crested by long, red nipples, as red as the ribbon that bisected her pale torso. He imagined the sensation of her flesh as it swelled either side of the tight bindings, soft and defenceless.

That was what was different about Charlotte, he realised with a jolt. The Charlotte who lay in that other room was totally helpless for once. He grunted with desire as he recalled the vision of her sex, reddened like her nipples, wet and open, the protruding nub of her swollen clitoris easily visible, even from the slight distance from which he had been forced to view her. Raising himself to his knees, he looked down at Sophie's vulva. Hers was pink, pink and innocent compared with the indecent scarlet gash between his sister's widespread thighs.

Sophie *was* innocent, though. He was certain she had never been party to dark thoughts. Not like those entertained by him and Charlotte. Innocence was pink and white. Wickedness was black and scarlet. All at once he felt his erection diminish. He wasn't being fair to Sophie. She didn't deserve this treatment. At that moment he almost felt as though he loved her. And she deserved to be loved and desired in a soft, gentle way – not like this. The primeval need which had prompted his uncharacteristically uncaring behaviour was what he felt for Charlotte. He had allowed himself to vent his confusion on the one person who least deserved it.

'I'm— I'm sorry, Sophie. I shouldn't have done that to you,' he said, withdrawing slowly from her. He pulled her into a sitting position and cradled her in his arms.

Sophie felt confused. Why had he stopped?

'Done what? I was enjoying it.'

It was the truth but she understood deep down what he was getting at. At once the realisation made her feel elated, then sick. She hadn't been imagining it. He had intended to use her. Worse, he desired his own sister.

'I think perhaps we'd better get dressed.' Chas stood up and zipped his fly. Averting his gaze as much as possible, he walked over to the mirror and pulled the cord, shutting out the image that he no longer wanted to confront.

Sophie pulled her knickers on but didn't bother with her tights. They were ruined. Balling them in her hand, she shoved them into the pocket of Chas' jeans.

'Dispose of those for me, would you,' she said dully.

All at once the tights became symbolic in her mind, tattered beyond repair just as the relationship between herself and Chas seemed to be.

She allowed him to take her hand as they walked back to the west wing. His grip was light, almost brotherly, a fact which made Sophie laugh inside her head. Now there was an anomaly if ever there was one. She recalled the way Charlotte often looked at her brother. Her behaviour, which had seemed strange at the time, made sense now.

She couldn't help wondering exactly how far their sibling relationship extended. Up until a half hour earlier she would have assumed it was all one-sided. Now she wasn't so sure. However, she decided firmly, one thing was for certain, she wasn't prepared to give up on Chas without a fight. She had assumed Penny was her only viable opponent. Now, it seemed, she had a far more daunting rival to deal with.

Chapter Nine

For the duration of two glasses of port there remained an uneasy silence between Chas and Sophie. She regarded him thoughtfully over the rim of her glass. He was seated on the sofa opposite her, apparently enthralled by the bare patch of wall behind her left shoulder.

'Chas, what is it, what's going on?' she said at last. Her voice was soft and questioning, with no hint of reproach. 'What happened back there' – she jerked her head in the direction of the doorway – 'was a bit weird. With your sister and her husband, I mean. But that's not really anything to do with us, is it? What they get up to in private.'

Chas laughed then. A sort of cross between derision and irony.

'You call that private?'

She smiled. 'They don't have to know we saw them.'

Glancing up, he held her gaze steadily. 'No, I don't suppose they do.' To Sophie's relief he got up and took a giant step over the low coffee table that divided them to sit next to her. He draped his arm around her shoulders and hugged her to him. 'I'm sorry about the way I reacted, I really am. I was just a bit shocked, I suppose.'

'And a bit turned on,' Sophie added. 'Oh, don't worry, I should think it's all perfectly normal. I was turned on too by what we saw. I'm not made of wood, you know.'

'I should say not.' Chas stroked his hand assessingly over her breasts before pretending to tap each of them with his knuckles. 'No, no wood there, definitely flesh and blood.'

Glancing up he gave her a winning smile. 'Do you mind if we start again?'

Letting out a sigh of relief, she turned sideways, flung her arms around his neck and pressed herself to him.

'I'll take that as a yes,' he said, grinning.

Half an hour later Sophie broke free of his clutches, pink-cheeked, dishevelled and smiling from ear to ear. It was all right. Chas had obviously just been shocked earlier. There was certainly nothing untoward about his behaviour now. Or, rather, there was, she was glad to say.

'I'm going upstairs to get changed for supper,' she said. She had already planned what she was going to wear. The black basque and stockings, with a little black velvet dress over the top.

Chas stretched. 'I think I'll stay as I am. We're not expecting company.' He glanced up at her as she stood up. 'You look perfectly delectable as you are, why bother changing?' The wink she gave him sufficed. 'Oh, right,' he said, rubbing his hands together. 'Well, roll on bedtime.'

Not surprisingly, after such a huge lunch, no one was particularly hungry. Sophie arrived back downstairs in the TV room first, closely followed by a smug looking Penny and Tim.

'Dare I say WATS?' Sophie said, copying Penny's habitual smirk.

'You can dare what you like.' Penny tossed her head airily. 'You're absolutely right and I don't give a shit.'

Their laughter was interrupted by the appearance of Charlotte and Robert. Chas studiously avoided looking at them, Sophie noticed, her laughter dying a little. However, she couldn't help feeling cheered by the couple's behaviour as soon as they sat down. Like the newlyweds they had only just ceased to be, they teased and toyed with each other constantly. Canoodling, her mum would call their behaviour. Sophie called it a blessed relief.

Even Chas seemed to thaw out quickly in the face of their renewed affection for each other. Perhaps Charlotte's reactions towards Chas had been merely the result of her own tension, Sophie mused. Now that the other woman appeared totally relaxed, the only person she had eyes for was her husband. She even volunteered their services for making supper.

'Cheese, salad and cold cuts, everybody?' Charlotte said, jumping to her feet. She was wearing a pair of blush-pink leggings, teamed with a lighter pink mohair jumper.

Sophie couldn't help thinking Charlotte's candyfloss look was a sharp contrast to her usual Cruella de Ville style. She tried hard to reprimand her devilish imagination which immediately cast Charlotte in all her favourite 'bitch' roles. Intense, the other woman may be, possibly even a little mixed up behind her confident facade, but Joan Collins she certainly was not.

'Hey, dreamer.' Chas prodded Sophie in the ribs causing her to glance up guiltily. 'Dinner is served.'

Sophie watched as Charlotte placed a platter of cold meats and cheeses on the coffee table between them. Next to the platter Robert placed a large crystal bowl of mixed green salad and a basket of water biscuits. In the midst of this Penny walked in bearing a couple of bottles of champagne and Tim immediately jumped up to get some glasses.

Moments later they were all seated more or less comfortably – Chas and Tim sat cross-legged on the floor – and ate from plates balanced on their laps. No one could manage to eat all that much but the champagne went down well. Within no time everyone was totally relaxed and in an appropriately festive mood.

Most of the talk that circulated the small gathering was of the 'do you remember when?' sort. Sophie bemoaned the fact that she couldn't participate properly in the conversation but enjoyed some of the tales that the others had to tell.

'Did Chas tell you he nearly got married a couple of years ago?' Penny said to Sophie.

'No.' She tried not to look as startled as she felt by Penny's unexpected disclosure. Although, she thought, glancing at Chas who was perched on the arm of the sofa beside her, he didn't look all that perturbed. In fact, he laughed.

'Oh, yes, thank you, Penny. The wedding of the decade.' His tone was deliberately ironic. Turning to Sophie he added, 'Everyone was thrilled about the idea apart from me, the supposed groom.' He glanced at Penny. 'Go on then, Pen, tell her all of it. Tell her about the lovely Laura Frimly-Smythe.'

Tim snorted. 'Lovely? She was a dog. Or rather a horse. Prime mating stock, wouldn't you say, Chas?'

'And how.' Chas grinned. 'I couldn't keep her off me. Every time we were left on our own together for five minutes she started braying on about how many sprogs she wanted. A boy first, of course, to be my son and heir, and then oodles and oodles of dinky little pinks and blues.' He put on a soppy voice which Sophie supposed – judging by the way the others fell about laughing – was an accurate imitation of that of his betrothed.

'So, do I take it this marriage wasn't actually a part of your agenda, Chris?' Sophie asked.

'Too right. It was all the brilliant idea of those two schemers.' He glanced at Penny and Charlotte who both stuck their tongues out at him. 'They led this poor girl on. Remorselessly, I might add. Telling her how mad I was about her. How I thought she'd make the perfect lady of the manor. Pair of sods.' He pretended to frown at the other two women, then smiled at Sophie. 'Now here's one woman I *am* mad about. Totally smitten.'

There was real feeling behind his words, Sophie noticed and a quick glance at both Penny and Charlotte told her that they bore her no hostility. Everything's going to be okay now, she thought, with an inner sigh of relief. All Chas and I have to do is enjoy our relationship for as long as it lasts.

It certainly looked as though it was going to last well into

Boxing Day. Shortly after midnight, Chas began to yawn and stretch enthusiastically, fooling no one.

'Bloody hell, I feel exhausted,' he said, 'it must be all the food and the champagne.'

'It couldn't be anything to do with Sophie and a four-poster bed, could it?' Robert laughed and winked at Sophie, who annoyed herself by blushing furiously.

He hadn't failed to notice that she was looking particularly lovely that evening. Although her innocence was undoubtably all on the outside, he thought, considering himself to be a good judge of women. The occasional flash of dark stocking top as she crossed her legs had conjured all sorts of images in his head as to what she might be wearing underneath her demure black dress. Not all that much, he supposed, and what there was of it was probably lacy and totally decadent.

'Well, don't do anything we wouldn't, Chas darling,' Penny trilled.

Chas grinned at her, wondering if she was even aware in her sloshed state that she had her hand down the front of Tim's trousers. 'Thank God *you* said that, Penny,' he said. 'That means we've got plenty of scope.' Hauling Sophie to her feet, he patted her velvet-covered bottom. 'Come on, sweetheart, I am in urgent need of your delicious body.'

'Chas!' She pretended to slap his hand away but didn't object when he placed his palm firmly on her buttocks and began to gently push her towards the door. Instead, she gave an exaggerated sigh, which was followed by a cheeky smile. 'Oh, all right then, if I must.'

Her playfulness disappeared as soon as Chas closed the bedroom door behind them. She was dressed for seduction and seduce him she would.

'Sit there.' She pointed to the edge of the bed. 'And don't you dare move until I say so.'

'Yes ma'am.' Chas saluted and jumped up onto the high bed. Tugging at the crotch of his jeans which had become uncomfortably tight over his fast-growing tumescence, he winked at her. 'Now look what you've done.'

'Stop complaining,' she admonished, 'I can guarantee you're going to be in a much worse state by the time I've finished.'

There was a small midi-CD system in Chas' room and now she took out her new Madonna CD and put it in the player. As soon as the music started up she began to dance. Moving sinuously, she danced her way over to Chas until she was standing just a foot or so away from him, then she began to gradually wriggle out of her dress.

'Christ!'

Chas' eyes widened as her basque-clad body emerged. Lightly boned, it moulded her curvaceous body in all the right places, the scanty lace cups uplifting her breasts. He licked his lips. A tasty offering if ever he saw one. As he reached out to her, she danced away from him.

'Naughty, naughty, look but don't touch,' she said.

The music changed rhythm and as it did so, Sophie turned around and began to gyrate her hips. Glancing over her shoulder she noticed that Chas seemed mesmerised by the sight of her bare bottom jiggling in front of him. Deliberately exaggerating every movement, she bent forward from the waist, arched her back and swung her hips from side to side.

Chas was on his feet in an instant.

'I thought I told you—' she began but he took her breath away by pushing her forwards until she was able to grasp the edge of the dressing table. Then she gasped again as he thrust a couple of fingers inside her moist vagina.

'Sod what you told me,' he growled in her ear. 'Wanton little hussy, I ought to thrash you for such lewd behaviour.'

She giggled. 'Thrash me?'

'Oho, you think I wouldn't?'

One moment she felt his fingers sliding out of her body, then the sharp sting of his palm connected with her right buttock.

'Ouch! That hurt!'

'Good.'

She could hear the laughter in his voice.

Then he smacked her again and again until she was half laughing, half weeping and pleading with him to stop.

'Fuck me, Chas. Please fuck me.'

'No way. Not yet.' Grasping her shoulders he pulled her upright, then turned her around. 'Sit on the edge of the dressing table,' he ordered gruffly, 'and open your legs.'

Trembling with barely suppressed excitement, Sophie did as he asked. Her buttocks seemed to flame as they came into contact with the hard wood, the heat quickly engulfing the lower part of her body. From the dark welts of her stocking tops to the lacy hem of her basque she was completely exposed.

Chas knelt in front of her, his fingers sliding up the insides of her thighs, parting them even more.

'Oh, oh God!' She felt the moisture trickling from her as he deftly parted her labia and flicked out his tongue.

Chas took great delight in savouring her. He laved her clitoris with the flat of his tongue until she began to writhe beneath him, then changed tactics, nibbling the luscious flesh of her labia and driving his tongue inside her vagina as far as he could.

'Please, please—' Her fingers sought her clitoris, desperate to assuage the desire that seemed ready to explode at any moment.

'No, now you're being naughty again,' Chas said, moving her hands. 'You can come when I'm ready and not before.'

'Beast!'

She tried to glare down at him but at that moment he flicked the very tip of his tongue back and forth across her swollen clitoris and she threw back her head and groaned instead.

If his mouth hadn't been full of her vulva, Chas would have smiled.

Downstairs in the TV room Charlotte and Penny were sprawled across each other on one of the sofas. They were alone, Tim and Robert having both claimed total exhaustion at the hands of their women and dragged themselves off to bed.

'So, Charlie, did you enjoy your walk this afternoon?' Penny took a swig from the bottle of Dom Perignon she was holding. 'I take it you and Robbo stopped off somewhere for a bit of nookie. Now, let me see, where could it have been?' She tapped her lips with her fingertip, pretending to consider the possibilities. 'The woodshed? The stables?' Her eyes gleamed wickedly. 'Yes, that was it, the stables. Darling Robert bent you over one of the stalls and beat your backside black and blue with a crop, is that it?'

Uncharacteristically, Charlotte blushed. She shook her head. 'No, not the stables. We didn't even make it as far as the back door.'

Penny took another swig of champagne, choking slightly as the bubbles crowded the back of her throat. 'You mean you just went up to your room and shagged like any other old married couple? Oh, that's a bit of a let-down.'

Charlotte laughed lightly at her friend's disappointment. 'We didn't go back to our room. We went up to *a* room. One of the bedrooms in the main house.'

'And what happened there? Not just straight in and out, I hope. Shame on you, Charlie.'

'Don't be ridiculous, Pen. How long have you known me?' Charlotte tossed her dark head airily. Even though she doubted that the sound of their conversation would carry through the thick stone walls of the old house, she lowered her voice a fraction. 'If you must know he tied me up in red ribbons and teased the life out of me with a vibrator.'

'Ooh, lovely.' Penny grinned. 'How many times did you come?'

Charlotte sighed and allowed her head to drop back against the soft cushioned arm of the sofa. 'Lots of times. I lost count after a while.'

Penny tried hard to imagine what it must be like to orgasm

so many times that you lost count.

'Lucky bitch!'

'Don't you come with Tim, then?' Charlotte eyed her friend from under the fringe of her long, thick lashes.

'Of course, but not that many times in one go. He seems to just miss the vital spot more often than not.'

'Poor you.' Charlotte sat up, turned around and lay with her head in Penny's lap instead. Taking the bottle of champagne from her friend, she raised her head slightly and took a long swallow before handing it back and lying down again. 'You should find yourself someone like Robert, he's turned making me come into an art form.'

She didn't bother adding that she didn't actually like her husband to know how much she enjoyed his attentions. This afternoon though there had been no escaping it, she recollected. Robert had taken great delight in extracting every ounce of pleasure from her that he could. And watching the results.

'You and Robbo are well into the kinky stuff, aren't you?' Penny said.

'If you mean a bit of spanking and bondage and so forth, yes. What's wrong with that?'

Penny shrugged. 'Nothing. I wouldn't know. Tim's too straight to indulge in that sort of thing.' She chuckled. 'I must say, I think I'd have a bit of trouble going for it myself. I mean,' she added, when she noticed her friend's interested stare, 'it all seems a bit silly, doesn't it? I'm sure I'd just crack up if Tim suddenly came over all masterful.'

'I'd bet you anything you wouldn't,' Charlotte said with conviction. 'I bet if he bent you over his knee and took a slipper to your bare bum you'd be creaming yourself in no time.'

'Huh!' Penny drained the last of the champagne and allowed the empty bottle to slip from her fingers to roll across the floor. 'I just can't see it. Now, on the other hand, if it were Chas playing the master—' She allowed her voice to trail off.

Charlotte shifted uncomfortably on the sofa. She didn't like to contemplate being chastised by Chas. It was too exciting for words.

'That got you going, didn't it?' Penny said incisively. 'You should see yourself, one mention of your darling step-brother and you're like a bitch on heat.'

'Don't, Penny.' Charlotte's voice took on a warning note.

'Don't what— don't tell it like it is? Come off it, Charlie, how long have we been best friends? And remember, I know all about your little virgin games with him all those years ago.'

Charlotte spoke through gritted teeth. 'I thought we'd agreed never to mention that again.'

'I know, it just slipped out, as the actress said to the bishop.' Penny paused to burst out laughing. 'Oh, lighten up, Charlie, for fuck's sake. This is me you're talking to now, not one of your arty-farty London friends who think celibacy is the *in* thing.' She paused and added thoughtfully, 'I wonder what they'd make of incest.'

Struggling to sit up, Charlotte glared at Penny. 'It was not incest. It was simple curiosity that's all. A bit of a game that went too far.'

'Oh, Christ, stop getting your La Perla's in a twist. All right, forget I mentioned Chas. Let's get back to the subject of spanking.'

Despite her annoyance with her friend, Charlotte laughed. 'OK, let's. What do you want to know?'

Penny sighed. Her hand came to rest lightly on Charlotte's stomach, her fingers playing with the long threads of mohair. 'Everything. Does it really hurt? Does pain really mean pleasure?' Her voice drifted off as though she were entering a dream.

'Yes, on both counts,' Charlotte said.

'Did Robbo spank you this afternoon?'

Charlotte glanced up, wondering whether it was worth lying. She decided it wasn't.

'Yes, he did. That is to say,' she amended, 'not spanked as

142

such, not this time. After he'd untied me he said he had a special Christmas present, a tawse.'

'What's one of those when it's at home?' Penny couldn't keep the excitement out of her voice. Her fingers began plucking more agitatedly at Charlotte's pink jumper.

'Well, it's a sort of whip. With lots of short leather thongs, some of them with knots tied in the ends to make it hurt more.'

'And did it hurt?'

'I'll say.' Charlotte grinned up at her friend. 'I'll be bloody sore for days.'

Penny seemed to ponder this new information for a moment. Then she spoke up hesitantly. 'Does it leave marks, this tawse thing?'

'Uh-mm.' Charlotte nodded.

The other woman gulped nervously. 'Can I— I mean— would you let me see?'

'What, see the marks on my bottom?' Charlotte couldn't disguise her amazement at her friend's request. The whole conversation seemed to have taken an odd, almost ludicrous, turn, yet she couldn't help feeling a flicker of excitement deep inside.

Penny's high colour and the anticipation dancing about in her hazel eyes told her the young woman was serious about her request, and every bit as excited as she at the way events were going.

'OK,' Charlotte conceded. 'If you really want to. But promise you won't laugh. Or tell anyone else about this, not even Tim.'

Charlotte deliberately tried to make light of it, hoping to cover her own embarrassment as much as anything.

Having extracted Penny's solemn vow of conspiracy she rose unsteadily to her feet, turned around so that her back was to Penny and slowly inched down her leggings. These were swiftly followed by her pale pink silk knickers which she pulled down to mid thigh.

'Oh!'

Penny's gasp of amazement told her that she had now witnessed what Charlotte already knew to be there. About a dozen thin red lines bisecting the taut ivory flesh of both buttocks. For a moment she simply stood there, unmoving, her back ever so slightly arched. Then she felt the questing glance of fingertips tracing the weals.

Charlotte held her breath. This was true excitement, real wickedness. Penny had been her best friend forever. They had shared their thoughts, their dreams, clothes, records, boyfriends – on occasion – and they had shared a bed quite a number of times. But they had never, ever crossed the unspoken divide between caresses which were friendly or consoling and those which were blatantly sexual.

Penny's touch was exploratory but it was also undeniably sexual. Her fingertips did not stop their journey at the extremities of the weals but carried on to the soft, wet place between Charlotte's legs.

'Ah!' Charlotte gasped as one of Penny's long finger-nails traced a path down the sensitive line of her perineum. It made a smooth circuit of the tight oval of her sex, rasping through the thick black hairs and cutting short its second journey to travel up the wrinkled slit between her compressed labia.

Unconsciously, Charlotte arched her back a little more, then with more deliberation shuffled her leggings and knickers down to her ankles and inched her feet apart. Bending right forward from the waist she rested her palms flat on the coffee table in front of her.

'Fantastic,' Penny breathed. 'I've never seen another woman this close up before. I can see everything, Charlie.'

Charlotte issued a sound that was somewhere between a moan and a plea. She waited for a split second that seemed like an eternity before Penny touched her again. This time, Charlotte noticed, her friend used the pads of her fingertips. They gently prised her labia apart, wider and wider until

Charlotte could feel a cool breath of air drying the moisture at the rim of her gaping vagina.

Then Penny, clever, knowing Penny, slid her fingertips between the thick fleshy pads of her outer labia and began to stimulate her clitoris with soft, intuitive caresses. Charlotte felt her knees buckling, turning to water. This was so bad, so wrong. She was a bad woman. Wicked, sinful Charlotte who enjoyed sadomasochism, who relished the physical attentions of her own step-brother, who wanted to lay with him and bear his child and who also, it seemed, appreciated the Sapphic pleasures of the flesh. She came in a rush, a tumultuous hurricane of heat and energy exploding within her womb.

As the tremors in her vulva abated, she sensed Penny moving behind her. One hand was kept lightly pressed between Charlotte's legs but the other was frantically unfastening buttons and shrugging off unwanted garments. In moments, Charlotte felt the soft warmth of her friend's naked flesh pressed up against her own.

The springy thatch of Penny's pubic hair caressed the sore flesh of her lower buttocks. It itched. Her vagina itched. Her whole body itched with need. She felt Penny's hands on her shoulders, pulling her upright, turning her around. Then the hands lifted her jumper pulling it up her cooperating arms as she raised them above her head, leaving her naked apart from the leggings and her knickers still wrapped around her ankles. In clumsy haste she kicked them off.

She had seen Penny naked lots of times. During puberty and beyond. And in all honesty her friend's figure had not altered all that much. It was still boyish and slight, with slim hips, a narrow waist and ribcage and small, firm breasts.

Wonderingly, she placed her palms flat against the other woman's breasts, not cupping them, simply covering them with her own flesh. Then she slid her hands down, over the flat plain of her stomach and the incongruously slightly swelling belly to rest upon the triangle of auburn hair at the apex of her thighs.

Gradually, feeling the soft, malleable flesh beneath her fingers and because her friend made absolutely no move, Charlotte allowed her thumbs to gently prise the outer lips of Penny's sex apart. She trapped the hard bud of her clitoris between the pads of her thumbs and worked it gently but insistently: compressing, pulling, circling.

In no time at all Penny began to whimper. She allowed her head to drop back and Charlotte found herself marvelling at the smooth sweep of her throat, the way her tiny breasts lifted and fell on her heaving ribcage as Penny began to pant with desire. Most of all, she marvelled at the fact that it was through her ministrations that her friend was transported on a rollercoaster of ecstasy that she, Charlotte, knew only too well.

Two women, the perfect combination some claimed. Perhaps it was true. Women knew what they liked and therefore what other women would like. It stood to reason. The pleasure was all there, all that was missing was the icing on the cake – a strong, thick cock.

They fell back on to the sofa, a tangled, perspiring heap of thrashing limbs and wayward hair. Their mouths clashed, ruby and ochre lipstick blending and smearing, pink tongues entwining, champagne-flavoured saliva mingling. Meanwhile their fingers were frantic, seeking out familiar yet unknown territory – hard little buds: nipples, clitorides, soft swelling folds, dark moist channels.

Penny raised her head and smiled down at Charlotte.

'I never realised it would be like this.'

'You mean, you've considered the possibility – with another woman I mean?'

'Oh, course, haven't you?'

'No, I— well, yes, I suppose so. But only in the abstract.'

'Come off it, Charlie.' Penny threw back her head and laughed. 'Only in the abstract. Who are you trying to kid?'

Charlotte laughed too, if nervously. In all the years she had known Penny, Charlotte had considered herself to be the leader. The stronger, the more adventurous, the wickeder of the two. Suddenly, she doubted it. Doubted herself.

'Do you find me attractive, Pen?'

Penny laughed again. 'Would I have my fingers up your cunt if I didn't?'

There! She was doing it again, Charlotte thought. Shocking her. Shocking the unshockable.

'What about me?' Penny added, 'do you fancy me?'

Charlotte wasn't about to be outdone. 'Tell me what you think when I stick my *tongue* up your cunt.'

Roughly pushing Penny backwards, she dived between her friend's legs. Just for a moment she hesitated, her mouth poised over the juicy pink folds that tantalised and yet scared the shit out of her. Then, taking a deep breath, she took the plunge.

She heard Penny gasp as her tongue drove into the intriguing hole and wriggled around, feeling the tautness of her friend's internal muscles give way with a silent, velvety sigh. Nectar flooded her mouth and dribbled down her chin. Penny tasted sweet and musky, much the same flavour as her own juices which Robert had induced her to lick from his fingers and from his cock. She loved the taste of herself. She loved the taste of Penny.

Penny began to writhe, grinding her sex urgently against Charlotte's face until she was forced to grab at Penny's hips to stop her moving quite so much and at the same time take a huge gasp of air. Penny's sex was suffocating, the wiry hair tickling her nose. Averting her face quickly, Charlotte sneezed.

'Oh, please don't stop,' Penny said breathlessly, 'please—'

Charlotte silenced her by flicking her tongue across her clitoris. It was fascinating, Charlotte thought, spreading Penny's labia wide open. Her friend's clitoris was long and hard, emerging from its hood of skin like a miniature cock. She wondered if hers looked the same in close up during full arousal. Usually, at the point Penny had obviously reached, Charlotte was too far gone to bother holding a mirror to herself any longer.

She worked the clitoris back and forth with the flat of her tongue, it seemed to have a life of its own, never still, slithering away from her oral caresses. It was frustrating yet pleasurable all at the same time. Pausing every now and again to suck lightly on Penny's labia, she brought her friend to a crashing climax.

'My turn again,' Charlotte gasped as she watched Penny's breathing return to normal. 'I want you to eat me.'

Penny grinned. 'My pleasure, I think. What's it like?'

'Lovely.' Charlotte licked her lips with obvious relish. 'You taste divine, just like me.' She had no sense of false modesty.

'Oh, goody, I love the taste of myself so this should be wonderful.' Penny struggled to sit up and motioned to Charlotte to lie back. Then she tucked a cushion under Charlotte's hips. 'Tim says this works much better for him,' she said, 'so we'll give it a try, eh?'

Charlotte nodded absently. She was too intent on the thought that at any moment she would feel her friend's lips caressing her most intimate flesh. She watched the tousled, auburn head dip between her thighs, marvelled for a moment at the smooth sweep of Penny's back and buttocks and then closed her eyes to sink into a haze of bliss.

Chapter Ten

Robert awoke to a strange sensation, the feeling of being all alone. The room was cold, the fire having died out hours ago he estimated, although he couldn't see his watch in the pitch blackness. Reaching out automatically for Charlotte his questing hand encountered only smoothness. The familiar hump of her body was absent, as were the rhythmic sighs of her breathing. For a moment he felt concerned, then irritation overtook him. Where the hell could she have got to at this time of night?

For a brief, mad moment he imagined she was somewhere locked away with Chas but, remembering the lovely Sophie, he decided it unlikely. He was suspicious of Charlotte's depth of affection for her step-brother. It seemed more than ordinary sisterly concern, or abiding loyalty, even more than the unique sort of love and understanding shared by children who had only had each other for friends most of the time. No, Charlotte's feelings for Chas were nothing to do with having the same father as him. He was sure the underlying nature of her sentiments was wholly sexual.

Well, damn her and her sainted brother, he thought, flinging back the duvet angrily, she could bloody well come and lie beside him where she belonged. On bare feet, he padded over the darkened room, stumbling over a pair of Charlotte's shoes and banging his knee against a chair. Tugging at the curtain cord, he managed to flood the room with the pale ghostly glow of moonlight.

It was a full moon, and for a moment he savoured the

view from the window. The hoot of an owl startled him and a moment later he saw its shadow, grey and feathery, illuminated against the silver coin that lit the sky. It was a magical, ethereal moment in his otherwise practical life and he felt instantly compelled to revert to the boyish impulse of wish-making.

Even his fancy took him by surprise. He wished that Charlotte would grow to love him properly, with all her heart and soul. Shrugging himself into his thick navy towelling dressing gown, he mused glumly that the likelihood of his wish coming true was about as substantial as the shadow of the owl.

Tucking a forbidden pack of cigarettes and a disposable lighter into one of his deep pockets he crossed the room and opened the door. Charlotte didn't know he smoked in secret. She didn't know a lot of things about him and would be surprised if she ever saw him with the evil weed between his lips. In everyday life he disapproved of the habit. It was unhealthy and it aged a person prematurely. Smoking certainly did not go with his image, but just occasionally it suited his restless nature to light a cigarette and enjoy the transient serenity that the drug bestowed.

Low-wattage wall lights illuminated the landing and the stairs. Robert moved as silently as he could. It was not fair to disturb the others and he didn't want to be caught out. His destination was the kitchen, where he could enjoy his secret vice over a cup of tea laced with brandy. But first he would just glance into the TV room, where he had left Charlotte hours ago, just in case she had fallen asleep on the sofa.

As he approached the bottom of the stairs he thought he heard voices, two female voices that made him sigh with relief. Charlotte's was one of them and the other no doubt belonged to Penny. That meant his wife was not in the act of seducing her brother after all, but merely indulging in the sort of schoolgirlish gossip that she and Penny always seemed to relish.

He stiffened suddenly as the voices stopped and he heard a moan. It was Charlotte's moan, he would know it anywhere. Now he was in a quandary. He wanted that cigarette more than ever and yet he was curious. Curious about what he would see were he to push open the door he was just approaching on his right.

Sophie also heard the owl. Its hoot woke her and drew her from the warmth of Chas' bed to the frosty air whistling through the aged window frame. She saw the owl's shadow pass across the moon and sighed with the simple pleasure the vision invoked.

For a little while she stayed there, watching thick grey clouds drift across the clear sky, gathering and melding together to form a dense blanket – the unmistakable indication of an imminent snowfall. Hugging the knowledge to herself, she crossed the room on whispering feet and slipped back under the covers again. With a second sigh, but this time of contentment, she snuggled up against the reassuring warmth of Chas' sleeping body.

In the midst of an orgasmic stupor Charlotte thought she heard a noise. Forcing herself to open her heavy-lidded eyes she glanced towards the doorway. The breath caught in her throat. There stood Robert, his dark, towelling-clad outline illuminated by the flickering glow of the fire.

'Charlie?' His voice was questioning, his expression disbelieving as he edged into the room.

Penny obviously hadn't heard him, Charlotte realised. Her head was still buried between Charlotte's thighs, her mouth and fingers working overtime to perfect her recently learned skills at pleasuring another woman.

Coming to his senses a little, Robert tore his gaze away from his wife's dreamy expression. It came to rest on the unexpected vision of Penny. Naked, her bottom thrusting into the air as she ministrated to Charlotte, she presented a sight so arousing that he could hardly bear to look. And yet neither could he look away.

Suddenly, sensing a change in the atmosphere and a surprising degree of tension in Charlotte's body, Penny looked up. She saw Charlotte looking towards the door and followed her gaze.

'Robert!' She sat back suddenly on her heels, her hands flying to cover her naked breasts.

He hesitated, wondering if he should simply make a tactful withdrawal, or ask Charlotte if she wanted to come to bed. He was in no doubt he had to fuck her. His cock was so hard, his groin so aching with lust, that he couldn't bear to deny himself his release of the desire that the sight of the two women had aroused in him.

Of the three of them, Penny seemed to recover from the shock first.

'Well, Robbo, what do you make of this then?' She glanced at Charlotte, who still lay passively – as though she had been stunned by her husband's unexpected appearance – and then at Robert. Her lips formed their familiar smirk. 'Perhaps you want to join us.'

He wasn't sure if it was intended as a question or an invitation. With shaking hands he closed the door behind him and then walked over to the sofa. Sitting on the edge of the coffee table he reached out and stroked Charlotte's breasts.

'Did you do this to her?' he asked thickly, pinching one of Charlotte's nipples quite hard and eliciting a moan. 'She likes it, you know. She likes a bit of pain.'

'So I believe if her bum's anything to go by.' Penny still sat with her hands covering her breasts but now she lowered them and stared challengingly into Robert's eyes. 'Charlie told me how much she likes it.' She laughed softly. 'I can't see it myself, but there you go, it takes all sorts.'

Her casual shrug diverted Robert's gaze away from her face. Reaching out with his other hand he cupped one of Penny's breasts. His fingers sought her nipple and pinched it hard, harder, until she let out a groan.

'You bastard,' she hissed, although her quick smile told him she wasn't really annoyed, 'how would you like it if I did that to you?'

He laughed then, feeling more in control at last. 'I wouldn't. But then I'm no masochist.'

'No, you're not are you?' Penny glanced slyly at him as she looked down at Charlotte. 'Do you want him to go away, Charlie? Or me?'

Charlotte shook her head dumbly. She wasn't sure what she wanted. It all seemed like a very strange dream. She whimpered as Robert's hand slipped between her thighs and began to stroke her sensitised flesh.

'I hope you haven't spoilt her for men now,' Robert said, still staring at Penny's breasts. His finger tweaked her nipple again and he waited until she gave a little grunt of pleasure. 'I would have to punish you if I thought you had.'

Penny gave a sort of strangled cry. God, she thought, what the hell is he doing to me? She wanted to laugh but her throat felt too tight. She wanted to get up and run upstairs to the safety of Tim but her body felt welded to the spot.

Robert gave a wolfish smile. 'Don't worry, Pen, no harm done, I don't think.'

Penny watched wide-eyed as his fingers slid inside Charlotte's moist vagina and began to move back and forth. Without realising it, the light of expectation that hovered in her eyes died a little.

Robert noticed. For a moment he delighted in the twin sensations of Penny's nipple between the fingers of one hand and the velvety walls of Charlotte's vagina enclosing the fingers of the other, before making up his mind what to do next. He moved his hand from Penny's breast.

'Stand up,' he ordered firmly. 'Bend over the table.'

Penny hesitated, then she felt the life flow back into her limbs. Moving slowly, as though in a dream, she stood up and allowed Robert to appraise her nakedness for a moment before stepping over his legs. She bent forward from the waist, palms placed flat on the top of the coffee table, in the same position Charlotte had assumed for her benefit hours ago. Then she waited, hearing Charlotte's prolonged gasp of pleasure as Robert swiftly brought her to orgasm with his fingers.

'OK.' He stood up and licked the creamy nectar slowly from his fingers before running an assessing hand over the taut flesh of Penny's behind. 'Let's see what naughty Penny makes of this, shall we?'

Winking at Charlotte he mouthed the words, 'Is this all right with you?' then smiled, as she nodded and he saw the unmistakable glitter of excitement reflected in the dark pools of her eyes.

Raising his arm he cracked his palm soundly across the quivering flesh of Penny's buttocks. She flinched but made no sound. He smacked her harder and harder until her bottom glowed as red as the logs in the hearth beside them and she began to moan.

Charlotte reclined lazily and watched Robert spanking Penny. At first she felt almost detached, although she gradually sensed her growing arousal. Penny had positioned herself so that her bottom was directly within Charlotte's line of vision and Robert stood to one side of her so that Charlotte could see the effect the chastisement was having on her friend.

She empathised with the sensations Penny must be experiencing. She knew how fiery her buttocks must be feeling, how urgently her sex must be craving attention. Months ago, Charlotte had experienced her first ever orgasm through spanking alone and couldn't help wondering if Penny's first time would be the first time for both experiences. If it was, she would be a lucky girl.

Robert nudged Penny's legs with his knees, silently urging her to open them wider and wider until they were splayed far apart. He applied a gentle pressure to her back, causing her to arch her back and so thrust her buttocks further into the air. She let her head drop forward so that the ends of her hair trailed across the warm pine table.

Penny groaned when she opened her eyes. Between her widespread thighs she could see the upside-down image of Charlotte's naked body reclining on the sofa. Her friend was aroused, she noticed, seeing the hard nipples, the casual hand rubbing between her thighs and the rapt expression on her face. My bum's on fire and I'm enjoying it, she thought, amazed at the way events had turned out that evening and at her own capacity for sexual gratification. No wonder Charlie had raved on about Robert for months before the two of them had finally married.

Robert turned to glance at Charlotte. 'Leave yourself alone, greedy little bitch,' he said, his voice gruff but veiled with tenderness, 'touch your friend instead.'

Charlotte obeyed instantly. Moving to sit upright on the edge of the sofa she found she was able to caress Penny's exposed sex quite comfortably. Gently she pushed a couple of fingers into the creamy flesh in front of her, driving them right inside the other woman's vagina until they could reach no further.

'Now finger-fuck her properly,' Robert said.

Again Charlotte obeyed and Penny began to churn her hips, whimpering with pleasure as she felt the heat in her sex grow to match that of her bottom.

Robert sat on the coffee table and reached under Penny's shuddering body to caress her breasts. He squeezed the small handfuls of flesh, his fingertips drawing out her nipples until they doubled in length. After a while he stopped what he was doing and gently tugged at Charlotte's wrist to make her withdraw her fingers.

'Lie down on the table,' he instructed Penny. As soon as she was lying flat on her back, he moved her arms and legs as though she were a doll, forcing her to grasp her bent legs under her knees and pull them back to her chest. He glanced at Charlotte who stared in horrified fascination at the other woman's lewdly displayed body. 'Now get down there and lick her,' he said.

The table wasn't very long but, with Penny almost doubled up, Charlotte managed to kneel on the edge of the table and nuzzle her friend's widespread sex. She kept her bottom thrust into the air, half hoping, half knowing what Robert would do next. He didn't disappoint her. As she began to lap at Penny's swollen clitoris Charlotte felt Robert's cock nudging the moist rim of her own vagina.

He slid smoothly inside her, his hands holding her firmly by the hips as he began to gyrate his pelvis, his penis stroking every part of her grasping channel. She could feel her internal muscles working, drawing his hardness in deeper and deeper. Every so often the tip of his cock glanced across her G-spot and she groaned with desire. He knew how to touch her and where to touch her to give her the maximum pleasure. Feeling herself sink into the welcoming depths of ecstasy, she heard Penny's voice.

'Are you in her cunt, Robbo? Are you fucking Charlie?'

'You bet.' His voice was grim with concentration. 'So you like to talk dirty, do you, Penny? I suspected as much.'

'Did you?' Penny gasped. It was difficult to carry on a conversation when Charlotte was doing such wonderful things to her with her mouth, but it was stimulating to think that Robert had harboured certain concepts about her sexuality. 'What else did you suspect?'

'That you're a horny little bitch,' he said, slowing his circular movements and changing to short, sharp thrusts. 'If Charlie doesn't object, I'm going to fuck you afterwards.'

The idea of changing from one woman to another, and the very fact that he could see his darling wife lapping at her best friend's vulva, conspired to push him over the edge. With a series of hard thrusts and grunts he came.

When Sophie and Chas finally emerged from their room at eleven o'clock the next morning they were surprised to find that no one else was up and about.

'And I thought we were a couple of lazy sods,' Chas remarked, leading Sophie by the hand into the kitchen. It looked like a bombsite, dirty plates and glasses littering every surface. 'Oh, shit. I forgot about all this.' He sank down on to a chair and pulled Sophie with him so that she straddled his lap.

'Don't worry, we'll soon sort this lot out in no time,' Sophie said. She cupped the back of his head with her hands, her fingers delving into the silky mass of his hair.

She had been right about the night sky looking dense enough for snow, she mused, gazing over the top of Chas' head and through the kitchen window. Outside everything was white, a thick blanket of pristine snow covering the grass and paths and bending the bare branches of the trees. She found her active mind wandering as Chas caressed her bottom and nuzzled the upper swell of her breasts. What would it be like to make love in a snow drift? Would it be too cold to bear – or bare, she grinned inwardly – or would the heat of passion keep them warm?

Well, she decided on the spur of the moment, there was only one way to find out. Disengaging herself from Chas' exploratory clutches, she stood up and began to strip off her clothes.

'What on earth are you doing now?' Chas stared at her in amazement. 'Do you usually wash up in the nude?'

'Balls to the washing up.' Sophie put out her hand and hauled him to his feet. 'Get your clothes off and come with me.' Turning away from him she walked purposefully towards the back door.

Chas shook his head and then began to pull off his boots and socks. His fingers fumbled with the belt around his jeans. There was no telling what Sophie would do next. It was one of the things he loved most about her.

Loved? The realisation that he had even thought such a word brought him up short. Did he love her, really love her, or was it just infatuation, or sexual attraction? They definitely had chemistry going for them and a liking for the same sort of things: music, art, books, plenty of sex . . . Still, he mused, that didn't mean they were in love with each other. Did it?

'Come on, I'm starting to get the shivers.'

Sophie turned her head and glanced at him over her shoulder. She wrapped her arms around her torso and hugged herself dramatically. As soon as she saw that Chas was naked, she reached up and unbolted the door. Flinging the door open, she gasped as a sharp blast of icy air hit her.

'Oh, Christ, Sophie,' Chas said in amazement. 'What are you doing now, are you crazy or what?'

Although her teeth were chattering, she giggled and held out her hand. 'Come with me, we're going to find out what it's like to fuck in the snow.'

Chas opened his mouth to protest, then closed it abruptly. Fuck in the snow? She was mad. Mad but totally irresistible.

Despite her bravado Sophie hesitated about actually putting her bare foot into the snow. Only Chas' presence behind her, the warmth of his breath upon her shoulder, prompted her to move forward. She raised her right foot and put it down. The snow crunched beneath her foot as it sank into the icy mass up to the ankle.

'Shit, it's cold!' she exclaimed, half shivering, half laughing.

Glancing over her shoulder she watched Chas give her a look that said, 'Well what did you expect?'

'Go on, big baby.' He prodded her gently between the shoulder blades. 'This was your bright idea, remember?'

No one called her a baby and got away with it. Teasing and dares were the only things guaranteed to make her do the opposite of what she wanted. Steeling herself she ran across the snow and flung herself headlong into it.

She rolled over, gasping with the shock of the cold. She had been caught out by wayward showers before, the sort that went from boiling to freezing in a millisecond, but she had never experienced anything as physically thrilling as this.

Well, not in this context anyway. Certainly nothing as cold.

Chas followed her, picking his way across the snow-covered lawn more slowly. He shook his head in disbelief when he saw her throw herself full length onto the icy blanket and roll over. Her eyes glittered brightly. She looked freezing.

'Thank God for your body warmth,' Chas lay down far more cautiously on top of her, his knees digging into the snow. He started in surprise as her cold arms enveloped him. 'Christ! This is sheer, bloody madness.'

'Fuck me,' Sophie urged, wrapping her equally cold legs around his waist. 'If you f-fuck me, we'll w-warm up quickly.' Her teeth started to chatter.

Chas was amazed that he managed to get a hard on in such detrimental conditions. It was a tribute to Sophie, he supposed. He took a perverse delight in watching her tremble as his numb fingers sought the tropical heat of her vagina. Moments later, he replaced his fingers with his cock, sliding it right inside her up to the hilt. For once he didn't perspire as he got into his stride, although he did start to feel a lot warmer.

Anxious to create her own warmth and encouraged by her body's enthusiastic response to Chas' lovemaking, Sophie began to buck and squirm energetically. Soon they were rolling over and over in the crisp, white snow, their ardent passion melting it in patches. With a final stereo groan of pleasure and relief, they both came. For the briefest of moments they lay panting, then Chas stood up and helped her to her feet.

'Come on, let's get back inside before we get double pneumonia.'

The kitchen seemed almost tropical compared with the temperature outside, Sophie noticed as she made a beeline for the Aga and pressed her frozen bottom against it. Glancing down she noticed how hard her nipples still were.

'I'm not surprised,' Chas said when she remarked on it, 'they'll probably drop off through frostbite in a minute.'

'Oh, don't.' Sophie laughed nervously, her teeth still

chattering slightly. She glanced up at him. 'You don't think
they will, do you?'

''Course not, idiot. Shove over.' Chas nudged her hip with
his, as he too pressed his buttocks against the blissful warmth
of the oven.

They had just started to play fight, nudging and prodding
each other, when to their complete horror the back door
opened and Mrs Lavender stepped into the kitchen. For a
moment the old woman busied herself, stamping clumps of
snow from her fur-lined ankle boots, then she glanced up.

Her hand flew to her mouth and her eyes widened. 'Oh,
my lord!'

Covering himself with his hands, Chas grinned sheepishly. 'Hi, Mrs L, I forgot you were coming over to prepare
lunch.'

'You are joking, aren't you, Chas?' Charlotte gave her brother
a narrow-eyed stare as he recounted the story to the others
over a plate of turkey stir-fry.

He shook his head, looking totally unabashed. 'Nope.' He
shrugged his shoulders and held his hands up in a gesture of
innocence. 'Now how could I possibly make up something as
bizarre as that?'

Charlotte sighed and pushed her hair out of her eyes. 'You
are the limit, Chas. What do you suppose Mrs Lavender
thought, walking into the kitchen and seeing you two standing
there starkers?'

'That we'd run out of clothes?' Chas helped himself to a
second glass of white Bordeaux. 'Oh, come on, Charlie.
Lighten up. She saw the funny side eventually.'

'How many glasses of sherry did it take?' Charlotte asked
drily.

'Two.' 'Four.' Chas and Sophie answered simultaneously.

'All right, four,' Chas conceded, 'but only small ones.'

His sister frowned at him and then at her plate. 'No wonder
this turkey has all the texture of old boot leather.' Then, to

everyone's surprise, she started to laugh, and kept on laughing until tears ran down her cheeks.

Later that afternoon Robert received a phone call, when he came back to join the others in the TV room he looked glum.

'What is it, darling, bad news?' Charlotte said. She patted the sofa next to her. 'Come and sit here.'

He sat down and put his arm around her, hugging her to him for a moment before glancing around apologetically.

'Sorry, everyone, it looks as though my holiday's over already. Or at least for a few days.'

Charlotte looked at him aghast. 'Oh, no, Robert. Not work. Why didn't you turn it down?'

'It was the agency,' he said. 'One of their largest advertising agency clients has an urgent gap to fill. The model they had booked has gone down with food poisoning and they need someone with the right look. Apparently only I fit the bill.'

Charlotte sighed. 'What is it then?'

He grinned. 'A commercial, national TV. Would you believe I've got to play the part of a city analyst?'

'I can actually,' Charlotte conceded. 'You've certainly got the right image.' Reaching up she stroked her fingers tenderly through the thick hank of blond hair that had flopped over his forehead, pushing it back into place.

It seemed ironic really, she thought, that for the past twenty-four hours or so she had actually felt herself falling in love with him properly. And now he had to go and leave her just when she felt they were truly getting to know each other.

'You'll be all right here on your own, won't you?' he said. 'You could come back to London with me but it would just mean sitting around the flat, or shopping, or whatever. It wouldn't be much fun for you.'

'We'd have the nights together,' Charlotte murmured suggestively, oblivious for once to the presence of the others.

Robert shrugged. 'You know how tiring these shoots can be. I'll probably come home late and have to get up early. I wouldn't be much fun. But, as I said, it's completely up to you.'

Charlotte considered her options for a moment. It would be boring back in London at the moment. As far as she knew all her friends were away, either staying in the country with family or loved ones, or enjoying a tropical break somewhere. At least at Bickley Manor she had Penny and Tim, and Chas, of course. She shivered inwardly. For once, her dreams about Chas had taken a back seat to the reality of Robert. With her husband parted from her she might find herself reverting to her former self.

'I'll stay here if you really don't mind, Robert,' she said decisively. 'At least I'll have friends and family around me.' She smiled at him. 'Don't worry. We'll survive, and you will be back for New Year's Eve, won't you?'

'Oh, yeah, absolutely,' Robert agreed. 'The shoot will probably only take a few days, four at the most. I'll ring you every night and let you know how things are going.'

'When do you have to leave?' Tim cut in.

Robert pulled Charlotte closer to him, his fingertips massaging her upper arm. 'I could go tonight but I decided that I'd rather stay here with Charlie and get an early start in the morning. The roads will be practically empty so it should only take me a couple of hours to get from here to the City. That is provided you don't mind me taking the car, Charlotte?'

'No, of course not.' She nestled against him. 'I'm not planning on going anywhere and I daresay Penny will take me if I decide to go into town to do some shopping.'

'Natch,' Penny said. 'You can count on me and Tim. Don't worry, Robbo,' she added, giving him a knowing smile, 'you know Charlie will be in good hands.'

Robert couldn't help colouring slightly. 'Yes— er— well, that's all right then, thanks Penny.'

Reclining against the back of the sofa he closed his eyes and allowed his mind to wander over the events of the night before.

Charlotte hadn't been too keen on the idea of him actually fucking Penny but she hadn't objected to him caressing her, nor when her friend finally took his cock in her mouth. She had sucked him greedily and with obvious relish and he had ended up coming convulsively a second time, his semen splattering all over Charlotte and Penny's breasts as they knelt at his feet.

Now, although he was excited about the TV commercial, he was disappointed that he had to return to London. He had been hoping that another, similar session might have been on the cards. Now it looked as though his wife and her best friend would be playing without him. Now which one of his smart London friends had mocked his holiday plans, saying that the countryside was boring? Well, more fool them.

Chapter Eleven

The bed seemed strangely empty without Robert beside her, Charlotte thought, stretching out her hand and feeling the rumpled sheet. It was still slightly warm from where he had lain earlier and between her legs she felt the merest trickle of his juices.

He had left her with a goodbye present, the best kind and she fervently hoped it would sustain both of them during the next three or four days. She didn't really think Robert would succumb to the temptations of the models he would be working with on the shoot, however luscious and available they may be. No, the person who concerned her the most was herself.

Despite her recently awakened feelings for her husband, Charlotte still couldn't stop her mind wandering in the direction of her step-brother. It made it extra difficult that he was there all the time and at the moment seemed to exude a particular air of sensuality that she'd never really noticed before.

She supposed that was due to his relationship with Sophie. She seemed to have a way with her, that girl, naturally warm and sexy, good humoured and kind natured. It was a difficult combination for any woman to try and outdo. But, Charlotte reminded herself with a grim smile of satisfaction, she wasn't just any woman, and who knew her brother better than she?

Chas left Sophie sleeping off another delicious bout of lovemaking and, having showered and dressed, quietly closed the bedroom door behind him and went downstairs to the kitchen in need of urgent sustenance. That was the trouble with using up so much energy, he mused, recalling how Sophie liked to fuck every which way and at every available opportunity, it meant he always felt starving hungry afterwards.

The atmosphere was deathly silent and he assumed that all his houseguests were otherwise occupied upstairs. He had heard Robert leaving at about six that morning and imagined that Charlotte would spend the rest of the morning entertaining herself in her room – having a long bath, or reading, or whatever – and was therefore surprised to find her sitting at the kitchen table.

She was gazing down into the mug of coffee in front of her and seemed oblivious to his entrance until she suddenly spoke up.

'Sophie still sleeping, is she, Chas?'

He whirled around, surprised at the way her dry tone seemed to echo in the stillness that surrounded them.

'Um, yes, she is.'

Charlotte laughed thinly. 'Don't look so guilty, little brother. What you and your girlfriend get up to is no concern of mine.'

Chas studied her face closely. For some reason he got the feeling that she was not being strictly truthful. Perhaps it was something in her expression, the way her face looked slightly pinched, as though she was struggling with something mentally.

'I would like to think you meant that, Charlie,' he said gravely. Pausing to help himself to a mug of coffee from the glass jug keeping warm on the Aga, he walked over to the table and sat down opposite her. 'So how come I don't believe you?'

She laughed again then. The same thin laugh. And this time when she spoke her voice was tinged with irony.

'You flatter yourself, don't you, Chas? Do you honestly imagine that every single woman on the face of this earth is lusting after you?'

He shrugged. 'You know I don't. The only person I'm not sure about is you.'

'Me?' She clapped her hand to her breast and pretended to look surprised. 'You really have got an inflated ego, haven't you?' She shook her head in apparent amazement.

'Well, if I'm wrong, I'm glad,' he said. 'Obviously, I've been reading you all wrong.'

'Obviously.'

They both fell silent, occasionally sipping their coffee and listening to the drip, drip, drip of melting snow. Outside the sun was bright, casting a wintry warmth over the earth and turning the snow to slush. Typical bloody Britain, Chas mused wryly to himself, not only are the summers pitifully short but we can't even get our winters right.

'Snow's melting,' he observed, draining the last of his coffee and standing up to get another one. 'Would you like some more?' He held the glass jug aloft and looked questioningly at Charlotte.

She nodded. When he sat down again she leaned across the table and lowered her voice to a conspiratorial level.

'Are you and Sophie a serious item?'

'It depends on what you mean by serious,' he hedged, knowing exactly what she meant. 'I seriously fancy her, and like her.'

'So you two are not in love with each other, then?' she cut in.

'Well—' He searched around in his mind for the right words, remembering that Charlotte didn't know he and Sophie had only met the day before Christmas Eve and had originally agreed to just pretend to be boyfriend and girlfriend. Then he grinned sheepishly. 'I'm not actually sure. I've never been in love before.'

'I see.' Charlotte paused to sip her coffee. 'Perhaps you just don't feel ready to settle down yet.' She glanced up at him and gave him a steady, appraising look. 'Maybe you've still got a few wild oats to sow.'

He laughed then. 'Wild oats? Only teenagers have wild oats. Mine are a bit more refined.'

'Are they?' Charlotte gazed at him until Chas was forced to turn his head away. She laughed. 'You're embarrassed!'

'No, I'm not.'

Despite his automatic, almost childish denial, it was true he felt distinctly uncomfortable. The way his sister was looking at him was unnerving. As carbon copies of their late father, their eyes were the only feature that they didn't have in common – aside from the obvious. His were bright sapphire blue and hers as dark as coal. Her mother's eyes.

'Are all the rooms in the main house ready to be used on New Year's Eve?' she asked, deftly changing the subject.

Chas felt a surge of relief. 'Yes, although Mrs L said she's going to get a few women in from the village to give them a final going over before the party.'

'The bedrooms are still covered with dustsheets,' Charlotte said.

'I know.'

Suddenly, Charlotte glanced up at him. 'How do you know? Have you done a spot check lately?'

'Yes— the— er— the other afternoon.' Chas felt himself colouring slightly, an uncomfortable warmth suffusing his throat and creeping up to stain his cheeks.

Charlotte experienced a horrible realisation as she watched his change in demeanour.

'When, exactly?' she demanded.

He tried to shrug casually. 'Oh, er, sometime, I can't remember.'

'Yes you can.' Her tone was as uncompromising as her gaze. 'You saw Robert and me, didn't you?'

He didn't answer. His throat felt closed up tight and wished his mind would do the same. But no, contrary as ever it opened out, forcing him to recall in graphic detail the image of Charlotte tied to the bed and bound in red ribbons.

'You did,' she gasped in a low voice, 'you saw it all.'

'I saw— something,' Chas said hesitantly, 'but we didn't stay.'

'We? You were with Sophie?'

He nodded. 'Yes, she saw it too. But as I said, we left pretty sharpish.'

'Why, didn't you like what you saw?' Charlotte was taunting him now. 'Didn't you like seeing my naked body again after all these years? Did the familiar sight of my cunt upset you?'

'Stop it, for Christ's sake!' Chas stood up abruptly. Going over to the sink he rinsed his cup under the hot tap. He turned around and glared at her. 'I'm going up to see Sophie. We'll probably go out for lunch.'

'That's it, run away, little brother,' Charlotte taunted. 'What is all this, if you can't stand the heat get out of the kitchen?' She paused to grimace at her own irony. 'Or is it that you're so turned on now you've just got to run upstairs and fuck that little bitch stupid?'

Chas rounded on her, his eyes blazing. 'How dare you, you filthy-mouthed—' He raised his hand, then came to his senses just as quickly and allowed it to drop.

Charlotte's eyes glittered. 'My, my, you are confused aren't you, little brother? One minute you want to fuck me and the next you want to hit me. It must be true what they say then. Love and hate *are* the same emotion.'

'I don't hate you,' Chas said, fighting to control the angry tremble in his voice, 'and I don't want to fuck you either.'

He watched as Charlotte sat back and folded her arms, appraising him steadily. 'Oh, yes you do, Chas. You want to fuck the arse off me but you daren't.'

'Bitch!' He glared at her. 'Stupid, lying little bitch. You live in a dream world.'

'No, I don't, Chas,' she said calmly. 'I leave the dreaming to you.'

Sophie was startled awake by the sound of Chas slamming the bedroom door behind him. Struggling to sit up she watched wide eyed as he stomped across the room and smashed his fist against the far wall.

'Chas?' Her voice was soft. She got out of bed and padded over to him. Wrapping her arms around him, she pressed her naked body to his fully clothed back. 'What is it— what's happened?' She knew it must be something serious, she had never seen him look anything more than mildly irritated before.

At first he didn't answer her. She could feel his shoulders heaving, his heart beating rapidly under her palms. Then gradually he seemed to calm down. After a moment he turned around in her arms and pulled her fiercely against him.

'I love you, Sophie,' he muttered into her hair, his hands feverishly roving her naked back. 'Will you marry me?'

Tipping her head back, she gazed at him in amazement. 'Do you mean it?'

Her eyes roamed his face, looking for some indication that he was merely joking with her. Chas was a great one for jokes. This time though, she was forced to admit, she had never seen him look so utterly serious.

'I never say anything I don't mean,' he said gruffly, pausing to kiss her forehead, her cheeks, her throat. He looked up and caught her hazy-eyed expression, the passionate currents of his uncompromising gaze drawing her deeper and deeper. His voice became husky as he stroked her hair. 'I love you and I want to marry you. All I need now is for you to say yes.'

Sophie wavered for a moment, then started to laugh. 'Of course my answer's yes, you fool. How could you doubt it, even for a minute? You know I'm crazy about you— love everything about you— can't get enough of you—'

As she spoke her fingers began to work the buckle of his belt undone and then grappled with the waistband of his jeans, trying hastily to free the bottom of his T-shirt.

Turning her swiftly around, Chas lifted her up by her buttocks, pressed her back against the wall and fucked her fiercely, with every ounce of passion he felt stored up inside him.

* * *

Penny heard the sound of a car starting up. For a moment she thought it was her own car and wondered if Charlotte was borrowing it without asking first. That would be typical of her friend, but then she realised that the engine of her car didn't make that strange pinking sound. Walking over to one of the tall windows that graced her and Tim's room she saw a red Peugeot turning around in the driveway. She instantly recognised Sophie's blonde head and saw that Chas was in the passenger seat beside her.

'It looks as though Chas and Sophie are going out somewhere,' she said, turning away from the window. She glanced over at Tim who was still sitting up in bed reading a thriller. Although they had both showered, neither of them had bothered to dress yet and, a swift glance at her watch told her, it was almost lunchtime.

She couldn't help wondering if it was the country air which made Tim so uncharacteristically ravenous for her body. Although she had come to bed very late the night before last, totally exhausted from her session with Charlotte and then Charlotte *and* Robert, Tim had woken up and immediately pounced on her. Last night he had been positively rampant as well, and then this morning he had fucked her twice, once in bed and then again on the floor of the bathroom.

Penny stretched, luxuriously. She certainly wasn't complaining about her husband's rejuvenated sex drive. Whenever and wherever Tim might be ready for it, so was she.

'Do you want to go out somewhere as well?' she added.

Tim didn't bother to glance up from his book. 'Not really,' he said. 'Unless you particularly want to. I'd rather just lounge around. We've only got another four days of this idle luxury and then it's noses back to the grindstone time. I plan to make the most of it.'

'Fair enough, suits me.' Penny walked over to the dressing table, sat down and began to brush her hair. Thanks to Ozzie,

Oxford's acclaimed and highly-talented gay Peruvian hairdresser, her auburn locks fell neatly into their deliberately unstructured style. 'Do you think I should have my hair cut short?'

Realising she was determined not to let him read any longer, Tim put down his book and glanced at her reflection.

'You know the answer to that. I love your hair the way it is. In fact, I'd prefer it a little longer if anything.'

'A lot longer, you mean.' Penny fingered a strand of hair thoughtfully, twisting it between her neatly manicured fingers. 'You'd prefer it if I had a wild mane of hair like Charlotte's, or Sophie's,' she added drily. 'Oh, don't look like that, darling husband of mine. I've seen the way you keep looking at her. I'm not blind.'

'I haven't been looking at her,' Tim protested. 'Well, not in the way you mean, anyway.'

'Liar!' Smiling, Penny turned around on the stool and threw the hairbrush at him. Fortunately, he ducked and the brush missed its target, which would have been his head. 'I'm not annoyed about it, but I wish you'd be honest for once.'

'OK,' he conceded, straightening up and eyeing her warily in case she threw something else. 'I am a little bit taken with her, but only because she's so nice and because it's good to see Chas with someone decent for a change.'

'Indecent, more like,' Penny snorted. 'Her body's like an open invitation for sex. She even has a "fuck me" smile.'

Tim grinned. 'What the hell is a "fuck me" smile?'

'This.' Penny lowered her eyelids a fraction and curved her lips. Leaping up from the stool she ran across the room and flung herself onto the bed. 'Now fuck me, you randy bastard.'

Charlotte wandered around the grounds of Bickley Manor, idly deadheading roses as a battle raged inside her head. She bitterly regretted her outburst that morning and felt more than a little foolish. Now, not only was Chas thoroughly annoyed with her but he had run straight into Sophie's willing arms.

All at once she felt herself missing Robert, his good looks, his easy smile. She wanted to feel his arms around her, his cock inside her. Worse still, she ached to feel the sting of his palm on her buttocks. That's the trouble with being a masochist, I suppose, she thought wryly, you have to go around making everyone want to hit you.

She wished Penny would hurry up and surface. Personally, she had no appetite for lunch but the idea of sitting down at the kitchen table with her best friend, and Tim, was far more appealing than moping about on her own. She had seen Chas leave with Sophie and felt a familiar knot of envy at their obvious togetherness which made her annoyed with herself. She had Robert – young, handsome and very, very sexy – she had a comfortable home, half the legacy of Bickley Manor, a great circle of friends and a challenging career, now why couldn't she just be content with all that?

Just as she reached the kitchen door she heard Penny's voice calling to Tim to ask him if he wanted a turkey sandwich. She didn't hear the reply but assumed he would groan about the prospect of eating yet more turkey. Fixing a smile on her face she pushed open the door and stepped into the kitchen.

'Hi, Charlie, how are you doing?' Penny glanced up. She was just filling the kettle. 'Want some tea?'

Charlotte nodded. Shrugging off her coat, she hung it on a peg by the back door and sat down at the table. 'That would be great, thanks.'

For a moment they were silent, each of them wondering whether to mention the events of the night before last now that they were alone for the first time since then.

'I— er— was everything OK with you and Robbo before he left?' Penny spooned sugar into one of three mugs which she had taken out of the cupboard in front of her.

'Yes, shouldn't it have been?'

172

Penny shrugged. 'Yeah, of course. I just— you know— wondered that's all.'

'You mean after the other night?' Charlotte decided it was time for one of them to come straight to the point.

Pausing to pour boiling water into the teapot, Penny blushed slightly.

'Keep your voice down, Tim doesn't know.'

'Oh, doesn't he?' Charlotte gave Penny a look that intimated she was filing the knowledge away for possible future blackmail purposes.

'No, he doesn't, and I'd rather keep him in the dark for now, if you don't mind.'

'Oh, I don't mind.' Charlotte flicked a thick strand of her hair over her shoulder in an airy fashion. 'It's none of my business if you want to keep secrets from your husband.'

'Oh, Charlie, don't, for fuck's sake.' Pouring out the tea into the three mugs, Penny placed one in front of Charlotte, one in the empty place opposite and carried the third to the door. 'I'm just taking this in to Tim. He's watching some golfing programme on TV. When I get back we'll talk properly, OK?'

'OK.' Charlotte picked up her mug, warming her hands around it, and waited until her friend returned a couple of minutes later.

Penny pulled out the chair opposite Charlotte and sat down. 'So,' she said, leaning forward on her elbows. 'We need to discuss this, do we?'

'Only if you want to,' Charlotte said. Cautiously, she sipped her tea.

'Well, to be perfectly honest, I want to know if you're angry about what happened.'

'Angry?' Charlotte glanced up in surprise.

'OK, then. Not angry. How about regretful?'

'No, I don't regret it. Why, do you?' Charlotte eyed her friend thoughtfully.

Penny shook her head and sat back. 'No. I don't. I enjoyed it, to be frank. All of it.' The tone of her voice was meaningful.

'At least you have the balls to admit it,' Charlotte said. Her expression softened and she reached out a hand across the table towards Penny. 'Look, Pen. As far as I'm concerned what happened the other night was wonderful, fucking fantastic. OK, so I didn't actually want Robert to put his cock in you but I had no problem with the rest of it.'

'I can understand why you didn't want Robbo to fuck me,' Penny said, taking Charlotte's proffered hand. 'He is your husband, after all. I don't think I'd particularly like it if Tim fucked you.'

A response sprang to Charlotte's lips which she immediately squashed. Tim was a nice guy but he didn't do anything for her physically.

'Good,' she said instead, 'well, at least we're on common ground.'

'We always were.' Penny smiled at her. Letting go of Charlotte's hand she picked up her mug of tea and sipped from it. 'Do you think we could get together again soon?' She rolled her eyes meaningfully to which Charlotte laughed.

'I don't see why not. I enjoyed it. I enjoyed *you*, Pen. You've got a lovely, responsive body and what you can do with your tongue is out of this world.' She sighed and felt her sex tingle just at the thought.

'I'll have to make sure Tim is otherwise engaged,' Penny said. She gave a low, throaty laugh. 'I don't know what's come over him lately, he's as randy as a young pup.'

'Oh, as randy as Robert, you mean,' Charlotte quipped.

'Yeah,' Penny laughed again. 'Exactly, but without the spanking part.'

'You really enjoyed that, didn't you?' Charlotte looked at her questioningly.

Slowly, Penny nodded. 'Yes, I did. I surprised myself.' She glanced at Charlotte, noticing the way she was grinning. 'OK, yes. You told me so. Go on, I know you're dying to say it.'

'I never intended to say any such thing.' Charlotte pretended to sound amazed at the suggestion. 'Oh, all right then,' she conceded, 'but I was right, wasn't I?' She paused as Penny nodded again. 'Well, if you enjoyed it so much, why don't you ask Tim to spank you?'

Penny snorted, spilling her tea everywhere as she hastily put her mug down. 'You must be joking, ask Tim? He'd either have me committed, or crack up himself. He's so unkinky he thinks Batman is a perv for wearing all that leather and rubber and stuff.'

Charlotte joined in the laughter. 'I'll tell you what, Pen,' she said, wiping the tears from her eyes with the tips of her fingers. 'I've got a magazine I can lend you. Just leave it lying around the bedroom and see what he says.'

'I hope you don't expect this magazine back,' Penny said, giggling. 'He'll most likely take one look at it, tear it into bits and flush it down the loo in disgust.'

'I'll bet you he doesn't.' Charlotte's tone was confident.

'How much?'

'Ooh, huge stakes, you couldn't afford it.' Charlotte racked her brains to try and think of something. Money didn't mean all that much to either herself or Penny so she would have to think of something else.

'What? Five hundred quid, a thousand?'

Charlotte shook her head slowly. 'No, not money. Something worth betting for.'

'What's that then?' Penny was totally intrigued now.

'Loser has to fuck someone of the winner's choosing at the New Year's Eve party,' Charlotte declared, feeling inspired, 'and in one of the mirrored rooms. After all, the winner has to be sure the bet's been honoured.'

'Christ! That's some bet, Charlie.' Penny looked dumbfounded.

'Are you being a scaredy-pants?' Charlotte deliberately used one of their old childhood taunts.

'No. Of course not.' Penny felt a sickening feeling inside. 'Just, let's make the bet on the grounds that Tim refuses to spank me, not that he goes as far as tearing the magazine up.'

Charlotte pondered her suggestion for a moment, then nodded. She reached out her hand again. 'OK, it's a deal.'

Both feeling slightly nervous about the possible outcome of their bet, they shook on it.

Sophie and Chas returned to find Penny and Charlotte in the kitchen, giggling over a half-empty bottle of Bollinger. Another completely empty bottle poked its head defiantly through the swing top of the waste bin.

'Still feeling festive, are we, ladies?' he said, sitting down at the table. He reached for the bottle of champagne as Sophie handed him a couple of clean glasses. She sat down opposite him, next to Charlotte.

For a moment Chas felt a shiver run down his spine. It was like seeing the fly innocently enter the spider's web. However, it soon became apparent that his sister's earlier bad humour had deserted her. She laughed and joked along with Penny and soon Sophie began to join in.

'Do you know the Wheatsheaf at all?' Sophie asked, glancing first at Charlotte, then at Penny. The two women nodded.

'Is old Jerky still the tapman there?' Penny asked.

'Er— there was an old man working behind the bar but I think his name was Burt,' Sophie said. 'He was quite a character, kept winking at me when he thought Chas wasn't looking.'

'You're lucky he only winked,' Penny said, to which Charlotte snorted with laughter.

Sophie looked from one to the other and then at Chas who was grinning from ear to ear.

'Oh, come on,' she pleaded, 'what's the joke?'

There followed more laughter, then Chas finally took pity on her.

'Burt, as you call him, is renowned for his habit of exposing himself to young women and then masturbating in front of them.'

'That's why we call him Jerky,' Charlotte cut in. 'Old Jerky

Jerk-Off. He's practically an institution around here.'

'Should be in one, you mean,' Penny said drily.

'That's cruel,' Sophie protested. 'He seemed all right to me. A little bit familiar, perhaps, but then country folk are like that, aren't they? They're not all standoffish like us Londoners.' She glanced sideways at Charlotte for confirmation.

'Well,' she said, 'I'm not strictly a Londoner. Chas and I were born here the same as Penny. But I know what you mean, Sophie. Still, take it from us that Jerky is a total perv. It's got more to do with what's in his jeans, than what's in his genes.' She stressed the words to mark the difference. 'Speaking of pervs, Penny. If you come with me I'll get you that magazine.' Four-and-a-half glasses of Bollinger had loosened her tongue.

'Oh, right, thanks, Charlie.' Penny scraped her hair back hastily and turned her head to hide her blushes.

'I see, what's all this then, you two?' Chas glanced from his sister to her friend. 'Porn before suppertime?'

'It's not porn, it's artistic,' Charlotte said, tossing her head huffily. 'I thought you would appreciate the difference, little brother. Some things are sensual and some are just plain back to basics.' She glanced pointedly at Sophie, who gazed innocently back.

Chas narrowed his eyes. 'I'm warning you, Charlotte, don't start again.'

'Again?' Penny glanced at her friend and then at Chas.

'We just had a bit of a disagreement earlier, that's all,' Chas said. 'But it's all sorted out now, isn't it, Charlotte?'

She shrugged. 'Search me.' Then she chuckled. 'Whenever you like.'

He chose to ignore her suggestion but Sophie gave him a questioning look. She couldn't help remembering the anger he had displayed earlier than morning. Obviously Charlotte had been the cause. Nevertheless, she couldn't make sense of his sister's blatant remark. Was she trying to suggest something physical? No, Sophie admonished herself inwardly, Charlotte was just drunk, that's all. Drunk people didn't know what they were saying at the best of times.

'I'm right behind you, Charlotte,' Penny interrupted, hastily shoving her friend out of the kitchen. 'Let's just go up to your room and have a little lie down.'

As soon as the two women had left, Chas glanced at Sophie. She looked a bit shell-shocked, he realised, as though she had finally realised that Charlotte's feelings towards him were more than just sisterly affection.

'What did she mean, Chas?' Sophie said, as soon as she was certain that Charlotte and Penny were out of earshot. 'It almost sounded like, like—'

'Like she'd had too much to drink,' he interrupted. 'Yes, you're right. She had.'

'You know that's not what I meant.' Sophie spoke in a low voice. 'I know this sounds ridiculous but— well— do you think she fancies you?'

Chas wanted to laugh, to reassure her that her notions were totally ludicrous. However, he found to his dismay that he was unable to put on an act with Sophie.

'I think she's a bit confused,' he said carefully. 'She's always been highly strung, even as a child. What with never knowing her own mother and everything.'

'You haven't ever— I mean— have you?' Sophie gazed at him wide eyed.

'No.' He shook his head. Vehemently denying what he knew to be the truth. To assuage his own guilt he added, 'I have never had sex with Charlotte. What a thing to suggest.'

'Oh, Chas, I'm sorry.' Sophie was instantly contrite. 'I don't know what came over me to say a thing like that. Of course you haven't. She's the one who's confused, not you. You're the most honest, straightforward man I have ever met.'

Penny followed Charlotte up to her room and reclined on the bed while her friend rifled through a stack of magazines.

178

'Here it is,' Charlotte said triumphantly. She threw a glossy magazine on to the bed.

Penny picked it up. The front cover depicted two women and a man all dressed in leather. One of the women wore a corset that left her ample breasts exposed, the other was wearing what looked to be a leather string vest, her tiny breasts peeping through the holes, while the man was merely sporting a studded jock strap and carrying a whip.

'Wow! These outfits are— um— different, aren't they?' Penny glanced up at Charlotte who sat down beside her on the bed.

Charlotte kicked off her shoes and tucked her legs under her. She was wearing a long black wool wraparound skirt and now the front of the skirt fell open to reveal her slim thighs clad in sheer black tights.

'Take a look inside if you think those are bizarre,' she suggested.

She watched with interest as Penny began to flick through the pages and stopped at one which was simply a full colour photograph of a young woman in schoolgirl's uniform. She was bent forward over an old fashioned desk, her navy serge knickers around her ankles and the rounded globes of her buttocks exposed. By the side of her stood a very stern looking man dressed in a traditional gown and mortar board. His hand was raised in the air, obviously about to spank the girl.

'Shit!' Penny's exclamation hissed from between her parted lips. Her eyes glittered brightly as she turned to look at Charlotte. 'This should make me laugh, it's so ludicrous, but all it's doing is making me feel as horny as hell.'

Shamelessly, she thrust her hand between her legs and began to caress herself.

Charlotte glanced down to the place where Penny's hand was moving feverishly. Despite the cold weather her friend was not wearing tights under her dark green rib-knit dress, and now Penny's fingertips eased under the crotch of her black satin knickers.

'Let me do that,' Charlotte said huskily. Gently pushing Penny back against the green silk coverlet, she pushed her short dress up to her waist and began inching down her knickers.

Suddenly, there was a knock at the bedroom door.

'Penny, Pen, are you hungry? Only Chas and Sophie are currying the last of the turkey for anyone who's interested.'

'Tim!' Penny sat up hurriedly and pulled down her dress. 'Hang on to those,' she said to Charlotte who knelt on the bed holding her knickers.

She got up, walked over to the door and unlocked it. As Tim entered the room, Charlotte hastily shoved the magazine and Penny's knickers under a pillow.

'Hi, Charlie,' he said amiably. 'What are you two up to? You look as guilty as a couple of schoolgirls caught behind the bikeshed with your pants down.'

Penny glanced at Charlotte and stifled a giggle.

'Do we?' she said with an air of innocence that made Charlotte want to explode with laughter. She turned to Charlotte. 'Are you hungry, Charlie – shall we go down and polish off the last of that damned turkey?'

Feeling unable to speak, Charlotte replied by nodding enthusiastically. Too much champagne on an empty stomach immediately made her regret it: her head began to swim and she became aware that she had broken out in a cold sweat.

'I'll be down in a minute,' she muttered, clapping a hand over her mouth as a wave of nausea washed over her. She stumbled from the bed to head for the bathroom. 'I must just use the loo.'

As soon as the bathroom door swung shut behind her, Tim turned to glance at Penny.

'I hope you're not feeling sick as well,' he said, caressing her bottom over the top of her dress, 'I've got great plans for us later.'

The rest of the week passed in a leisurely but mainly relaxed fashion. Chas kept the peace by avoiding Charlotte as much as possible without arousing suspicion but he had to admit, on the few occasions they did find themselves alone together, she didn't behave in anything other than a sisterly manner towards him. It was as though the conversation between them in the kitchen had never taken place.

Just to make sure that Charlotte couldn't get to him, he spent every available minute with Sophie, either in their room or away from the house. Every morning, after a late breakfast, they would go for a long ride and in the afternoon go out somewhere in the car, either to a pub, if it was early enough, or simply sightseeing. On the day before New Year's Eve they decided to go completely mad and drive into town to spend the afternoon at the cinema.

'What's on?' Sophie asked, searching in her handbag for her car keys.

Chas shrugged. 'Who knows and who cares? Just so long as I get to spend the afternoon with you in a darkened room.'

Chuckling at his reply, Sophie came across her keys at long last and jangled them in her hand.

'Have you ever done anything naughty in a cinema?'

'No, can't say that I have,' Chas said. 'Why, have you?'

Sophie shook her head. 'No, but I've often fantasised about it.'

'Oh, yes, tell me more.' Chas looked interested.

'Well, I—' She glanced up and smiled at him. 'I just sort of imagine what it would be like to be doing something and then suddenly being illuminated by torchlight. It would be a bit like being caught in one of those searchlights they used to have during the war. There I'd be, with my legs wide open and my companion's fingers up inside me, or else down on my knees with his cock in my mouth and then suddenly . . . POW! We're right there in the spotlight in all our lascivious glory.'

'Sounds wonderful,' Chas murmured hoarsely, feeling his cock stir. 'Let's go for it.'

'Do you mean it, shall we?' Sophie glanced coyly at him from under her eyelashes. Her lips were curved in a devilish smile.

'Do bears shit in the woods?' Chas asked as he took her hand and literally dragged her out of the door.

'I don't know,' Sophie giggled. 'Do they?'

Chas grinned. 'Oh, absolutely. All the ones around here do, anyway. Come on, wanton wench, let's get in your car before my cock freezes and drops off.'

Sophie's eyes widened in mock alarm. 'Oh, God, don't say that,' she said with feeling. 'Don't even think it.'

Life without Chas and his wonderful thick, hard cock, she mused as she slid into the driver's seat of her Peugeot and reached for the seat belt, would be unbearable. Thank goodness he had asked her to marry him. Now they could forget all the crap that had mucked up their lives before and concentrate on living happily ever after.

Chapter Twelve

The small Cotswolds market town to which Chas directed Sophie was only a mile from the boundaries of the Bickley Manor estate as the crow flies, but by car took a good half an hour to reach. Sophie recognised it as the place she had visited with Penny and Charlotte, where they had done their last minute Christmas shopping. Now the shops had taken down the 'Christmas Countdown' notices and instead all the windows sported bright red-on-white SALE banners.

Chas noticed Sophie was distracted by various displays in the shop windows and asked her if she'd rather take advantage of the sales instead.

In reply, she shook her head. 'No way, I want to get you inside that cinema. My nipples are rock hard just at the thought of what we might get up to. Feel.' She took his hand and placed it on her left breast.

Blatantly ignoring the shocked gaze of the female passenger in the car which had just pulled up next to them at the traffic lights, Chas massaged Sophie's breast thoughtfully.

'Mm,' he murmured, tweaking her nipple over the soft jersey fabric of her black button-through dress. 'I see what you mean. Or, rather, I feel it.' Deftly he unfastened the top two buttons of her dress and slid his hand inside the warm gap. She was not wearing a bra and he felt a surge of pleasure at the warmth of her bare breast under his palm.

Sophie shivered. 'Your hand is cold,' she said, not making any move to deter him from caressing her. 'And that woman is staring at us.'

'Let her eat her heart out.' Chas cupped her breast and began fingering her nipple, rolling the hard bud between his fingertips. 'She looks as though she could do with a good fuck to put a smile on her face.'

Blushing, Sophie glanced out of the corner of her eye at the grim-faced middle-aged woman. Next to her sat a man who looked to be about the same age. He had a thick grey moustache and wore a flat tweed cap.

'I bet her husband's moustache tickles,' she mused aloud. 'I wonder if he takes his cap off when he goes to bed.'

'We'll never know,' Chas said, pinching her nipple until she squealed in protest. The lights changed and Sophie slapped his hand away.

'Stop that now, I've got to concentrate. I don't know where I'm going remember.'

'Oh, it's just over there on the right.' Chas withdrew his hand and pointed at a dirty white nineteen-thirties building which bore a battered red ODEON sign.

Sophie glanced up at the cinema's display board as she managed to cut across the line of traffic and park right outside the building.

'Oh, look, they've got an adult's only afternoon showing. That's handy.'

'You mean you were actually planning on watching the film?' Chas murmured drily, noting the showing's triple-X symbol.

'Well, I wasn't,' she admitted, 'but I'll make an exception in this case. It might give us some ideas.'

'I've already got plenty of those.' Chas winked at her as he opened the car door and started to climb out. As he straightened up he shrugged. 'Oh, well. I suppose a few more wouldn't hurt.'

Sophie smiled at him as she locked the car, then she walked around to the pavement and tucked her arm through his.

'Come on, big boy, let's put a few of those ideas into practice.'

* * *

The darkened cinema contained the motley assortment of men in long macs that Chas had expected. He and Sophie found a couple of seats over at the far side of the cinema, three rows forward from the back. There was no one else seated in the same row, nor the rows in front and behind. Chas had instructed Sophie in advance to bring her coat and now he draped it casually over their laps.

'It gets a bit chilly in these places, doesn't it?' he whispered to Sophie, making her chuckle.

He heard the nervous excitement in her laughter and had to admit he felt more than a tingle of anticipation wondering what, if anything, they would actually be able to get up to before being thrown out.

They sat quite primly as they watched a series of adverts. Then, under the cover of the coat, Sophie reached for his hand and squeezed it. The lights dimmed even further and the opening credits of the main film began to roll. She squeezed his hand again then deliberately stroked the bulge of his cock over the outside of his jeans. He watched a smile curve her lips as his tumescence grew.

On the screen a bosomy young woman with bleached-blonde hair wiggled across the set of a penthouse flat and sat down in an armchair. Her tight white dress rode right up her thighs, making it obvious first that she was wearing no knickers and also that she was not a natural blonde.

Sophie found her eyes drawn to the thatch of dark curly hair just peeping from beneath the hem of the young woman's dress. A man came onto the scene – naturally, Sophie thought, what was the point of sitting around with no knickers on if you were all alone? He was tall, dark and broad with the air of a gangster about him. Without any preamble the man knelt in front of the woman and buried his face between her legs.

Sophie gasped aloud, feeling the moisture trickling from her naked sex. Chas didn't know it yet but she wasn't wearing any knickers either.

Chas felt under the coat and stroked Sophie's mound over

the fabric of her dress. With a slight moan she parted her legs and slid a little lower down in her seat. His fingers sought the buttons on her dress. Starting at the hem he unfastened each one until the backs of the fingers brushed the curls of her pubic hair. He tickled her lightly, delighting in the way she squirmed and gave a soft 'Ooh!' of pleasure.

'Naughty girl,' he whispered in her ear. 'No knickers either, are you training to be a porn queen or something?' He smacked her sex lightly and heard her sigh again.

'I thought I'd surprise you,' she whispered back, rubbing herself against his fingers.

'Surprise me?' He laughed softly. 'You haven't stopped doing that since the moment I first met you.'

Sophie smiled in the darkness and pretended to concentrate on the film while Chas' fingers burrowed between her labia.

The woman on the screen was now in the throes of a very dramatic orgasm, throwing her blonde head back and thrusting her breasts – which had somehow become bared – into a second man's face. Now where the hell had he appeared from? Sophie wondered idly as she felt herself being drawn into the realm of lust.

She felt her vagina moisten as a couple of Chas' fingertips skated around its slick rim and then slid inside. His thumb was rubbing her clitoris, circling around and around. Feeling warm and shaky, she thrust her hand back under the coat and sought his fly. She had a little trouble unzipping it, but when she did she was delighted to feel his hard cock spring into her hand.

Staring straight ahead – now at the woman's bare bottom which was being fondled by both men – she began to caress Chas' cock. Soon she felt a little drop of moisture emerge from the little slit at the tip of his glans and she smeared it all over the taut surface, sliding her fingertips around and around the bulbous head.

Beside her, Chas turned a low groan into a cough. Grinning, Sophie continued to stare at the screen. The gangster-type man was fucking the woman now, taking her from behind while the other man – Scandinavian by the look of him – fondled her breasts. They were huge and pendulous with dark areolae and big brown nipples the size of acorns.

Remembering the gold acorn hanging around her neck, she fingered it thoughtfully. Barely a week ago Chas had given her this gift, now he wanted to give her a wedding ring. Was she really in love with him, or just infatuated? Could events really change the course of one's life as quickly and decisively as it appeared?

Her thoughts quickly dissipated as she felt Chas' fingers thrusting deeper inside her, stimulating her G-spot. His thumb was still caressing her clitoris in a circular motion, but now he changed direction and she felt a lusty heat build up inside her. Despite the loud gasps and moans coming from the film's soundtrack she could hear the wet, squelching sounds her own body was making as Chas fingered her. And beneath her own fingers she could feel his cock becoming engorged, the veins standing out from the surface of his delicate organ like tramlines.

Leaning over sideways from the waist, she buried her head in his lap. Chas quickly made sure the coat shielded her oral activity from prying eyes and gave himself up to the sensation of having his cock sucked in a public place. In front of his heavy-lidded eyes lewd images danced and melded together in a blur of bare breasts and bottoms, flaccid cocks and gaping wet orifices.

It's not fair on women, he thought idly, having to suffer at the hands of the censors and being forced to make do with floppy dicks. Especially when the woman portrayed in the film was so obviously ready for sex. The noble thought didn't stay with him for too long. Sophie's mouth was working its magic on his cock, drawing the very life out of him as she sucked hard. Just at the last moment, he pushed her head away and came all over her face instead of in her mouth.

Sophie gasped with surprise within the little black tent that was her coat. She licked her lips and then lapped the traces of semen from his cock. Then she mumbled, 'Hanky, coat pocket.'

Chas felt around in her pockets and pulled out a clean tissue. Passing it to her under the coat he waited for a minute or so and then she emerged, smiling. Even under the dim lighting he could tell her eyes were shining and her face looked flushed. Tendrils of her hair were plastered to her forehead and cheeks with a mixture of perspiration and semen. He found another tissue and cleaned her face properly.

She gave him a self-satisfied smile as she sat up straight again. His hand was still between her legs although he had stopped caressing her for a moment while he came and while he was cleaning her face. Now he started to finger her again. In no time she was panting softly, her eyes glazed as she stared straight ahead at the image on screen of two couples copulating on the same bed.

Her sex was really moist, her vagina oozing with creamy nectar which coated his fingers. He longed to suck them clean, to taste her sweetness but he didn't want to stop what he was doing. She was obviously close to orgasm, her internal muscles grasping at his fingers as she ground herself against his hand. Her clitoris felt huge. Hard and swollen. He could almost feel it throbbing. Almost hear her body begging for release. Then it came. Or rather, Sophie came, with a strangled cry and an expression on her face of pure ecstasy.

Sophie felt thankful that her cry was drowned out by the soundtrack of the film. One of the women on screen climaxed at the same time as her and let out a hearty yell which echoed around them in the darkness. Far from feeling satisfied by her orgasm, she craved more of the same. Her clitoris still pulsed with need, her vagina hungry for another finger or two. Between her legs she felt awash with her own juices, all hot and sticky and throbbing.

She glanced pleadingly at Chas. 'Don't stop,' she hissed, 'I'm going to come again.'

His confident smile told her that he had already worked

that out for himself and had no intention of stopping. Oh, thank God, she breathed silently, just let me come one more time . . .

Robert arrived back at Bickley Manor to find the place apparently deserted. The commercial shoot had gone extremely well and he was confident of getting more work from that particular client. He felt happy, he felt successful, he felt glad to be alive and most of all, he felt incredibly amorous. Just wait until I get my hands on Charlotte, he mused as he walked up the stairs to their room, she won't be able to walk for the next week.

To his disappointment Charlotte was nowhere to be found. She wasn't in any of the downstairs rooms, and when he went upstairs she wasn't in their room either. Swiftly he began to unpack, putting his dirty clothes in a pile for Mrs Lavender to deal with and hanging his clean ones up again in the capacious mahogany wardrobe. Just as a matter of interest he opened Charlotte's wardrobe and noticed straight away that her fur coat was gone. Shit! That meant she had gone out. Penny's car hadn't been parked in its usual place, so presumably the two women had gone somewhere together.

Wondering if Tim was still around, he walked down the landing and rapped lightly on the door to their room. There was no answer. Turning the brass doorknob he found that it was unlocked.

'Robert, what a— er— surprise!' Tim glanced around and hastily tucked his erection back into the gaping fly of his navy-and-maroon-striped boxer shorts.

Penny was lying face down on the bed, totally naked and, instead of looking perturbed, glanced up.

'Hi, Robbo, back already? Charlotte's gone shopping, by the way.'

Robert wasn't sure whether to say something, or just nod and flee, but Penny put out her hand to him, blatantly ignoring Tim's look of annoyance.

'I— er— gathered she was out,' he said, edging into the room. 'I just wondered— oh, well, never mind.' He turned around to go.

'No, Robbo, don't go,' Penny insisted, 'I'm glad you're here. You can settle an argument for us.'

'Oh, yes?' Robert glanced warily at Tim, who seemed to hover halfway between him and the foot of the bed where Penny lay as though torn by indecision.

'Penny, I don't think—'Tim spluttered but she interrupted him.

'Oh, Tim, for goodness sake, don't be such an old prude. Robert has seen a naked woman before.'

Blinded by ignorance, Tim wanted to say, 'Yes, but not you,' but decided it wasn't worth arguing about. He and Penny had already spent enough time disagreeing with each other that afternoon and they had just been on the point of making up when Charlotte's husband had put in his untimely appearance.

Robert decided to ignore Tim's expression and listen to Penny instead. For one thing he craved company and for another he was enjoying looking at the young woman on the bed. He sat down cautiously on the padded stool in front of the dressing table.

'OK,' he said, 'what's the problem?'

Tim blushed. 'Look, Pen,' he mumbled, 'I don't think this is a good—'

Penny interrupted him again. 'Trust me, darling, Robbo knows about this sort of thing.'

'Really, how would you know?'Tim raised an eyebrow and glanced at Robert who gazed back, wondering what on earth the two of them could have been arguing about.

Penny ignoredTim's question and sat up instead. Reaching out, she grabbed a magazine that was lying in the middle of the bed and threw it at Robert.

'We were discussing S-and-M, Robert. Or at least, I was trying to discuss it.Tim would rather pretend it doesn't exist.'

'Of course I know it exists, Penny,' Tim interrupted, 'I just don't see what it has to do with us, that's all. What other people do in the privacy of their own homes—'

'Oh, Tim, for Christ's sake stop sounding so fucking pious.' Penny glared at him. Then she glanced at Robert. 'Robert, you tell him. Tell him that these people aren't pervs. That a bit of bondage and so forth can be very enjoyable for some folk.'

Robert nodded. 'It's true,' he said, looking candidly at Tim. 'Charlotte and I enjoy it.'

'Oh, I might have known.' Tim stomped across the room and flung himself into an armchair. 'Your friend' – he glanced at Penny then switched to Robert – 'your *wife* is a bit too keen on going around putting mad ideas in other people's heads. Especially yours, Penny.'

'Oh, now hang on a minute!' Penny and Robert both spoke in unison and glared at him.

Tim put his hands up in self defence. 'OK. OK. I'm sorry. I like Charlie, I really do. But she does have the habit of—'

'Being honest,' Penny finished for him. 'Yes, she does and I admire her for it. Always have.'

'I was going to say being outrageous for the fun of it,' Tim concluded. He glanced down, looking and sounding defeated.

There was an uncomfortable silence for a moment until Robert felt as though he had to say something.

'I happen to know Penny has been talking with Charlotte about this subject. They— er— that is to say, Charlotte, told me Penny is curious about being spanked.'

Tim laughed harshly. 'Oh, wonderful!' He looked pointedly at Penny who forced herself to look abashed. 'Why didn't you discuss this with me? Why is it that you can go around talking to the whole world about your secret sexual fantasies but can't even let me in on them. I know you think I'm a mind reader but—'

'Tim, darling,' Penny cut in softly, 'the reason I find it difficult to talk to you about anything like that is because you invariably go off the deep end. This is a prime example. Look at the state you got yourself into this afternoon.'

'I was not in a state. I just don't understand why you can't be happy with the way things are.'

Penny sighed. 'Because there's more to life than the bleedin' obvious.' She put on a funny, Monty Python voice. 'We've been married for seven years and in all that time you've never wanted to try anything the remotest bit kinky.'

'Oh, so now you're telling me our sex life is boring.' Tim ran his hands through his hair.

Although he sounded angry, Robert thought, the other man looked totally distraught.

'Tim, I don't think that's what Penny's trying to say,' Robert cut in gently. 'Like most women, well, most human beings come to that, she's curious about different aspects of life. I expect that goes for the non-sexual as well.'

Penny nodded encouragingly and Robert stood up. He walked over to where Tim was seated and held out the magazine.

'Have you actually looked at this?' he went on. 'Have you seen the expressions on the faces of the people in here? They're not models, most of them are real S-and-M devotees in real situations. Look' – he thrust the magazine right under Tim's nose – 'tell me they don't look as though they're having a bloody good time.'

Unwillingly, Tim glanced at the series of photographs on the pages in front of him. One of the bare-bottomed young women looked remarkably like Penny. He glanced over to his wife, wondering for the first time what it would actually be like to smack her delectable behind. He wouldn't like anyone to do the same to him, but he supposed it wouldn't hurt to give it a go if it would make Penny happy. In a halting voice he said as much.

Robert walked back to the stool and sat down again and Penny breathed a sigh of relief. She smiled and held her hand out to Tim.

'Come on, darling, just give me a little tap on the bottom, see how you feel about it. I know I'd love it.'

Tim didn't bother asking her how she knew, he just watched her get onto her hands and knees on the bed and wriggle her bottom at him. He glanced at Robert meaningfully.

'I'll— er— go then,' Robert said, starting to rise to his feet.

'No, don't.' Penny's quick response made him sit down again. She glanced at Tim who now stood behind her. 'If you don't mind Robbo staying, it could be handy.' She paused to giggle at her unintentional pun. 'I mean, he could give you a few tips.'

To both Robert and Penny's surprise, Tim grinned.

'OK, stay if you want to, Robert. Knowing you do this sort of thing all the time makes me feel less of a fool. Now' – he raised his hand – 'how hard should I actually do this?'

He brought his hand down swiftly but the actual contact with Penny's buttocks was tentative.

'Harder than that,' Penny and Robert both said in unison.

Tim smacked her again, much harder this time. Penny groaned.

'Did I hurt you, darling?' Tim sounded anxious.

Penny nodded, her eyes glazed. 'Yes, it was wonderful. Do it again.'

Charlotte returned to Bickley Manor in a foul temper. The dress hire agency had totally scuppered her plans to be the most outstandingly devastating woman at the annual New Year's costume ball. This year the theme was *Dangerous Liaisons* and she had chosen a super gown in ruby-red silk which she intended to wear with a high powdered wig the same colour as her own hair.

But the fools at the agency had mixed things up and could only supply her with a blonde wig. Worse still – and the ultimate insult as far as Charlotte was concerned – the only dress they had been able to supply for Sophie at such short notice was one that was almost identical to her own.

How can I possibly stand out, Charlotte raged silently, when that little bitch will be dressed almost identically? Slamming the gearstick into neutral she turned off the ignition and flung open the driver's door of Penny's BMW. She was tempted not to bother going to the ball. At least that way she wouldn't be humiliated but even she had the sense to realise that too many people would be curious as to the reasons for her absence. Well, this was one time she was really going to pull out all the stops. She *would* be the queen of the ball come what may, and Sophie, precious little Sophie, could eat her dirt.

Flouncing across the gravel driveway, she called out to one of the handymen, who was busy repairing a lawnmower, to get her things out of the car and bring them into the house. Then she went in search of Penny, knowing that her friend would understand her distress and be able to commiserate in the appropriate fashion.

In the kitchen she paused to take a bottle of Bollinger from the fridge. Uncorking it, she poured out a glassful for herself and drank it down in one go. Then she drank another and another . . .

By the time she started to make her way upstairs she was weaving unsteadily. She hadn't eaten all day and now she felt all woozy, the bubbles from the champagne fizzing and fermenting inside her head it seemed.

'Pen, Penny?' She bumped against a couple of bedroom doors as she staggered unsteadily down the landing. 'Penny!'

Robert couldn't mistake the clipped tone of his wife's voice, although Tim and Penny seemed oblivious to it. Tim had really got into his stride now. Penny's bottom was beacon red and she was loving every minute of her chastisement.

Getting swiftly to his feet Robert rushed to open the bedroom door just as Charlotte did the same on the other side. Consequently, they collided with each other on the threshold.

'Oops!' Charlotte clutched at him as she wobbled

unsteadily. From the fingers of her right hand dangled an open bottle of champagne. Sensing her balance return a little she grasped him around the neck and planted a kiss somewhere just below his left ear. 'Robert, darling, I didn't see your car. How lovely' – she paused to kiss him again, this time almost hitting the target of his mouth – 'how wonderful. How absolutely, absolutely—' Words seemed to desert her.

Smiling at her drunken state, Robert tried to usher her backwards but although she teetered slightly on her high heels, Charlotte refused to budge.

'Must see Penny,' she slurred. 'Must tell her about that little— little slut.'

'Who's a little slut, darling?' Robert said soothingly, still trying to push her back down the landing. 'Come and tell me all about it.'

'No!' She shook her head vehemently. 'Must talk to Penny. She's my friend.' She smiled up at Robert. 'She's my very good friend. You know that, don't you, darling? You know what good friends we are. Intimate. Very intimate.' She giggled.

Suddenly, to Robert's surprise, she slipped out of his grasp and ducked under his arm. Within moments she was inside the room.

'Well!'

Tim and Penny both turned their heads to see Charlotte standing in the doorway, hands on hips. She was still wearing her fur coat and underneath it a wine-coloured knitted suit, the skirt of which ended at mid-thigh. Black suede high-heeled shoes and barely-black stockings completed her outfit.

Without the benefit of any clothing at all and with her glowing bottom thrust into the air, Penny glanced over her shoulder and challenged her friend with a steady gaze.

'Charlie, how nice, do come in.'

Tim sighed. He gave up. If Penny wanted to invite the whole world to watch their sexual antics it was obviously no business of his. He would just go along with it.

Robert stepped back inside the room and gave Tim a look which said, 'I tried.'

'Take a seat,' Tim said in a resigned tone. 'Robert was just showing me how to spank Penny.'

'Oh.' Charlotte flopped down into the nearest armchair. Then her eyes widened. 'Oh!'

Penny nodded, a catlike smile curving her lips. Silently, she mouthed the words, 'You win.'

Charlotte glanced from Penny, to Tim, to her husband. 'That was kind of you to lend a hand, Robert,' she said, reiterating her friend's earlier pun. 'Mind if I join in?' So saying she shrugged off her coat and began to unbutton her jacket and slip out of her skirt.

Underneath she was wearing a black satin boned bra which made the most of her small breasts, and matching knickers and suspender belt.

Tim's eyes widened considerably. He had seen Charlotte lots of times in various bathing suits and bikinis but this decadent underwear was something else altogether. Immediately, his cock sprang to attention and peeped through the fly in his boxer shorts.

'Oh, how sweet,' Charlotte drawled. 'Tim's thingy wants to come out to play.'

Penny glanced over her shoulder again. Her husband's erection certainly looked impressive and it would be a shame not to do something with it. Besides, the spanking that Charlotte had interrupted had left her feeling unbearably hot and wet. Wiggling her bottom at Tim, she invited him to fuck her.

'Yes, go on, Tim,' Charlotte said, sitting back down in the chair and allowing her long legs to sprawl wide open. 'Fuck Penny.' She glanced up at Robert and graciously extended a hand. 'Why don't you come over here, darling, and do the same to me?'

Robert had no compunction about making love to his wife in front of an audience, but he could see that Tim was totally out of his depth.

'Perhaps we should go to our own room,' he suggested. 'Tim and Penny might prefer to be alone.'

'No, don't be silly.' Charlotte wasn't to be deterred. In all honesty, she was creaming herself at the thought of watching Tim fuck her friend. Wriggling out of her knickers, she nodded in Tim's direction. 'Go on, go for it, Tim darling.'

Chapter Thirteen

Tim only hesitated for the briefest of moments. Forcing himself to tear his eyes away from the sight of Charlotte's naked sex, he pulled his boxer shorts down and kicked them off. Turning to Penny, he grasped her around the waist and without further preamble succumbed to the enchanting temptation of her willing body.

Charlotte smiled at Tim's eagerness and, as Robert approached her, slid forward in the chair so that she could spread her legs as far as possible. Her body was a candid invitation to him, wet and open, her clitoris already hard and clearly visible among the blossoming rose-pink petals of her vulva.

'Come on, darling,' she breathed huskily, 'come and give it to me hard.'

Robert divested himself of his clothing as he moved. Standing in front of Charlotte, between her parted thighs, he slowly unbuttoned his dark navy trousers, a lustful smile playing about his lips and eyes.

'Not so fast, baby,' he crooned, 'first I need a little persuading.' He dropped his trousers, stepped out of them and folded them neatly. Underneath he was naked save for a small gold hoop piercing his navel.

Charlotte felt herself transfixed by the hoop. 'When did you . . .' Her voice tailed off as she pointed to it.

He glanced down. 'It was part of the deal,' he said, referring to the commercial shoot that he had just been on, 'they wanted a young bit of blond beefcake with a pierced navel. All that was missing when I arrived was the piercing bit, but they soon sorted that out.'

'Ooh, darling.' Charlotte reached forward and fingered the hoop thoughtfully, pulling it slightly and wincing as the skin around it gave. 'Didn't it hurt?'

Robert smiled down at her upturned face. 'Not as much as I expected, but I'll admit I did anaesthetise myself first with a couple of whiskeys.' Moving her hand down to his eager cock he added, 'And the girl who did it was very pretty. Looking at her kind of took my mind off things.'

'Yes,' Charlotte said drily, stroking his cock, 'I can just imagine what effect that had on you.' She grasped the base of his shaft and began to tease his glans with her tongue.

'I'd be lying if I said it didn't,' Robert admitted. He reached down and thrust his hands into her hair, gently forcing her head forward so that her mouth engulfed him completely. 'But I saved it all for you, baby. It's all yours.'

Sighing around his cock, Charlotte began to lick and suck him in earnest. She believed him. Believed that he had held himself in check until he returned to her. And she was going to let him know just how much she appreciated his show of faithfulness.

Across the other side of the room Penny began to pant as she felt herself approaching orgasm. The spanking Tim had given her had sparked off an intense lust that she was desperate to assuage. She was still kneeling, although now she rested her upper body weight on her forearms, her hands clasped in front of her as though in prayer. Her back arched as she thrust her hips against him. She could feel Tim's balls slamming against her as he moved, the vibrations sending ripples of pleasure through the whole of her sex.

The dark vortex of climax was dragging her down, spiralling her into a secret place where only pleasure and sensation resided. There were no need for fantasies, no room in her feverish mind for them to crowd in. This was all she'd ever wanted, a glowing, well-spanked bottom and then Tim's wonderful cock inside her. Pounding and pounding . . .

'Aah!' The power of her orgasm forced the gasp from her lips. She churned her hips frantically, feeling another wave of hot emotion rolling in, obliterating the last.

Robert and Charlotte both glanced in Penny's direction when she came.

'You're remembering the last time, aren't you?' Charlotte said in a low voice, to which Robert replied with a nod.

His whole body felt suffused with passion for his wife. She had brought him swiftly to orgasm and now she was slathering her breasts with the product of his release. A blob of viscous fluid lingered on one nipple and she caught it with her fingertip and held it to his lips. Sucking her finger deeply into his mouth, he wrapped his tongue around it, tasting himself mingled with her own musk. While she fellated him, she had fingered herself, working her body into a state of feverish anticipation that was so familiar to him that he could have wept.

Charlotte was beautiful. The most beautiful woman he had ever met, and he'd worked with some very attractive women during his career as a model. But she was different. Mysterious, exciting, dangerous. She excited him beyond reason. Always demanding more.

He would die for her, he thought, pressing her further back into the chair and kneeling so that he could bury his face into the open flower of her sex. He breathed in her special scent, delighting in the warmth emanating from her dewy flesh. The sound of her breathing touched his ears, so delicate, so anxious, filled with wanting.

Pressing the soft flesh of her labia open even further, he leaned forward and flicked his tongue across the hard nub of her clitoris. Waiting until he felt the residual ripples of her excitement, he licked her again. He knew she was anxious for release and yet he wanted to extend each moment, to make it last. He had been looking forward to this for days and, despite the presence of Penny and Tim, felt inspired to give Charlotte the best orgasm she'd ever had.

'Oh, oh, oh my God!' Charlotte's exclamation came out as a long sigh.

Trembling she gripped the arms of the chair, her red-painted fingernails digging into the soft blue velvet. It was becoming impossible to deny the urge to give in completely to her passion and allow Robert to witness the effect he had on her. It was pointless anyway, she decided, her champagne-fuddled brain trying to make sense of why she had wanted to shield her pleasure from him in the first place. He loved her, that much was obvious. And slowly, she was beginning to trust in her love for him. He wasn't about to run off with a younger woman. It was she he wanted. She he desired. If only Chas could disappear from her thoughts, she would be able to love her husband completely.

Chas! Almost against her will her mind took an alternative direction. He was an unfeeling, ungrateful bastard. She had let him have everything, Bickley Manor and all its contents, her pubescent body— Oh, God, she trembled again as she recalled that night. Stop it, she admonished herself, stop it now, for Christ's sake!

'Robert. Robert fuck me please.' She looked at him through heavy-lidded eyes. He seemed slightly out of focus, his face magnifying then receding in front of hers as he raised his head from between her thighs. Around his mouth glistened the proof of her arousal. 'I want to come again with you inside me.' She reached for his cock, her expert fingers swiftly restoring it to its former hardness. 'Please,' she breathed again. 'Please.'

He didn't think he could ignore such an impassioned plea. The most recent version of Charlotte that he had come to know was much more vocal about her needs and satisfyingly responsive. The old Charlotte had held back from him, he had sensed it; but now, it seemed, she was willing to let passion fly in the face of whatever had stopped her from being true to her desires.

'Where do you want it?' As he knelt up and edged even closer to her he glanced around the room, making sure his eyes carried hers on their swift journey. 'The dressing table, up against the wall, on the floor, next to Penny on the bed?'

Charlotte pulled his erection towards her, guiding his glans to the soft, wet place between her legs that silently begged to be filled.

'Right here,' she said earnestly, 'and I want it hard and fast.'

He raised his hand in a mock salute. 'Yes, ma'am.' Moving her hand he entered her as deeply as he possibly could, grasping her buttocks and pulling her hard against him. Ignoring her request for hard and fast, he fucked her slowly instead, alternately grinding his pelvis and then changing to a carefully paced thrusting.

The arousal she felt was plain for him to see and feel. Her vagina felt wide open and soaking wet, her ruby nipples hard and uptilted. From her open lips she emitted little sighs and whimpers and her fingers clutched repeatedly at the arms of the chair, clenching and unclenching in perfect harmony with the tightening and releasing of her internal muscles.

Churning her hips she came convulsively, the unmistakable power of her orgasm forcing Robert to do the same.

The drive back to Bickley Manor from the cinema seemed to Sophie to take half the time it had taken to get there. She felt exhilarated by the knowledge that she and Chas had got clean away with their public display of sexual antics. No one had noticed them or, if they had, no one had bothered drawing attention to their secret fumblings and muffled gasps.

They had left before the film ended, both anxious to finish what they had started – but in style. The undeniable opulence of Chas' four-poster bed was a far cry from the threadbare moquette of a couple of flip-up seats. It had been cold in the cinema too, she reflected, looking forward to reclining naked in front of a blazing log fire. After the heat of her passion had abated a little she had begun to shiver, and that was when Chas suggested that they left.

'I propose a selection of titbits and a bottle of claret in our room for supper,' Chas said as they turned into the long, winding driveway that led up to the house.

Sophie nodded her agreement. They had both eaten a huge lunch, prepared in advance by Mrs Lavender and so neither felt particularly hungry.

'Sounds wonderful,' she sighed. She took her hands off the steering wheel for a moment to allow herself to stretch luxuriously.

'Hey, watch it, you nearly had that bush then.' Chas caught the steering wheel and pointed the car back in the direction of the house. 'Shortcuts across the lawn are not allowed,' he added with mock severity.

'Sorry.' Sophie took the wheel again and gave him a sideways glance. 'I can't help wondering how come you never learned to drive.'

He shrugged. 'I've never felt the need. Horses are my passion, next to you of course.' He winked at her and squeezed her thigh. 'The local suppliers deliver to the house, and if I have to drive anywhere I either ask one of the estate workers to take me, or I order a chauffeur-driven car through a local firm.'

'Oh, chauffeurs, eh?' She smiled at him, although she kept her eyes fixed firmly ahead. 'You don't know you're born, do you, my lad? I wonder what the poor are doing.' She mimicked her grandmother who came from West Yorkshire and prided herself on her canny origins.

'If, by the poor, you mean people like you, they're driving me around and playing fast and loose with my body in cinemas,' he said, smiling back.

Sophie drove around the side of the house and parked her car outside the kitchen door.

'I'll give you fast and loose,' she warned, pretending to punch him. The punches turned to tickles, to which Chas responded in kind. 'Oh, no, stop,' she begged after a few moments of relentless torment, 'I can't take any more.'

'Oh, dear. Can't take any more,' he mocked. 'That's a shame. A very big shame, because I was planning on fucking you senseless tonight.'

A wave of heat flooded Sophie as she looked up at him. 'You know I mean the tickles,' she said, 'don't think I've given up in any other respect.'

Chas grinned at her, then pulled her into his arms for a long, searching kiss before suggesting that they got out of the car and went up to his room.

'The others will get fed up with us, the way we keep sneaking off,' Sophie said as she reached into the back of the car to get her coat. She stood up, closed the car door and then locked it. Giving him a cheeky wink over the roof of the car, she couldn't resist adding, 'But who cares?'

As they walked along the landing to Chas' room, Sophie spotted that, further down, the door to Tim and Penny's room was slightly ajar. Just as Chas put out his hand to open the door to his own room, she heard the distinctive sound of voices, coupled with collective gasps and sighs.

'What do you suppose is going on in there?' she said, inclining her head.

Chas laughed. 'Oh, three guesses.'

Pursing her lips, Sophie pretended to glare at him. 'But I thought I heard Robert's voice just now.'

'Really?' Chas was intrigued now, she noticed.

As he started to creep down the landing she shadowed him, feeling like a criminal. Just as they approached the door, she tugged at his sleeve.

'We shouldn't,' she hissed, 'it's not—'

'Shush.' He put his finger to his lips, then crooked it and beckoned her forward.

Reaching out, he pressed the door open with the palm of his hand. Sophie gasped as the door swung back on its hinges.

There, right in front of her, just yards away, were Charlotte and Robert making love. Glancing wildly at Chas she suddenly noticed Penny and Tim. Slowly, she backed away, her hand over her mouth.

'Come on,' she whispered to Chas behind her hand. 'We can't stand here and watch them.'

Sophie just felt grateful that all four people inside the room seemed oblivious to the fact that she and Chas were standing on the threshold watching them. Turning resolutely around she began to head back in the direction of Chas' room.

Pausing to take one last look at the copulating couples, Chas turned and followed her. As soon as they were inside his room, with the door firmly closed and locked, they both gave way to the laughter and gasps of amazement they had been trying so hard to suppress.

'Oh, my God, how embarrassing!' Sophie cried, flinging herself onto the bed. She lay back, her arms outstretched, staring at the canopy above her.

Chas crossed the room more slowly and stood looking down at her. 'Do you know how beautiful you are?' he said, his expression suddenly becoming serious.

'No. Am I?' She shook her head as she struggled to sit up. Reclining on her elbows, she regarded him thoughtfully. 'Are you sure about this marriage thing?'

He sat down and began to stroke her legs, his fingers inching under the hem of her dress.

'I don't say anything I don't mean,' he said, 'I thought you realised that by now.'

'Yes, but' – she sighed – 'we've only known each other such a short time. It seems, oh, I don't know.' She paused to shrug, and in the meantime Chas cut in.

'It seems right,' he murmured, 'at least to me it does. Why? Aren't you happy about it?'

'Yes, you know I am. I couldn't be happier.'

'Well, where's the problem? I love you and like you. You feel the same about me. We want to be together and we have terrific sex. It sounds like the ideal basis for marriage to me.'

Sophie had to admit that, put in those terms, it did. Yet there was something troubling her, something she couldn't quite put her finger on. Hastily, she shook the feeling off. Chas was there beside her doing magical things with his fingers and she was the luckiest young woman alive.

'All right, conversation over,' she said, inching her legs apart, 'let's just concentrate on picking up where we left off, shall we?'

She sighed with pleasure as Chas pushed her dress up to her waist. Raising her hips slightly off the bed, she made him a wanton offering of her naked sex.

'Kiss me there,' she ordered softly, adding, 'please,' as an afterthought, remembering that she was supposed to be a nicely brought up, well-mannered young woman.

Chas' lips curved into a wolfish smile. 'How could I resist such a tempting request? Especially when it was so delicately put.'

She watched as he lowered his head and a moment later felt the tip of his tongue burrowing between her labia. Her clitoris seemed to jump and tingle as he touched it. Jolts of excitement zinged through her body, setting alight her breasts, her sex, her mind. She felt his hands on her inner thighs, stroking softly as he pressed them wider apart, moving his hands to her shins he pushed gently against them so that her legs bent at the knees. He carried on pushing, forcing her knees back towards her chest.

'Hold your legs there,' he murmured, 'that's it, wide open now.'

Despite the number of times they had made love, she felt a flush of shame creep over her throat to stain her cheeks bright pink. She couldn't help noticing the confident smile that stole over his lips as she lay there blushing and trembling.

'Wider,' he said gruffly, 'let me see all of you. Hmm—' He paused to study her exposed vulva for a moment before glancing up to her face which, she felt sure, was now bright red with mortification. 'You look delicious. All soft and juicy like a ripe peach.' He stroked her, his fingertips delving into the wide open entrance to her vagina. Then he raised them to his lips and licked them. 'Just as I thought. Good enough to eat.'

'Oh!'

Sophie felt a wave of heat engulf her as Chas pressed his lips to her vulva and began to kiss her exposed flesh. It seemed as though he nibbled gently on the thick, fleshy lips of her outer labia before drawing them into his mouth and sucking them. She felt the moisture gathering inside her and oozing out, trickling down the sensitive, fully-stretched skin of her perineum, tantalising her even more.

The silky ends of his hair tickled and teased her belly and her groin as he moved his head to suck and lick every part of her. Just for a moment he stopped what he was doing and glanced up. His fingers massaged her heated flesh as he spoke.

'You're so wet, sweetheart, so very, very wet.'

She gasped as he spoke and she felt his fingertips skate around the slick rim of her vagina. Then she groaned as his fingers entered her, searching, scissoring, plunging deeply before withdrawing. Leaning over her he held his fingers to her face so that she could see the dewy moisture glistening on them, thick and creamy. Then he brushed them across her lips and her mouth opened automatically, her tongue drawing them deep into the wet cavern of her mouth.

Her juices tasted as good as they looked, sweet and creamy with a hint of musk. She gobbled greedily on his fingers, lapping up every last drop, and then moved her hips, rubbing her upturned buttocks against his thighs.

He was still fully dressed, in faded jeans and plain white T-shirt with a slight V-neck, although he had discarded his boots, socks and leather jacket at some time during this latest seduction of her.

Sophie sighed with pleasure. Even though she often made the opening moves, Chas always made her feel as though she were being seduced by him. Or courted. Every time was like their first time. And each seduction a little bit more wonderful than the last.

'I want you,' she breathed huskily. Letting go of her thighs she wrapped her legs tightly around his waist and urged her pelvis up to rub her tender, feminine flesh against the cold metal of his belt buckle. 'Oh, God, I want you so much.'

Straightening up, Chas pulled his T-shirt off over his head and threw it carelessly in the air so that it landed on the floor somewhere. Then he gently loosened the grip of her legs to unbuckle his belt and remove his jeans. He kicked them off with a similar carelessness and positioned himself over her, his arms taking his weight as he nudged her vagina with his cock.

Sophie wriggled and tilted her pelvis and he entered her smoothly. For a moment he simply allowed his cock to rest inside her and she revelled in the sensation, feeling its length and breadth filling her. For a moment they simply gazed into each others' eyes, their mutual gaze speaking volumes, before their natural instincts for gratification took over and they began to move their bodies slowly and in perfect harmony.

Several hours later, Chas and Sophie roused themselves and wandered downstairs in search of sustenance of the edible kind. They found Charlotte, Penny, Tim and Robert all seated around the kitchen table looking as though butter wouldn't melt in their mouths.

Chas glanced at Sophie and winked at her.

'Hi, folks,' he said casually, pulling out a chair at one end of the table and sitting down, 'everyone OK?'

'Mm, yes,' Tim mumbled, his mouth full of pasta. 'Penny and I just made some spag bol. There's plenty left if you two would like some.'

'I wouldn't mind, actually,' Sophie said, hovering by Chas' side, 'where is it?'

'In the Aga, keeping warm. We've only just made it so it

should be OK.' Penny glanced up at her and gave her a warm smile.

Sophie couldn't help marvelling at everyone's cool. She was sure that, in the unlikely event of herself and Chas indulging in some sort of orgy, she wouldn't be able to act so self-possessed afterwards. She chuckled inwardly. If only they knew she and Chas had seen them all at it, there'd be some red faces then.

'You sort the food out and I'll get us some plates,' Chas directed, standing up again. He opened a cupboard and put down a couple of plates on the work surface by the Aga. And as Sophie stood there, ladling out the pasta and thick meaty sauce on to the plates, he moved a lock of her hair aside and whispered in her ear. 'Don't they look the picture of innocence?'

Pursing her lips, she forced herself not to laugh aloud but she knew Chas could read her expression. Without saying a word, she picked up the plates and walked over to the table. Just as she leaned forward to put them down, she suddenly recalled the sight of Tim's bare backside wobbling as he thrust inside Penny. A gurgle of laughter rose in her throat and, knowing she wouldn't be able to suppress her amusement this time, she pushed past a startled Chas and ran out of the kitchen.

'What's the matter with her?' Charlotte asked, glancing towards the door which slowly swung closed behind Sophie's retreating figure.

Fighting his own urge to burst out laughing, Chas forced himself to shrug casually.

'Who knows? Urgent call of nature I expect.'

For a full five minutes Sophie leaned against the wall and shook with silent laughter, then she managed to compose herself enough to go back into the kitchen.

'Sorry about that, everyone,' she said brightly. Without offering any further explanation she sat down at the other end of the table opposite Chas and picked up her fork.

They had all stopped talking when she returned but now they picked up the thread of their conversation.

'I was just telling Chas that I've got your costumes for the party tomorrow night,' Charlotte said to Sophie.

'Oh, costumes, I didn't realise it was fancy dress.' Sophie twirled her fork and transferred some spaghetti to her mouth.

'Hardly fancy dress, darling,' Charlotte said drily. 'That's for children. This is a costume ball.'

'Oh, what's the theme?' Sophie asked.

'*Dangerous Liaisons.*'

Charlotte looked steadily at her, Sophie noticed, as though she were trying to convey something significant.

Sophie coughed and picked up the glass of wine which someone had thoughtfully poured for her in her brief absence.

'What fun,' she said. 'I love dressing up.'

'I rather thought you would.' Charlotte sipped her own wine and continued to gaze unwaveringly at Sophie, who eventually lowered her eyes and forced herself to concentrate on her supper.

After a while, when Sophie didn't look up again, Charlotte turned her attention to Chas.

'The agency made a stupid mistake, actually,' she said. 'They ordered me a blonde wig.'

'Oh.' Chas smiled easily at his sister. 'That'll be interesting. I've often wondered what you'd look like as a blonde.'

'Really?' Charlotte tried hard not to look pleased by his comment. So what if he'd imagined her with a different hair colour, she told herself firmly, it didn't mean anything. 'And the only dress they could come up with for Sophie,' she went on, 'is very similar to mine.'

Chas smothered a smile. Knowing his sister as well as he did, he knew she wouldn't like that one little bit. Charlotte liked to be different. To stand out in the crowd.

'Oh, wonderful,' he enthused wickedly, 'with your blonde wigs and wearing the same clothes you'll look just like twins.'

Charlotte glared at him. 'Hardly.'

She smoothed her hands down her sides, deliberately conveying the message to him that Sophie's figure, voluptuous in comparison, was no match for her own slender form.

'No I suppose not,' he countered, 'there's no faking a woman who's all woman. All men like a body they can really get to grips with, don't they, Tim?'

Tim glanced up in surprise. He had secretly been making his own comparisons between Sophie and Charlotte and so far Sophie, with her generous breasts and sinuous figure, was winning hands down. He groaned inwardly as he imagined putting his hands down her top, or her knickers.

'Er— what was that, Chas?' he said.

Chas repeated his question.

'Oh, absolutely,' Tim replied, averting his eyes from Penny's angry glare. 'Although there's a lot to be said for women who look good in clothes.'

He tried to smile winningly at his wife but could see that his hasty amendment had cut no ice with her. Oh, shit! he thought dejectedly, she would make him pay for this later.

Chas seemed determined to continue to be provocative.

'I can't agree, old man,' he said, reclining in his chair and clasping his hands casually behind his head. 'I think most men prefer women who look sensational in the buff. Sophie does.' He winked at her.

Sophie blushed and tried hard not to catch anyone's eye. She could sense definite waves of antipathy emanating from both Penny and Charlotte and could equally feel all three men undressing her with their eyes.

Robert broke the uncomfortable silence. 'More wine, anyone?'

He held a bottle of claret aloft and, as everyone nodded, stood up and began to circulate the table. When he reached Sophie's side, he deliberately allowed the back of his hand to brush against her breast as he poured. Feeling her tremble he smiled inside and glanced over at Tim who seemed to be in some sort of trance.

'Whoops!' Robert deliberately allowed a few drops of wine to trickle down Sophie's cleavage as he raised the bottle. Immediately, his index finger followed the trail.

Sophie blushed as Charlotte glared at them both. Then she glanced at Chas who, she noticed, merely looked amused by Robert's deliberate clumsiness. Why oh why does everyone seem intent on winding Charlotte up? she wondered, groaning inside. And why pick on me? She dislikes me enough as it is.

Suddenly, she felt gripped by annoyance. She was fed up with Charlotte always trying her hardest to make her feel inadequate. Instinctively realising that Chas would understand her motives, she smiled up at Robert and wriggled provocatively. If Charlotte thought she was a sex-mad bimbo, she would damn well act like one. Just for the hell of it.

'Ooh, Robert, that tickles,' she breathed girlishly.

Tim made a sort of strangled sound as Robert grinned and delved into the neckline of her dress again.

'We don't want any traces of wine staining that lovely flesh of yours, do we?' Robert said, glancing slyly at Charlotte who looked as though she were about to blow a gasket. He rubbed his fingers slowly up and down the valley between her breasts.

Sophie pouted as he withdrew them with obvious reluctance.

'Spoilsport,' she simpered. At the opposite end of the table she noticed Chas was grinning widely. Her eyes sparkled at him for a moment before she glanced back up at Robert. 'You have a very delicate touch.'

All of a sudden the tense atmosphere was shattered by the sound of Charlotte pushing back her chair.

'That's fucking well it!' she hissed angrily. 'When you've quite finished playing your little games, Robert, you'll find me in bed – asleep.' She stressed the last word and without looking back flounced out of the kitchen.

For a moment there was complete silence, then Chas burst out laughing. His laughter was followed by Robert's, and soon everyone joined in, not least Sophie who was forced to wipe away tears from her eyes.

'Oh, God, you've done it now,' Penny said, glancing at Sophie and Robert and then at Chas. 'You don't imagine Charlie will take this lying down, do you?'

Chas gulped back his laughter. 'Well, she is at the moment, isn't she?'

Robert put down the bottle and squeezed Sophie's shoulder reassuringly.

'Sorry about that,' he said, 'it seemed like a good idea at the time.' She smiled to let him know she didn't mind. 'Well,' he continued in a resigned tone, 'I'd better go and smooth my darling wife's ruffled feathers. See you all in the morning.'

Everyone wished him a subdued goodnight, and as soon as he'd gone, Chas said, 'I don't envy him. Charlotte can be a right bitch.'

'Oh, really?' Penny pretended to seem amazed. Then she added, 'I hope he succeeds in calming her down. I dread to think how she's going to behave tomorrow otherwise.'

Chas felt suitably chastened by her observation. It was true, his sister could be a bitch at the best of times and now she had what she would see as good reason to be angry with Sophie, she would be hell bent on revenge.

'Come on, sweetheart,' he said, standing up and holding out his hand to the object of his desires, 'let's go to bed before we do any more damage.'

Sophie stood up and walked around behind Tim and Penny to take his hand.

'I was only playing along,' she said, sounding genuinely upset.

'I know, I know, darling, don't worry.' Chas smoothed her hair with his free hand and tipped her chin up so that he could deposit a light kiss on her downturned lips. 'Come on, I know the best way to cheer you up.'

She grinned then and squeezed his hand. 'That's true,' she

said softly, fluttering her eyelashes provocatively at him, 'but would you mind reminding me how – I think I may have forgotten?'

Chapter Fourteen

New Year's Eve dawned early for Chas who got up and showered straight away, saying that he had to go and check on the preparations for the party.

'I want to make sure the main house is clean and I need to tell the contractors where to put all the tables and chairs. Then at nine-thirty' – he glanced at his watch to reassure himself that he still had plenty of time – 'I've got to meet with the musicians who have been booked to play tonight.'

'Great, a live band.' Sophie smiled up at him as she propped herself up against a pile of pillows.

'Not exactly a band,' he said, returning her smile. 'More like a small orchestra. We want to keep everything authentic, you see, right down to the music.'

She frowned. 'Oh, dear, I can't dance. Well, not properly anyway. I can't waltz or anything.'

'Oh, dear.' Chas' tone teased her but his eyes twinkled. 'Then you'll just have to trust me to lead. It's quite easy really.'

Sophie privately disagreed with his blithe statement. She'd tried ballroom dancing before and still couldn't tell a foxtrot from a fandango. Never mind, she consoled herself, spending all night in Chas' arms wasn't a bad prospect even if her feet wouldn't know what they were supposed to be doing.

'How long do you think you'll be?' she asked.

'I should be finished by ten-thirty, eleven at the latest. By that time I expect you to be up, dressed and ready for the surprise I have in store for you.'

'Surprise?'

Noticing the childish animation on her face Chas gave her a tender look and sat back down on the bed. For just a moment he allowed himself the luxury of pulling her into his arms and kissing her. He let her go with obvious reluctance.

'Much as I'd love to stay here with you, I really must push off,' he said.

Sophie pouted. 'Oh, but I don't know what the surprise is yet.'

'No and you won't ever find out if you don't let me get going.' Dropping one last kiss on the top of her head he straightened up and headed for the door. There he paused and turned around to look at her. 'By the way,' he added casually, 'I want you to wear warm outer clothing but with very little underneath.'

He didn't give her the chance to ask why. Before she had even managed to open her mouth he was gone.

Sophie tried to go back to sleep but after half an hour gave up and treated herself to a long soak in a hot bath instead. Afterwards she dressed carefully in a knee-length dogtooth-check skirt, black polo-neck jumper and thick opaque hold-up stockings. True to Chas' wishes, she left off her underwear and, having applied a little makeup and brushed her hair, she picked up her coat and went downstairs.

Her entry into the kitchen was tentative. She half expected to find Charlotte there and was dreading the thought of running into her again after the misunderstanding of the night before. Fortunately, the kitchen's only occupant was Tim, who sat at the table nursing a mug of coffee.

'Oh, hello there, you're an early bird,' he said, glancing up.

'Chas had to get up early to see to the preparations for the party,' she offered by way of explanation. Helping herself to a mug of coffee, she sat down beside him. 'I think we're going out somewhere when he comes back.' She glanced at her watch and saw that it was barely a quarter to ten. 'Oh,' she groaned, 'it'll be ages yet.'

Tim felt unaccountably cheered by the prospect of having

Sophie to himself for a little while. Although they had been sharing the same house for the past week they had hardly spoken to each other. Only the odd comment, or joky remark, nothing of any significance. As she sat beside him, elbows on the table, sipping her coffee, he appraised her surreptitiously. She was looking as good as ever, he thought. His eyes followed the curve of her breast and waist, over her hip to her crossed legs. Just below the hem of her skirt he could make out the darkly shadowed welt of a stocking top.

He felt his stomach clench at the sight and, although he tried hard not to think about it, the vision of Sophie reclining on the sofa masturbating came back into his mind. If he was honest, it was that image which had lurked in the back of his mind ever since the day he and Penny had arrived at Bickley Manor and had been responsible for boosting his flagging libido. He knew Penny was enjoying the new, revved up and raring to go version of him but he felt guilty all the same that it wasn't actually his wife who was responsible.

Just at that moment Sophie raised herself slightly from her seat to reach across the table for the daily paper. Tim felt his gaze fixed to the tops of her legs. As she stretched further, so her skirt rode up her thighs revealing first the tops of her stockings, then the creamy flesh of her thighs – so deliciously pale in comparison with the dark stocking tops – and a moment later, as she stretched just a little bit more, the plump flesh of her lower buttocks.

Naked, she was naked under that skirt! Tim sat back, feeling his heart racing. When Sophie sat back down she glanced sideways at him with a quizzical expression.

'Are you all right, Tim, you look a bit funny?'

Tim paused, took a deep breath, then he lunged at her. One hand grasped for her breast and the other shot up the hem of her skirt.

'Tim, Tim, get off!' Sophie pushed him with all her might with one hand as she tried to steady herself with the other. She was leaning right over the edge of the chair, her hand holding onto the wheel-back for dear life, the ends of her hair trailing the kitchen floor. 'Tim, stop!'

Her shout shocked him into stopping. Slowly, he sat back, removing his hands as Sophie straightened up. She pulled down the hem of her skirt and ran her fingers through her hair. They were both breathless and shaking, their faces bright red but for different reasons.

'Well,' she gasped, when she got her breath back a bit, 'what on earth was all that about, Tim?' She gazed at him questioningly. 'Tim, oh, come on, it's OK. Just a bit of New Year's Eve madness.' Putting her hand on his shoulder, she tried to jolly him out of the apoplectic state he seemed to be in.

'Oh, God, Sophie, I'm so sorry,' he said at last. 'I don't know what came over me. Please don't tell Penny.'

'Of course I won't tell Penny.' Sophie felt concerned, he was still bright red in the face and his chest was heaving. Oh, God, she hoped he wasn't about to have a heart attack or something. 'Are you sure you're all right?'

To her relief he nodded. 'I'm OK. It's just that— just that' – he shrugged helplessly – 'I can't stop thinking about you. Ever since I saw you that first day on the sofa—' He stopped abruptly, realising he had gone too far.

'On the sofa?' Sophie tried to think back. Suddenly, a terrible realisation struck her. 'You don't mean—' She gazed at him in horror.

Again, Tim nodded. 'Yes, Penny and I— well, we couldn't get any answer at the door, so we— er— we walked around the side of the house. You were lying on the sofa when we looked through the window. You— well— you didn't look as though you wanted to be disturbed, so Penny and I went and sat in the car.'

He didn't think there was any point mentioning that he and Penny had watched her for some time, or that they had been so turned on that they done more than merely sit in the car and wait for Chas.

Sophie went bright red. As Tim spoke she could feel the flush starting at the tips of her toes and spreading like wildfire through her whole body. Now her cheeks flamed and, self-consciously, she put her hands up to cover the burning flesh.

It seemed it was Tim's turn to reassure her. 'Look, Sophie, don't be embarrassed. Penny and I haven't mentioned it since. Christ! It's hardly crossed my mind.' He raised his eyes to the ceiling, hoping that God, or whoever lurked up there, would forgive him for lying so blatantly.

'More secrets,' Sophie murmured, lowering her hands and picking up her coffee again. She tasted it. Ugh! It was cold. She picked up Tim's mug. 'Fancy another?'

For one brief, mad moment, he imagined she meant another grope. Then he came to his senses.

'Yes, please. If you don't mind.' His gaze followed her as she walked over to the Aga, picked up the glass coffee jug and began to pour. 'What did you mean just then, about more secrets?'

Sitting back down, she placed the mugs on the table and turned in her seat to look at him.

'Ever since you all arrived, well, since Charlotte arrived, I've got the distinct impression that there are things going on here that I don't know about. Undercurrents, if you like. There certainly seems to be a lot of unexplained tension between Charlotte and Chas. I know they don't really get on but—'

She was interrupted by a burst of harsh laughter from Tim.

'Don't get on,' he said, 'I wouldn't put it like that exactly.'

'So, what is it then between those two?' she prompted, feeling more confused than ever.

Tim averted his gaze. 'I don't think it's really my place to say anything.'

'Oh, come on, you can't start hinting at things and then leave me dangling like this!' Sophie felt a frantic clutching at her stomach. She lowered her voice. 'Don't make me resort to blackmail, Tim.'

He glanced up suddenly. 'You wouldn't?'

'I don't want to,' she admitted, 'but I can't marry Chas under these circumstances.'

'He asked you to marry him?' Tim sounded as amazed as he felt. He was certain that Chas was destined to live out his days as a crusty, rather eccentric bachelor. Taking a gulp of his coffee, he sighed. 'I suppose, if you must know, Charlotte and Chas used to be very close when they were much younger. Very close.' He stressed the words.

Sophie took a few moments to allow the implications to sink in. Then she spoke slowly.

'I actually suspected as much the other day, but when I asked Chas if he'd ever made love to his sister he denied it categorically.'

'Oh, Christ, don't get me wrong, I don't believe they actually had— well, sexual intercourse.'

She breathed an audible sigh of relief. 'So whatever happened between them was just childish games then?'

Tim shrugged. 'More or less, that's what I gathered from Penny, anyway.' He paused. 'The thing is, it seems Charlotte can't let it go at that. She seems hell-bent on finishing what she and Chas started all those years ago.'

'But that's ridiculous!' Sophie thought back to the times when she had bathed her younger brother, Jimmy. Nothing had happened between them, but she had heard tales of similar cases from her friends. 'Sexual games between siblings or close friends are normal when you're a child.'

'She was eighteen,' Tim cut in.

'Eighteen?' Sophie digested this new bit of information. Then she shrugged. 'It still doesn't make any difference, people mature at different ages.'

'Well, I'm glad you can look at it that way,' Tim said, adding, 'the sensible way, that is. Just take my advice and watch out for Charlotte, that's all. She's dangerous at the moment but she'll get over it. Robert will see to that. He really loves her.'

'I know, I can tell.' She glanced up as the kitchen door suddenly opened and Chas walked through it.

'Hi, guys, having a cosy chat?'

Sophie and Tim both nodded in unison. Scraping his chair back, Tim excused himself.

'I'd better go and rouse that lazy good-for-nothing wife of mine,' he said amiably.

'OK.' Chas glanced at him and smiled, then looked at Sophie. 'All ready to go?'

'As ready as I'll ever be.' She stood up, grabbed her coat and took his hand. 'See you later, Tim. Thanks for the chat.'

As she and Chas walked around the side of the house Sophie said, 'He's a nice man, Tim.'

Chas nodded. 'Yeah, one of the best. Now' – he glanced at her – 'close your eyes and don't open them until I tell you to.'

Stumbling slightly on some cobblestones, she allowed Chas to guide her. Finally, they stopped and he told her that she could look now. When she opened her eyes she saw that they were standing in front of a parked car.

'Wow, she's a beauty!' Sophie gazed at the curvaceous lines of the open-topped vintage car and reached out to run her hand over the gleaming gold-painted bodywork. 'What is it?' She glanced at the bonnet badge.

'It's a nineteen-forty-eight Jaguar XK120. It used to belong to my father,' Chas said with obvious pride.

'Is this the surprise?'

'Yup. Somehow it reminded me of you.' He walked around Sophie to open the driver's door. 'Get in, you're taking me for a drive.'

'Really?' Her eyes shone as she gazed back at him. 'You're going to let me drive this?'

'Absolutely. I wouldn't trust anyone else.'

'Then I'm honoured.'

She slid into the driver's seat. The interior of the two-seater car was softly upholstered in red and white leather, with red leather trim. It took her a few minutes to acclimatise herself to the huge steering wheel, fragile gearstick and simple fascia, all of which seemed very strange and spartan in comparison with her Peugeot. She turned to Chas and smiled as he got into the passenger seat beside her.

'Where would you like to go, sir?'

'Just follow my directions,' he said mysteriously. 'I have somewhere very special in mind.'

Sophie was very glad that they encountered no other cars as she grappled with the gears and clutch and made kangaroo jumps up the driveway. By the time they reached the lane she felt a bit more confident and once they got out on the open road she felt able to put her foot down and let the car fly.

The cold wind whipped through their hair and bit into the exposed skin of Sophie's hands. Soon they felt numb with cold and her toes began to tingle, making her wish she'd worn gloves and several pairs of socks.

'Refreshing, isn't it?' Chas called out.

Sophie glanced sideways at him before reverting her eyes to the road ahead.

'Freezing, you mean.'

She had to admit, once she got into her stride it was an exhilarating drive. The speedometer inched towards 110mph and she eased her foot off the accelerator, knowing that they were approaching a series of tight bends.

'Just turn left at the next crossroads,' Chas instructed, 'then first right again.'

The crossroads was half a mile further on, and when Sophie went to turn left for a second time, she realised the road led up to a farm.

'Are you sure you mean this one?' she said to Chas.

'Yes, left just here.'

'But it only leads to a farm.'

'I know,' Chas said firmly, 'turn right into the farmyard and continue on into the barn.'

Taking his instructions as read, she shrugged. Chas was a law unto himself but she had never known him to be unsure about what he was doing.

The double doors to the timbered barn stood open and,

having successfully negotiated a gaggle of geese who waddled imperiously across the farmyard, she drove straight in. Sheltered from the wind, the interior of the barn seemed luxuriously warm in comparison, and she gradually felt the life returning to her frozen extremities.

Chas got out of the car and closed the barn doors, then he flicked on a light switch and walked over to a huge space heater which roared into life at the flick of another switch.

'Soon have you warmed up,' he said, blowing on his hands and rubbing them together. 'Then we can get on to the next part of your surprise.'

'The next part?' Sophie felt her stomach clenching with excitement as she opened the car door and swung her legs out.

Chas glanced up. 'Stay there, just as you are,' he ordered.

She sat and waited until he crossed the barn and came to squat down in front of her. Her heart started to race as she watched his hands slide slowly up the length of her legs. He pushed her skirt up, further and further until it was bunched around her hips.

'Good,' he murmured, 'very good, Sophie.' His eyes darkened as he stroked the soft bands of flesh of her upper thighs. 'I like these.' He twanged the elasticated top of one of her stockings.

'I thought you might,' she gasped, watching as his fingertips began to explore the compressed purse of her sex.

To her surprise he suddenly stood up and grabbed her hand. 'Come on,' he said gruffly, 'stand up and strip for me.'

She glanced around the shadowy interior of the barn, illuminated only by a single bulb hanging from the central rafter.

'What, here?'

'Yes, here,' he said, his voice gruff with barely restrained desire, 'where did you think I meant?'

Feeling very self-conscious, she began to unzip her skirt.

'What about other people?' she said glancing around again,

expecting an irate farmer to come bursting through the doors toting a shotgun.

'Oh, you expected an orgy did you?' Chas winked at her and started to pull off his T-shirt. 'I didn't realise.'

'Silly!' Sophie chuckled as she took off her skirt and folded it neatly, placing it on the driver's seat of the car. Her jumper swiftly followed, her breasts bouncing as she moved.

'Christ! I love your breasts,' he said, moving forward to cup them in his hands.

'Oh!' Sophie gasped, realising his fingers were still cold. Her nipples sprang to attention, and a moment later she watched his head dip and felt the warm wetness of his mouth as he enclosed first one nipple and then the other.

He stroked her breasts and bottom, at the same time depositing featherlight kisses on her neck and throat. Sophie arched her neck, sighing with pleasure as he tantalised her body with delicate caresses.

Moving his mouth to her ear he whispered, 'Climb on to the bonnet.'

She had ceased to be surprised by his instructions and on trembling legs she moved, conscious of the fact that her bottom swayed in front of him and her breasts dangled as she climbed awkwardly on to the front of the car. The metal was smooth and warm, a comforting heat emanating from the huge engine beneath.

'Beautiful,' Chas murmured as she lay down and cupped the back of her head in her hands.

Bending one leg at the knee, she posed for him. 'Do I look like a model?' she asked.

'Absolutely,' he said, unzipping his jeans and allowing them to drop to his ankles. He kicked them off, his eyes concentrating on the sight of her reclining naked on the car. 'But lucky me, I get a private viewing.'

Her giggle turned into a sigh as he climbed on top of her and began to stroke her between her legs. His fingers found her moist vagina and thrust inside, making her gasp. She felt his hardness nudging her belly and reached down with one hand to grasp it. Was it her imagination, or was his penis bigger than ever?

'Is it me or the car that's turning you on so much?' she whispered hoarsely.

'You, definitely you,' he said. 'The car is beautiful but you're sensational. There's no comparison.'

'Flatterer!' She moaned as she felt his thumb caress her clitoris. 'That sort of talk will get you everywhere.'

He grinned wolfishly. 'I know.'

Steadying himself on his forearms, he took possession of his hard cock away from Sophie and guided it inside her body. He thrust very gently, realising that they were in a very precarious position. The bonnet of the car was humped slightly in the centre and they had to balance themselves carefully. It didn't take anything away from their pleasure though, he thought, as he felt his passion rising and heard Sophie's soft whimpers of arousal. No, it didn't take anything away at all.

Back at Bickley Manor, preparations for the costume ball were almost complete. Charlotte stalked around the vast ballroom, playing the lady of the manor to the hilt. Heels clicking on the black-and-white marble floor, she crossed to the far side of the room and gazed up at her favourite portrait. It was of her great-great-grandmother. A very fine lady, by all accounts, and certainly the ancestor Charlotte most resembled. In more ways than one, she mused ruefully.

It was a well-known fact, at least locally, that her great-great-grandfather had disgraced himself by getting one of the parlour maids pregnant. Unlike the custom in those days, though, he hadn't sent her packing with a fifty pound note in her purse, but had publicly declared both his love for the girl and paternity by setting up a home for her and their son in the village.

For the tightly-knit community that surrounded Bickley Manor it had been the sensation of the new century, and her great-great-grandmother had further scandalised everyone by taking a series of young lovers. More than one similarity between us then, Charlotte thought, smiling inwardly as she concentrated on the portrait. She didn't hear Chas come in until he spoke softly in her ear.

'Admiring your ancestral role-model again?'

'Chas!' She whirled around and treated her step-brother to her most engaging smile. She gestured around the room, where tables draped in the finest linen and rows of deep-buttoned brown leather chairs lined three of the walls. A dais had been erected in front of the fourth wall. From the high ceiling, eight chandeliers glistened like clusters of icicles in the bright wintry sunlight that flooded the room through huge leaded windows. 'What do you think?'

'Wonderful,' he said, wandering around and checking that the silverware and groups of crystal glasses had been polished to perfection. 'In fact I think this evening will be sublime.'

'Oh, I'm sure it will be.' Charlotte smiled knowingly. Then she glanced at her watch. 'Well, much as I enjoy standing around talking to you, brother dear, I must go and attend to my toilette.'

'But it's only two-thirty, you've got hours yet,' Chas said, shaking his head.

'I know,' she replied, a mysterious look darkening her eyes, 'but the sort of preparations I have in mind will take every last moment. Trust me, darling' – she paused to lean forward and place a kiss on his cheek – 'I shall be the belle of the ball.'

He shook his head wonderingly. 'Oh, I don't doubt it, Charlotte. I don't doubt it for a minute.'

By six-thirty Sophie was starting to feel anxious. Chas had disappeared hours ago, and she was bathed and made up just as he'd instructed, but he'd forbade her to dress until he returned. Snuggling into the comforting warmth of her bathrobe, she curled up on an armchair in front of the fire and tried to concentrate on a back copy of *Country Life*.

'De-DAH!' Chas flung open the doorway to the bedroom and advanced purposefully into the room. With a casual air he tossed a gift-wrapped package on to her lap.

Sophie glanced up in surprise. 'What's this, more presents? Christmas was last week.'

'I know,' Chas said smiling, 'but I wanted to get you something special to wear.'

'But I've got my costume,' she protested, gesturing towards the garment bag that hung from the door of the wardrobe.

'Yes, but this is to wear *under* your costume,' he said. 'Go on, open it, try it on.'

He seems as excited as a young boy, Sophie thought as she carefully lifted the glossy purple lid of the package. Underneath were layers of tissue paper.

'Hurry up,' Chas said. He was almost hopping from one foot to the other in anticipation. 'I want to see what it looks like on you.'

Delving into the tissue, her fingertips came into contact with the unmistakable feel of silk. Excited herself now, she drew out the wine-red garment and held it up in front of her. It was an old-fashioned corset, boned and laced and breathtakingly exquisite.

'Wow! It's beautiful,' she breathed. Standing up, she hurriedly shrugged off her robe and held the front of the corset to her body.

'It will look all the more ravishing when it encases your delicious body,' Chas said. He inclined his head in the direction of the bed. 'Over there, grasp the foot of the bed like they used to do in the old days and I'll lace you up.'

Deliberately wiggling her hips as she walked across the room, Sophie did as he asked.

He huffed and puffed as he laced the corset.

'Go easy, Chas,' Sophie said, glancing at him over her shoulder. 'I can hardly breathe as it is.'

'It will be worth it,' he assured her, placing the sole of his booted foot against the solid oak bed and tugging hard on the laces, 'no pain, no gain.'

'Yes, but it's me who has to suffer, not you.'

Sophie knew her protests were useless and concentrated on regulating her breathing. The corset felt very tight indeed, constricting her ribs so much that she felt sure they would feel bruised when she took the corset off again. Beautiful though the garment was, she was already looking forward to that moment of blessed release.

'There! Turn around, let me see.' Chas took a step back and waited while Sophie straightened up.

As she turned around and posed in front of him, his breath caught.

'Christ! You look stupendous.'

'Do I?' Gasping for breath, she tried to glide elegantly over to the full length mirror in the corner of the room. Her eyes widened when she caught sight of herself. 'Gosh, I do, don't I?'

Chas came up behind her and they both gazed at her reflection. Already curvaceous, her body now had a very defined hourglass shape. Her luscious breasts swelled over the cups and were compressed together to form two enticing globes with a deep valley between. Her waist looked tiny, barely more than a handspan, and her hips flared out in an exaggerated fashion – lush and rounded.

'Oh, shit!'

Sophie turned around to glance anxiously at Chas. 'What's the matter?'

'I just want to fuck you now,' he said hoarsely. His hands came up to clasp her breasts, his breathing warm on her skin. 'I must, I must. I know it's getting late but—'

'Shush.' She put a finger to his lips and stroked his urgent tumescence with her free hand. 'We've got plenty of time. And anyway, it won't matter if we're a little bit late. Charlotte will be there to greet the first arrivals.'

'You're right, of course, as always.' He pushed her down

on to the carpet as he spoke, his knees forcing her legs wide apart. 'God, Sophie, I can't get enough of you.'

She thrilled to the passion in his voice and the way he looked at her. His gaze wondering, almost adoring. Feeling herself moisten instantly, she bent her legs at the knees and raised her pelvis, offering her body to him. The bones of the corset dug into her as she moved but she couldn't care less. Fucking with Chas was such a heady experience that nothing else mattered.

He came almost instantly, his arousal was so great, but ever the gentleman, he continued thrusting and stroking her clitoris until she came too.

'Oh, Chas, I do love you.' Sophie wrapped her arms and legs around him and hugged him tightly. 'I can't wait until we get married.'

'Nor can I,' he said, gently detaching her limbs. Leaning forward he kissed her for a long, delicious moment, then he gave her a rueful grin. 'I suppose we'd better get a move on.' As he stood up and helped her to her feet he said, 'Do you think a June wedding would be too soon?'

'June? Oh, yes, that would be perfect.' Her face glowed as she looked at him. 'Will there be a lot of guests? I have quite a large family and—'

'And we can discuss all this later,' he said, interrupting her.

'Yes, of course we can, sorry.' She walked over to the wardrobe and took down the garment bag.

He came up behind her, wrapped his arms around her waist and deposited a few featherlight kisses across her bare shoulders.

'Don't apologise,' he murmured. 'I'm glad that you're so happy.'

'Oh, I am,' she breathed, delighting in the soft caress of his lips, 'I'm the happiest woman on earth.'

Charlotte glanced up as Chas and Sophie made their entrance.

And what an entrance it was, she thought, with more than a flicker of irritation. Sophie looked lovely in her long red gown, her fair powdered wig making her look much taller. And as for Chas, well, he looked devastating. Unlike most of the other men, he had declined to dress in period costume and instead was wearing a superbly tailored dress suit, with wing collar and bow tie, that she hadn't seen before.

'Hello, darling,' she said, walking up to Chas and kissing the air beside his right ear, 'practising for the wedding already?'

She tried to make light of the news that she had gained that afternoon from Penny. It annoyed her that she was the last to know. Surely Chas should have told her before Sophie blurted it out to all and sundry. Penny had been almost beside herself with glee, the bitch, and Charlotte had been forced to retaliate with a comment about Tim and Sophie enjoying intimate tête-à-têtes. To her annoyance, her friend had merely laughed off her implied suggestion that Tim was attracted to the newcomer in their midst.

'Charlotte, you look lovely,' Sophie said, interrupting her thoughts.

Charlotte was taken aback by the generous compliment. 'Oh— er— thank you, so do you.'

'Yes, she does doesn't she?' Chas slid his arm around Sophie's waist in a possessive gesture that made Charlotte want to scratch the other woman's eyes out. 'And so do you,' he added but with less conviction. 'I told you you'd look good as a blonde.' He eyed her wig thoughtfully.

'Thank you, Chas.' She nodded at him. 'If you don't mind, Sophie dear,' she continued, smiling falsely, 'I must whisk my brother away from you for a moment. We have certain duties to perform.'

Chas gave Sophie a consoling look. 'Sorry about this, sweetheart. We gentry have to greet the serfs now.' He winked at her and kissed her lightly on the lips. 'Go and enjoy yourself. I'll catch up with you as soon as I can.'

'OK.' Sophie smiled at him. 'I'll go and see if I can fit any food into my stomach.' She patted the stiff, flat panel on the front of her dress and winced as she imagined how compressed her internal organs must be.

'I'm sure it wouldn't hurt you to fast for one night.' Charlotte couldn't resist the jibe and only looked vaguely contrite as Chas flashed her a warning look.

'Come on, sister dear,' he said thinly, 'let's just get this over with so that I can start to enjoy myself.'

With a nod of agreement Charlotte slipped her arm through Chas' and they turned and walked away.

For a moment, Sophie remained rooted to the spot, watching their retreating figures. She felt a familiar sinking feeling that she always got when something awful was afoot. It was obvious that Charlotte hadn't forgotten the previous evening, and certainly wasn't about to forgive either. And it seemed she had eyes only for Chas. Oh well, Sophie thought, trying to dismiss her premonition as her fanciful imagination at work again, Chas is a big boy now, no doubt he can take care of himself.

Chapter Fifteen

Penny and Tim hovered in front of one of the buffet tables, each deliberating the choice between caviare and oysters.

'I think I'll go for the caviare,' Penny said decisively. 'Although oysters make me feel decadent, they always remind me of—'

'Yes, OK, Penny, don't say it,' Tim cautioned. 'I used to love them until the first time you made that particular comparison.'

She laughed. 'Stop complaining and pass me the crackers, would you, darling.'

Turning around she rested her bottom against the edge of the table and popped a caviare-laden cracker in her mouth. As she ate, she glanced interestedly around the room. She was feeling in a very lighthearted mood. The decor and the music were wonderful and everyone present looked resplendent in their costumes. Even Tim, who had thrown up his hands in horror at the notion of dressing up.

He was wearing a gold embroidered jacket over tight cream breeches and matching hose. Around his neck he wore a cravat with a little gold and emerald stick pin which she had bought him for Christmas.

'Have I told you how marvellous you look, darling?' she said as Tim turned around and stood next to her. He offered her another caviare-topped cracker from his plate. 'Thanks.'

'You have, several times,' he mumbled, his mouth full, 'but I don't mind hearing it again.' He smiled down at her. 'You know you look absolutely gorgeous too, don't you?'

'Yes,' she said patting her red wig immodestly. She glanced down at the tight bodice and voluminous skirts of her dress. 'Do you realise the colour of this dress exactly matches the emerald in your tie pin?'

He nodded. 'I had noticed. By the way, where have Chas and Charlotte got to? I can see Robert over there talking to that Liz whatshername and Sophie's dancing with someone.' He paused to take a better look at the distinguished grey-haired man who he envied for having Sophie in his arms.

'Oh, that's Michael Brent, the MP,' Penny said dismissively. She sighed as she glanced around again. 'I don't know where Charlie and Chas are. I should think all the guests have arrived by now, so they should be in here circulating.'

Tim felt a sense of unease. Supposing Charlotte had drugged Chas and was, right at that moment, having her wicked way with him in one of the upstairs rooms. Although he felt a bit foolish for doing so, he shared his concerns with Penny.

Thankfully, she laughed them off. 'Don't be silly, darling. She wouldn't do anything as underhand as that. What you must realise is that Charlotte wants Chas to want *her*. It would be no good if he was drugged and didn't know what he was doing.'

'Oh, so you wouldn't put it past her to drug someone, then?'

'Not entirely.' Penny's eyes glittered as she smiled. Opening her fan, she used it to shield her words from eavesdroppers. 'She used to use cocaine, you know?'

Tim's eyes widened. 'No, I didn't. When was that?'

'Oh, when we were at college,' Penny said airily, waving her fan. 'I tried it, too, but I couldn't see what all the fuss was about.'

He tried hard not to look as astounded as he felt by his wife's surprising disclosure. She never would have struck him as the type to take drugs. Drink, yes, especially champagne, and by the bucketful if she could. Even the odd cigarette. But never drugs.

'You're shocked now, aren't you?' She grinned. 'Poor old Tim has been shocked rigid by his wayward wife yet again.'

'Don't call me poor old Tim,' he protested, 'especially not the old part.'

'Well, you're not poor either, are you?' She paused to wave at a couple she thought she vaguely recognised. 'Was that Sylvia Blenheim-Hindley-Jones?'

'Just Blenheim again now,' Tim said sagely. 'She dropped Rupert after he admitted a preference for dressing up in women's clothes.'

Penny rounded on him, her expression one of pure amazement. 'Are you telling me that hunky husband of hers came out of the closet – fully dressed and wearing high heels?' She laughed at her own joke.

'I didn't say he was homosexual. It just turned out he was a transvestite, that's all.'

'That's all!' Penny stared after Sylvia. 'Poor bitch, she must have been distraught.'

Tim shook his head. 'Apparently not. It turned out, after all the hoo-ha died down, that she was really a lesbian.'

'Really?' Penny's eyes became as round as saucers. 'So, if she's into girls, what is she doing with that chap on her arm?'

'He's not her bloke,' Tim said knowledgeably, enjoying the role of gossipmonger for once – which was usually Penny's forte. 'He's a male escort.'

'Really?' Penny said again, admonishing herself for sounding like an idiot and for not knowing all these fascinating details already. 'I didn't realise you could get such good-looking ones.'

She sounded thoughtful, Tim noticed.

'Well, don't go getting ideas on that score. You've got me.'

'*Moi?*' she said, looking amazed, 'I wouldn't dream of it.'

'You can dream all you wish,' Tim said drily, 'just don't try turning your fantasies into reality, that's all.'

Before Penny could think of a suitable response, they were interrupted by the arrival of Charlotte.

'Pigging it, are we, darling?' she said, eyeing Penny's plate.

Penny gave her a superior smile. 'Bollocks!'

Tim sighed. Sometimes his wife displayed all the charm and *élan* of a stevedore.

'I'll leave you two ladies to it,' he said in an ironic tone, 'I'm going to see if I can find a damsel in distress who would be willing to dance with me.'

Charlotte and Penny watched him for a moment as he walked off.

'What's the matter, not dancing yourself?' Charlotte said.

'No, I can't.' Penny lifted the hem of her dress to reveal a very high pair of cream stiletto heels. 'My feet are absolutely killing me.'

'Well.' Charlotte took her by the elbow. 'Come with me and take the weight off them. I need to talk to you in private.'

'Where are we going?' Penny hobbled to keep up with her friend as she stalked proudly across the ballroom.

'The conservatory,' Charlotte hissed over her shoulder. 'We shouldn't be disturbed in there.'

As she followed Charlotte, Penny had the sinking feeling that her friend wanted to discuss her forfeit. She had lost the bet they'd made. Tim had ended up spanking her and now she would be forced to pay the penalty.

The conservatory was a euphemism for a rather grand, glass-domed room that led off what had originally been the morning room. In it were a profusion of plants and a number of white wrought-iron sofas and tables.

'Phew! It's like Kew Gardens in here,' Penny said, brushing her way past a rather over-enthusiastic yucca.

'Just shut up and sit down,' Charlotte ordered, closing the door firmly behind them. 'This is important.'

'I wonder what it could be about?' Penny countered drily. 'Time for you to extract your pound of flesh, is it? Or rather time for me to extract someone else's pound of flesh.' Mentally, she carried out a quick resumé of all the men she'd seen at the party that she fancied. 'Please don't make me go with

Henry Fortescue,' she added, with feeling, 'or that chap who looks as though he has two noses, or that one with the—'

'Oh, shut up, Pen, for Christ's sake!' Charlotte said with an exasperated sigh. She chose the sofa opposite her friend, her dress billowing out around her as she sat down. 'You don't have to fuck anyone apart from Tim if you don't want to.' She noted Penny's look of amazement, tinged with relief, and allowed a catlike smile to curve her heavily painted lips. 'Provided, that is, you agree to do something for me in return for letting you off the bet . . .'

'Excuse me, may I have this dance?' Chas' fingertips glanced across the bare skin at the nape of Sophie's neck and she whirled around in surprise. Immediately, her slightly downcast expression changed to one of smiles.

'Oh, Chas!' She clasped a hand to the creamy mounds of her overflowing breasts and pretended not to take any notice of his interested glance. 'I was wondering where on earth you'd got to.'

'Stray businessmen kept waylaying me,' he said, pulling her close and leading her into a slow waltz. 'It looks as though business will be booming next year.'

'It's nearly that now,' Sophie murmured. She glanced at an ormolu clock which graced the mantelpiece of a huge white marble fireplace as they danced past it.

'The first day of the first year of the rest of our lives,' he murmured as he nuzzled her neck and inhaled the delicate scent he had bought her for Christmas. 'I can't wait.'

She sighed with pleasure at his words and pressed himself a little closer to him. Just at that moment, the band stopped playing, and the conductor clapped his hands together smartly and called for silence. Everything remained still for a moment, then came the sound of all the clocks in the house chiming midnight. Suddenly, everyone started kissing everyone else and it was a full five minutes before Chas and Sophie could resume their dance.

'Happy New Year,' he said.

Sophie smiled. 'Same to you.' She kissed him again, then she added, 'What time does this shindig normally end?'

'Shindig?' He laughed lightly. 'Usually, not until the cock starts crowing.'

'Oh!' Sophie's face fell. 'I've been so looking forward to getting you into bed.'

Chas pretended to look affronted. 'But I thought you liked seeing me in these clothes. You said they made a wonderful change when I got dressed earlier.'

'I know,' she said, 'I do like seeing you in them and they do look wonderful, but I'd rather see you naked in your bed.'

'*Our* bed,' Chas corrected, 'what's mine is yours from now on.'

She thrilled to his simple statement. All at once it occurred to her that by marrying Chas she would be marrying into all this – she gazed around the vast ballroom – Bickley Manor and the grounds and the antiques and everything.

'Gosh,' she said, 'it's going to take a bit of getting used to. My whole flat could fit into this one room.'

'Well, you know this is only for show,' he reminded her. 'You'll have to make do with the west wing the same as I do.'

'I know that.' Her powdered cheeks dimpled as she grinned at him. 'I just meant— well, you know?'

'I know.' Chas kissed the exposed part of her shoulder. 'I suppose you're just marrying me for my money.'

'Chas!' She took a step back.

'All right,' he said hastily, 'calm down, I was only joking.' He pulled her firmly into his arms again. 'I only said it in the first place because you're the most unworldly person I've ever met.'

At that moment the waltz changed to a quadrille, a dance that was more in keeping with the theme of the party.

'I'll sit this one out if you don't mind,' Sophie said, eyeing all the guests as they started to sort themselves into rows. Taking his hand she walked over to a group of chairs, sat down and pulled Chas down on to the chair next to hers. 'I tell you what,' she murmured, using her fan to shield the suggestion she was about to make, 'why don't I pop upstairs to one of the bedrooms for a little rest and you *accidentally* discover me. We could play lord of the manor and innocent virgin.'

Chas spluttered with laughter. 'You – a virgin?'

'Rotter!' She pouted at him, her eyes twinkling with devilment. 'Just use your imagination. You've managed pretty well up to now.'

'All right, you're on. Third bedroom on the left, OK?'

'OK.' Sophie stood up and smiled down at him. 'And please,' she added in a serious tone, 'when you find me, promise me one thing.'

Chas gazed up at her. 'And what might that be?'

She paused and fluttered her eyelashes as she let out a long sigh. 'That you'll be gentle with me.'

Her earnest expression changed to a smile and with a mock-haughty flick of her billowing skirts, she turned and walked away from him without looking back.

Penny wandered back into the ballroom and glanced nervously around. Where the hell was Chas? Oh, God, she swallowed deeply, there he was. She was surprised to see him sitting alone.

'Hi, Chas, great party.' Crossing the room swiftly, she sat down next to him.

He smiled. 'Oh, hi, Penny. Yes, not too bad a bash, is it?'

For a moment she fell silent. Noticing that her hands were trembling in her lap, she hastily sat on them instead. She could bloody well kill Charlotte for this, she thought, it wasn't fair to do what she planned. Not fair to her. Not fair to Sophie. And especially not fair to Chas.

'I've come on a mission, actually,' she said, finding her voice at last.

'Oh, yes?' Chas glanced interestedly at her and raised one eyebrow.

Please, God, forgive me for this, she begged inside her head, only Charlotte *is* my friend and I don't really want to be unfaithful to Tim and . . .

'Go on, Penny, you were saying.' Chas' voice interrupted her hasty prayer.

'I— er—' She searched her memory banks wildly for a minute, her mind had gone blank. 'Oh, yes.' She cleared her throat. 'There's— er— someone who wants to see you. Up in one of the bedrooms,' she added, 'fourth on the left.'

Chas was surprised by this disclosure. He had only just arranged the rendezvous with Sophie and couldn't imagine why she'd asked Penny to come and tell him what he already knew. And it seemed, she'd already forgotten which room he'd suggested. He smiled to himself at Sophie's aberration. Over the past few days he'd often teased her about having the memory of a goldfish.

'OK,' he said affably, rising to his feet. 'I'll go and see her now.'

Penny gazed up at him wide-eyed, astounded by his eagerness. 'How did you know it was a *her*?'

He surprised her again with his grin. 'Don't come the innocent with me, Pen, it doesn't suit you. I know as well as you do who's up there waiting for me.' He glanced at the ceiling and then looked down again and winked at her.

'Oh, right, good luck then,' she said faintly.

She stared after him as he went, feeling her heartbeat gradually slow down to normal again. Whereas she had thought she was going to have to use all her wiles to persuade him to go up and see Charlotte, her mission had been laughably easy to accomplish. Oh, well, she thought with an inward shrug, perhaps she had misjudged him after all. Obviously he was as keen to get his hands on his sister as she was to get her talons into him.

Charlotte lay on the bed trembling. It was pitch black in the room, and despite the muted strains of the band playing on the floor below she was certain she could hear her heart thumping. Now she was actually here, waiting for Chas, she half hoped Penny would be unsuccessful in persuading him to join her. After all, she had Robert to think about and, to a far lesser degree, Sophie. Even the child who might or might not be the product of their union was a consideration.

She thought about her motives and her preparations. If all the months she had spent carefully monitoring her temperature and everything were anything to go by, this should be one of her most fertile days. The chances of her conceiving were high, and she'd taken the precaution of a pregnancy test to ensure that she wasn't already pregnant by Robert. That had been a risk she'd been willing to take, but to her relief the test this morning had been negative.

If she was successful in seducing Chas she would have to invent a reason why she and Robert couldn't make unprotected love for a couple of weeks – thrush, perhaps, Robert still didn't understand all the workings of the female anatomy and would be none the wiser.

She cursed the darkness, wishing she could look at her watch. She seemed to have been waiting for ages. Then, just as she began to despair, she heard the muted click of the door and a soft *swoosh* as it opened.

In the next room Sophie also lay on the bed, but she wasn't listening to her heartbeat, or having second thoughts about seducing Chas. She was humming softly to the music coming from downstairs – a polka – and listening expectantly for the sound of his footfall outside the bedroom door.

The curtain on the far wall was drawn, revealing a huge mirror. All it showed when she looked at it was her reflection, and she fervently hoped that no one was in the room next door. If they were, they would see the way she reclined voluptuously on the bed, her full skirts drawn up to her waist at the front, her fingers gently stroking the impatient flesh between her legs.

The room was lit by a single candle on the small table beside her. Fat and white, it flickered inside a brass-and-crystal holder, and reflected off the gold brocade coverlet on which she lay to flatter her face with a pale golden glow.

Suddenly her ears picked up a noise, a slight cough, low and definitely male. Then another sound, a tentative knock at the door. She almost giggled. Chas was certainly playing this part to the hilt, fancy knocking. Instead, she managed to compose herself and pretended not to hear. He must come across her by accident and be instantly aroused by the sight of her – the innocent virgin – playing with her own body.

A moment later she heard the slight creak of hinges as the door opened. She averted her face and closed her eyes, pretending to be transported into another world. One of mindless, self-induced pleasure. The soft tread of footsteps walking towards the bed was unmistakable, as was the slight give of the mattress as the 'interloper' sat down beside her on the bed.

She continued to stroke herself, her fingers sliding deep into the warm wetness of her vagina, her palm covering her mound. Every so often she emitted a small whimper of arousal, and presently felt a male hand covering her own, a couple of fingers joining hers inside the greedy vessel of her body.

'Mmm,' she moaned, turning her face to smile provocatively up at Chas.

'Sophie!'

'Robert!'

They gazed at each other in stunned amazement. Robert's fingers still caressed her vagina, but now he withdrew them hurriedly.

'I— er— oh, my God!' Sophie was the first to speak, or rather gasp.

She moved her own hand and pulled down the front of her dress hurriedly. A glance up at the mirror revealed to her that her face was at least the same shade as her dress and getting redder by the second.

'Sophie!' Robert repeated, looking thoroughly shocked. 'I thought you were Charlotte.'

'How could you possibly—' she began, then realised straight away that she and his wife were very similarly attired. Like twins, as Chas had pointed out the day before. And, with her face averted from him and her hand covering the blonde curls of her pubis, she supposed there was no reason why Robert should have assumed any different.

'Christ! This is so embarrassing,' he said. 'I'm sorry, Sophie. I really did think, well—' He shrugged.

'It's OK, really.' Sophie struggled to sit up. 'I was waiting for Chas. We were playing a little game and I just assumed—'

Robert took one of her hands and squeezed it sympathetically.

'Don't worry, 'nuff said.'

She smiled at him. 'I— er— I don't suppose you know where Chas is?'

To her disappointment he shook his head. 'I saw him talking to Penny earlier but—' He shrugged again. Letting go of her hand he stood up and tugged down the dark blue embroidered velvet jacket that he was wearing over cream silk breeches. 'I'm going to go and look for Charlotte. Someone told me they'd seen her come up here.' He paused to wink at her. 'I hope Chas doesn't keep you waiting too much longer.'

'So do I,' Sophie muttered fervently, 'so do I.'

Chas opened the door to the bedroom and was immediately stunned by how dark it was inside the room. He stumbled slightly as he started to make his way over to the window, intending to draw the curtain, but a whispered voice coming out of the pitch blackness stopped him.

'Leave it. Just come here, darling. I'm on the bed.'

'But we must have some light,' he protested, 'you can't have forgotten how much I enjoy looking at your delicious body.'

Charlotte shivered. He sounded so eager, so thoroughly in

control, it wasn't the way she'd imagined he would be at all. She had expected guilt, denial and bucketloads of shame to overshadow his lust for her.

'All right then, just a little light,' she conceded.

Fumbling, Chas felt for the tasselled cord and opened the curtains just a fraction. A path of moonlight travelled across the room and revealed the blonde-haired figure clad in red who lay in the very centre of the four-poster opposite. As an afterthought, he crossed to the mirror and drew the curtains there too, although he didn't bother to look through into the other room. Plenty of time for voyeurism later, he mused. All he had eyes and thoughts for at the moment was the sight of Sophie waiting patiently for him on the bed.

'So, you're my little virgin, are you?' he said, crossing to the bed and reclining next to the still figure. He propped his head on one hand, and with the other began to investigate beneath the opulent folds of silk which concealed the lower half of her body.

'Oh!' Charlotte gasped as she felt Chas' fingers discover how wet she already was.

Drawing her legs up, she encouraged him to delve further inside her impatient body. It was wonderful that he had obviously decided to pretend to pick up where they had left off all those years ago. Pretending she was still a eighteen-year-old virgin was inspired, and only served to increase her desire for him.

She kept her face averted from him, pretending to feel ashamed by what they were doing. It all added to the illusion that they had slipped back in time. The canopy above her head might have been the finest silk brocade, but in her imagination it was canvas.

Reaching down she felt for his fly, her fingers fumbling with the buttons. As she unfastened the last one and delved inside his trousers, she felt the heat emanating from his groin and then sighed with pleasure as her fingers curled around the delightful hardness of his penis. It was the first time she had touched him intimately. All those years ago she hadn't dared, but now it was just as she'd imagined.

Chas continued to caress the willing flesh that opened up around his fingers. With two fingers inside the hot, wet tunnel of her vagina he stroked the silken folds of her labia with his thumb, seeking out her clitoris which he knew would already be hard and pulsing with desire.

'Oh, oh, yes.' Charlotte almost swooned with arousal when Chas touched her there. There where her body craved his caresses the most. She orgasmed quickly. She was, had been so desperate, so excited. 'Fuck me,' she urged, rubbing his penis fervently, 'please, make love to me now. I can't wait.'

'Oho, an eager virgin. My favourite kind.' There was humour in Chas' low voice. Humour tinged with the throaty growl of desire.

In one lithe movement he was kneeling between her legs, pushing her legs back towards her chest, his glans nudging the moist entrance to her body. He glanced down, his eyes barely registering the thick bush of black curls framing the blushing folds of her vulva. He started to enter her slowly, reminding himself that she was playing the part of a virgin, and that she had made him promise to be gentle when the time came.

Just then the sight of her sex registered in his brain at the same moment as she turned her head and smiled up at him. Hers was not the sweet blissful smile that he had come to love, it was knowing and cat-like. The smile of a she-devil. The smile of . . .

'Charlotte!' He drew back quickly in alarm.

For a moment he simply stared at her face, almost unable to believe what was happening to him, what had almost happened. Then he glanced away. His mind whirled as his gaze drifted across the mirror. On the other side was a very familiar face, the face he had expected to see smiling up at him. Sophie was peering very closely at him, at him and Charlotte, but her eyes did not register the sight. She was intent on dusting her cheeks with powder.

'You— you—' Chas leapt up from the bed and began to button his fly hastily as he stared down at his sister.

With her legs still agape and bent back towards her chest, her vulva mocked him as much as the scarlet gash of her mouth. Suddenly he noticed how her confident smile wavered and crumbled.

'You didn't realise it was me?' Her voice sounded hoarse, incredulous.

'Of course not – I would never—' Chas gave her an anguished look, then he turned and strode out of the room, slamming the door behind him.

Stunned for a moment, Charlotte dissolved into floods of tears.

Sophie turned her head as the door to the bedroom opened.

'Chas, at last, where on earth did you get to?' She rushed over to him and clasped him in a fervent embrace, her lips covering his face with kisses as her hands clutched at his hair. Suddenly, she broke away. 'Oh, bloody hell, I forgot, I'm supposed to be a virgin.' For a moment she stood there in front of him giggling softly, then she noticed his odd expression. 'Chas, are you all right, has something happened?' Quickly, her mind ran through a whole catalogue of possible disasters.

Chas hesitated. Now was the time to tell her the truth if he was ever going to. Taking her by the hand, he led her over to the bed and made her sit down while he dropped to his haunches in front of her. Clasping her hands in his, he looked at her adoring expression and forced himself to commit it to memory. After what he had to say, it might be the last time she ever looked at him that way again.

Sophie gazed out of the window, her eyes surveying the scene taking place down below. On the gravelled driveway stood Chas, Tim, Penny, Robert and, of course, Charlotte. Unable to bear looking at the woman who had tried to seduce her step-brother – *my* lover, Sophie thought savagely – she glanced down beside her instead to where her suitcase stood packed and ready to be stowed in the boot of her car.

Walking away from the window, she sat in an armchair and waited. Presently, the door to the bedroom opened and she glanced up.

'They've gone,' Chas said needlessly, closing the door behind him.

Sophie gazed at him. Relief was plainly etched in his expression.

'Are they— is everything going to be OK, do you think?' she said after a few moments of silence passed between them.

He nodded. 'Yes, I think so. Robert seems to have calmed down and Char—' – he could hardly bring himself to say her name – 'Charlotte is more subdued than I have ever seen her. I think they must have rowed all night but—' He sighed. 'I really believe love will conquer all. Robert does love her, despite the way she is, or perhaps because of it, I don't know. And I think, in her own way, my sister loves him. It'll just take a bit of time, that's all.'

'Love does conquer all, doesn't it?' Sophie said softly. She held out her hand to him. 'Come here.'

Chas crossed the room and, as Sophie rose from the chair, he took her place and pulled her down on to his lap. Cradling her close to him, he spoke gently.

'I don't know what I would have done if you hadn't forgiven me— understood.'

She gazed up at him. 'There was nothing to forgive.' For a moment she nestled against him. 'Take me to bed,' she murmured huskily. 'Take me to bed and love me.'

They stood up, crossing the room, arms entwined around each other's bodies, feeling the heat, the anticipation, the desire.

Much later Chas glanced up, his gaze travelling across the

room to the window. He could see snow clouds gathering.

'I think you've missed your chance for today,' he said, stroking Sophie's nipple. The pink bud, already hard, hardened even more.

'Who cares?' She reclined and arched her back as she felt Chas' lips engulf her nipple. Sharp darts of pleasure coursed through her, igniting her womb for the umpteenth time that afternoon. 'I'll go tomorrow. I only need a day to pack up my stuff.'

'Are you sure you don't want me to come with you?' Chas' words were muffled as he laved her breasts with the flat of his tongue.

She wriggled delightedly as the silky ends of his hair trailed across her throat and stomach. His tongue had started to lay a damp path down the length of her torso and she had no doubt of its ultimate destination. Her sex moistened with anticipation, the dull pulsing of her clitoris increasing by degrees to an urgent throb.

'No, it's OK. I have to deal with Piers. I know he said on the phone that he wants to take over the lease, but I don't trust him an inch. I'm going to get him to my solicitor's office if I have to drag him there by the scruff of the neck.'

'And you would, wouldn't you?'

It wasn't the first time in the past twelve hours that Chas had come to marvel at her fortitude, her steely determination. She had overridden the truth about Charlotte with a pragmatism that had amazed him. He had expected hysterics, whereas instead he had received understanding. She was one hell of a woman. Raising his lips from her belly for just a moment, he smiled at her and voiced his thoughts.

'No, I'm not,' she said, 'I'm just an ordinary woman who happens to be in love with the most wonderful man on earth. Now,' she added firmly, 'stop complimenting me and start paying more attention to my clitoris, please. I think it's about to explode.'

'God, no!' He pretended to look horrified.

Sliding his hand down her body, his fingers sought the soft folds of her sex, opening her out until the core of her arousal was totally exposed. Hard and pink it beckoned to him. 'Is this the sort of thing you had in mind?' he asked, delicately flicking the pointed tip of his tongue around and across the swollen bud of flesh.

Sophie felt a wave of lust crash over her. 'Yes, oh, yes, that's exactly what I— oh, oh, God!'

The eighth climax of Sophie's New Year was just the first of many.